Storm's Passion
The fifth book in the Twelve Dancing Princesses Series

Christine Young

Credits

Cover Artist: Designs by Ms G
Editor: Christie L. Kraemer

Chapter One

The Year of our Lord: 1818

"No! I'd rather jump off hell's cliff north of here." Storm's hands were fisted at her side, her insides churning. What could her father be thinking? But it was her father, and she knew he thought only of himself.

"What?" Bradford appeared stunned at her revelation, his eyes narrowing. His cheeks turned red, and a small drop of saliva slipped down one corner of his chin.

"You heard me father." She turned from the old man who thought to call himself a man, unable to look at him, yet resigned to see this through to the bitter end if that's what it took. She would find a way to thwart his plans.

"You can't refuse. I have a signed contract." His slack jowls quivered, his cheeks flaming with the rage he wasn't holding in check. He shook his fist in the air as if to make his point clearer.

"This is not the Dark Ages. What kind of contract." Back stiff, she faced the man who'd sired her. He was mean-spirited and meant nothing to her. No familial feelings had ever existed between them.

"A written agreement, signed and notarized, promising you will marry Charles Robertson. In this matter, you'll do as I tell you." He moved forward in his chair as if this would accentuate what he said.

"I will never say the words and in the end it is up to me." Head high and fiercely determined, Storm faced her opponent. "Real fathers, real men don't betroth their daughters any more. It's archaic." So angry, her body shook with rage and the tempest brewing inside.

"It's my choice. I am your father and this marriage will be in your best interest. I have only your feelings at heart." His voice had regained a slight measure of calm, but his eyes had darkened.

"You have no feelings or a heart. Look what you did to my mother, your wife. She's in her grave now, because of you."

A few shattered seconds passed as Storm considered her biological father. A man who had despised her the second he knew she was not the male heir he'd coveted. More than anything, she needed to discover the truth about why he'd decided to sell her off like an animal to the highest bidder. "Why?"

His ensuing grin sent chills down her spine. "I can do whatever I want with you. It's time you were out of my home. You should have a husband who can control your impulsiveness. And children to keep you in the home."

"I'll leave." Her nerves snapped, and she tried to hold on to her fast-rising temper. Ravyn, her older sister, would give her a home. Storm had funds, one thousand pounds, her father didn't know about. Long ago, her survival instincts had become part of her everyday life, and she'd found a way to hide every extra penny.

"You'll do as I say," Bradford shot back, his temper flaring to life. "This is your fault. I don't have the funds to send you to London and the Duchess, Storm. For the last few years, I've asked you to find a husband, and you've blatantly ignored my wishes. Now, my health is not at its best, and I want to see you taken care of when I can no longer do it."

"To you, I'm a means to an end. I can take care of myself. And when have you ever cared about my well being?" Storm challenged, seeing the angry red splotches on his face. "What is this really about? For the same number of years you didn't care what I did. Why now?"

Bradford sat up straight, his hands on either side of his chair. "Charles Robertson has offered for you when no one else will have anything to do with you. You are wild, impulsive and have no manners. You've frightened away all the men who might have shown interest. I've had it with you and your willfulness. I will see you wed before I die."

Storm watched her father rub his fingers up and down his breastbone. She understood the signs of his failing health. That much he hadn't lied about. "The state of your health is nothing new."

"I care now, Storm. You cannot continue to run around the

countryside doing whatever only God knows." His voice was raspy, the color of his face growing white as death. "You're a woman who has past her twentieth year. All this time you have refused to listen to my requests. I gave you ample opportunities to find a husband for yourself. Since you have failed, I found one for you."

Storm pressed her mouth together, ready to defy her father again. "Bradford," she began, loathe to call the man in front of her, Father. "We have talked about this matter on numerous occasions. My feelings have not changed. I do not want to marry anyone. Ravyn has given you an heir, a male heir. There is nothing more to discuss."

"What Ravyn has done is no concern of yours. Charles wants an heir," Bradford retorted, his voice stronger. "Every girl wants a husband. Your sister Ravyn is happily married. You can be too."

"Not to Charles. I can't stand the man. And, what, can he find no one willing to marry him? Am I surprised? Hardly. He is as mean and as despicable as you, Bradford."

"I will have some respect."

"When you have earned it. If you acted like a father, I would both love and respect you. I am nothing to you, except a way to make money. So tell me, what will you gain from this marriage? I'm beginning to think this affair goes deeper. What have you done?" Storm approached her father. "Despite what you haven't told me, I don't like Charles and I won't marry him."

"It doesn't make any difference if you like Robertson or not. Many successful marriages are made every day between people who don't like each other." Bradford drummed his fingers on the table, his brows drawing together.

"I won't be one of them." Storm closed her eyes for a moment, trying to tamp down the rage threatening to explode. "Bradford, I want you to listen to me," she said, praying her words would reach him and change his stubborn determination to control her. "I loathe Charles and as I said earlier, I would rather jump off the cliff at hell's edge than wed that man."

"Storm, you must realize by now that a signed contract is binding.

I expect you to honor my wishes. I have no apologies. This is expected of you. You are my daughter whether you like it or not."

Strom faced the door, wishing she could run away from this conversation and what it meant to her future, but it was imperative she get to the real reason he was selling her to Charles. She wiped sweaty hands on the red day dress she wore while she paced the length of his study. "It can't be binding," she argued. "You can't do this without my consent and I don't give it."

Bradford sat forward, his forearms on his desk, and his hands clasped tight. "I never told you it was a betrothal contract."

She strode to the desk and rested both hands on the polished surface, knowing her fingerprints there would anger him. "Now we get to the truth. What is it then, the real reason for this travesty?"

He cleared his throat, and she watched his Adam's apple move up then down on his meaty throat. "More of a gentleman's agreement."

"You are not a gentleman. Did you gamble something away, me? Charles is a cheat. You should know that fact."

"I did not gamble with Charles but his father, Henry."

Storm sat on the chair in front of her father's desk in an effort to calm her escalating emotions. "Stop skirting the question, Bradford. Tell me the truth and not one lie."

Bradford grinned again. "A few days ago, Storm, I borrowed some money from Henry to escape a debt. I'd placed too much money on a horse race and lost. I was sure the beast would win."

"But he didn't. Was he a horse from your stables?"

"You told me he was the best. That he would win every race. It's your fault."

The facts became clearer. "You bet on Fiacre. He is not ready to race. When I spoke of him, I spoke of his future. Did you enter him against my wishes?" She held her breath, searching for an inner calm but found nothing remotely similar to tranquility.

Bradford cleared his throat then leaned back, folding his hands in front of him. "Henry wants his money, and I do not have that much. I lost a small fortune. Now he wants me to settle. But the real problem stems

4

back over fifteen years. I've owed him money and interest on what was borrowed."

"Settle?" Storm questioned. "What does that mean?"

"The translation is simple. He gave me a choice, the cash or..."

"Or agree to marry me off to his son," Storm finished, the despicable reality of the situation finally out in the open.

"Yes."

"You hate me that much, Bradford? Surely Mr. Robertson knows how I—no, how every girl in the town feels about his son."

"He doesn't care anymore than I do. Charles has told him how much he adores you and can't live without you. That's enough for Henry, and if I had a son, I would give him whatever he wished for."

"That sounds like obsession, not love. Do you know why Charles left last year?" The hair on the back of her neck stood on end.

"Not really," Henry said, "he was looking for adventure. Quite respectable for a young man."

"He...yes, I suppose it is acceptable for the male to find adventure." She knew what had happened and she'd agreed not to tell anyone, but Charles had forced her best friend and an illegitimate child had resulted from his action. He left to allow things to cool down, but now that he'd returned he was causing more trouble.

"Tell me if I'm wrong. You have signed an agreement with Henry Robertson that states he will forgive the debt if I marry Charles." Her father was worse than she'd thought. How could a father do that to a daughter?

Bradford grinned. "You are very bright for a girl. It's that or turn the stables over to him."

"Fine," Storm said, "then we will do just that."

"Good."

"We will hand over the stables. He can have them. He won't know what to do with them but that's his problem."

Bradford rose, his body quivering in anger. His hands fisted on the desktop. "You are a selfish bitch just like your mother. The stable and the brewery are all we have. If I turn the horses over to Robertson, I'll have nothing."

"What about the brewery?"

"The funds are controlled by my brother Tenley. I couldn't sell my interest even if I wanted. As the eldest, Tenley controls everything."

"Oh, you might have to sell the house?"

"You would be on the streets."

"I would find someway to support myself. I'm young and smart. I'll be fine." Her bravado was just her way of covering up the real fact. Other than begging on the streets, she didn't know how she'd survive.

Bradford's lips thinned when he glared at her. "You can't do that! I've arranged a fine marriage for you to one of the richest young men in these parts, next to Hadden Johnston."

"Charles is an ogre and the most odious creature I've ever met." Storm knew her arguments were not heard. Bradford's mind was made up, and she'd have to figure some way out of this situation or she was well on her way to becoming Mrs. Charles Robertson.

"If you won't do it to improve yourself and your status in the community then do it for me. I'm bound to honor the contract, and I know you don't want to lose the animals. Your selfishness will dishonor me. I don't think I could live with the shame."

Storm's fingers dug into the armrests on her chair. She tried to keep from screaming at her father. In a tight, controlled voice, she said, "I'm selfish? You accuse me when you fathered so many children on my mother, wishing for a son, that she died in childbirth. How dare you speak of selfishness? I did not gamble all my fortune on a horse and borrow money from Henry Robertson. I will not be bartered so you can pay him the money owed. I don't care if you sell the stable, sell the house, or sell your soul to the devil himself, but I will not marry Charles Robertson."

~ * ~

When anyone asked Storm to keep a secret, her lips were closed tight, but this had gone on far too long. Ella needed to step up and tell the world what Charles had done. But that wasn't going to happen. They were the best of friends but opposite in every way. This time Storm needed someone to listen to her woes. And it was this very difference that always prompted Storm, at every crisis, to turn to Ella for counsel and advice.

Ella Brummel and her new husband Lawrence lived in a plain brick house situated near the center of the village located near Berwick-upon-Tweed. Although Ella had wanted to live closer to Storm, Lawrence insisted they live close to the port where he kept the books for many of the merchants. Ella had confided that she didn't understand why this was so important to Lawrence, but she refused to question her husband. Ella had been grateful Lawrence had accepted the bastard child into his house. In return Ella would give her husband everything his heart desired.

After leaving her father's study, Storm had raced to the stables, saddled her favorite horse, Fiacre, and with hair flying behind her, sped to her best friend's home. Riding into the Brummel's yard, Storm jumped off the horse, and tossed the reins over the hitching post while muttering a few choice phrases, and praying Lawrence wasn't at home. She needed to talk to Ella about the situation her father had put her in, but it was private and she didn't want to hear Lawrence's opinion. She strode to the front door and pushed it open a crack, poking her head in and calling, "Ella? Ella are you home?"

"In the kitchen, Storm."

Her heart racing, Storm closed the front door and strode through the tiny living room into her friend's kitchen.

"What brings you visiting this afternoon?" Ella's voice was cheerful. She bent over and with a large mitten on her hand, opened the oven and brought out a loaf of freshly baked bread. "I didn't expect you today. I thought you were training the new filly at your stables."

Throwing her hands in the air, she said, "Everything has gone awry." Storm was curt and immediately regretted the way she sounded. "Bradford has done something cruel, and I have to talk to someone. I hope this isn't a bad time."

"I'd love to talk with you. Sammy is taking a nap and should be asleep for at least another hour. So out with it. What's on your mind?"

"Way too much and none of it good. I've a problem and it's the biggest I've ever faced."

"So what has Bradford done?" Ella's smile faded. She took her friend's hands in hers and led her to a chair. "Sit and I'll slice some bread and pour us a cup of tea."

Until Charles had forced Ella, she'd always thought a cup of tea would solve the world's problems. But Storm was too upset to sit. Instead she paced the length of the kitchen then back. With a reluctant sigh, she gave up and pulled out a chair. "What I need is a glass of wine or a shot of the best scotch you have, not a cup of tea."

Ella's eyebrows disappeared into her fringe of bangs. "Bloody hell, Storm, what could be so bad? You know I don't judge and there has been a number of times we've both indulged but..."

"Bradford."

Despite her concerns, Storm couldn't help but remember other times. Mostly the anxiety had come from Ella. But this time she was shocked when Ella rose and went to the sideboard where she pulled out a bottle of scotch and poured her a drink.

"Here you go. Now let's have some girl talk. Tell me what your father has done to upset you this much."

"He sold me." Storm told her friend. "He bartered me and signed a contract with Henry Robertson, selling me into marriage to Charles."

Ella hissed in a lungful of air. "Doesn't he know what Charles is capable of? If he did, he couldn't have done anything so despicable. Didn't you tell him what he did to me?"

"You swore me to secrecy. Besides, Bradford doesn't care about me, only himself. He would tell me that you had wanted it, and Charles couldn't refuse you or your advances."

"That much we both know is true. But why? This seems so sudden."

"It's a long story." Storm downed the scotch in a gulp, grimacing at the fire shooting through her insides. She slapped the glass on the table and poured herself another drink. "It seems Bradford entered one of our horses and bet on him, but the stallion wasn't ready. He wasn't old enough to race." Storm finished the tale, tears sliding down her cheeks. "And he did it to pay off another debt plus interest he accrued years ago."

"Well that's your father. I don't think he will ever change. He's a selfish man, but to betroth you to that scum of the earth, Charles Robertson." Ella paused, then, "You need to tell him."

"No." He wouldn't believe me and even if he thought there was a grain of truth in the story about you and Charles, his wishes would still come first on his agenda. I'm a female and can be used in anyway he pleases. He's proved many times what he thinks of women."

Ella gazed out the window for a moment, sucking her bottom lip beneath her teeth. "You know, Storm," she began, "he has a point. Not with Charles Robertson but with someone else. Wouldn't you like to be married and have children?"

"Not really...maybe if I loved that someone."

"You are wed to your horses and now you are about to lose them. What will you do? How will you take care of yourself?"

"I have thought about that very thing. I will go to London then on to America. Ravyn will take me in and give me a home."

"That would be running and that's not you. Honey, this is your home. I understand you're afraid, but I know you and you are determined and courageous. I've never seen you hide from adversity. You stand up and fight."

Ella was her supporter, but could she reveal Ella's secret to the world? No, she could not but maybe Ella could. "You said earlier that I should tell Bradford what happened to you. Did you mean it?"

Ella's face drained of color but she stiffened. "Yes, Lawrence knows the truth, but I don't believe he wants the entire village to learn of it. Telling your father would be a wild card."

"Charles would be dishonored, and his father would know him for the reprobate he is."

"Yes, yes..."

Looking at Ella's face, the lines of worry and despair etched across her forehead, Storm understood the secret had to be kept. She could not infringe on Ella's happiness. "I'll figure out another way around this. No matter what Bradford says or does, I won't marry Charles."

"I'm asking too much. I'm just as selfish as your father."

"No you are not. You have your family to think about, and they should come first. I feel better now just talking to you."

This time Ella poured herself a shot and Storm her third. They both downed the drink in one gulp. After a huge sigh, she said, "You have to tell Bradford everything. I will speak to Lawrence and if anyone would understand, he would. He's told me more than once how mean and despicable Charles is when he drinks. He would abuse you and cheat on you. Nothing in this world is worth that kind of pain. Your life would be a miserable one, and I won't have my dearest friend undergoing a lifetime of sorrow and misery."

"I can't do that. I won't lower myself to discuss something so...so private with him. Even if I did, he wouldn't believe me. As I said before, he wouldn't care. The debt is all important to him."

"But Storm you have no choice."

"No," Storm repeated. "When you told me about what Charles had done to you, you made me give my word I wouldn't speak of it to anyone. I feel like I betrayed you just thinking about telling Bradford. I don't know what Bradford would do with the information. Even if he went straight to Charles, you know the man would deny it, and I know who Bradford would believe. "

"What are you going to do?"

"I don't know yet," Storm said. "I thought maybe you had a better plan than running to London or the United States.

"You know," Ella said, tapping her glass on the table, slanting her gaze to the ceiling then back to Storm. "I just might."

Storm inhaled a breath of air, her nerves shattering while she waited for Ella's idea.

"What you need is to marry someone, and I'm not telling you that because I've found wedded bliss with Lawrence. You need to do this before Charles returns from his hunting trip. When will he be back?"

"I have no idea but that's not the answer to my problem. I don't want to marry anyone. I just want to go on running the stables."

"You and I both know that won't be possible, not unless you can find the money to pay back the debt and the only way to do that is to marry the wealthiest man in this part of the country."

Ella rose and for several minutes paced the length of her kitchen. She halted in midstride, her eyes lighting with excitement. "I've got it. You can marry Hadden Johnston.

Storm leaned back in her chair and laughed until tears ran down her eyes. "That's the most foolish idea I've ever heard. Hadden doesn't want to marry any more than I do. Besides he's always gone. He sails with his merchant ships. We see him in town every six months or so."

"Don't you see? That's perfect. He would be at sea, and you would be home in the stables doing what you love. You'd never stomp on each other's toes." She clapped her hands together. "What do you think?"

"Really? You're serious about this aren't you? You've lost your mind, is what I think."

"This calls for another drink." Ella sat down and poured them each another shot of Scotch. "My dearest friend, he's not only the answer to your problem, he's the perfect answer."

"At this rate I'm not going to be able to ride home." Storm downed her drink anyway then set the small glass on the table.

"Fiacre knows the way home."

"I might have to rely on that. Your scheme while worthy has too many flaws. Mr. Johnston is not going to suddenly ask me to marry him. Why on earth would he want too?"

"Well that is exactly what we are going to have to figure out."

"You are aware that every girl of marriageable age is after him. I don't stand a chance. And besides no one has received so much as an invitation to a dance, much less a wedding ring."

"That doesn't matter." Ella slanted her a huge grin. "It just doesn't make any difference what so ever. We can figure out some way to pique his interest."

"Ella," Storm said as if speaking to a stubborn child. "Hadden Johnston does not want to get married and neither do I."

"I understand all that. It's what makes this plan so flawless. The two of you could come up with some kind of agreement. You know, a marriage of convenience." She put a finger to her lips. "He doesn't want all that female attention, and you need someone to pay your debt. It's a bargain neither of you can deny."

"You've gone crazy, Ella. He would never agree to something so insane. He would never agree to this devil's bargain."

"He might, if we, if you laid out your plan in a way he couldn't refuse." Her eyes sparkled to life in a way Storm had never seen them.

"Ella, no."

"Storm, yes. All we have to do is figure out how to lay out our plan so Hadden Johnston is in agreement. After we do that, you can go to him and present the idea."

"Idea? It's more like a proposition which doesn't sound so good. I refuse to blackmail him."

Ella planted her hands on her hips and glared at Storm. "Would you please stop seeing something bad in every thought I have. I'm trying to help you out of a terrible place and I never said blackmail."

"I know you are," Storm gave her best friend a huge hug, "and I appreciate you more than I can ever say. But Ella, this idea or proposition is so ridiculous I can't take it seriously."

"I really think you should, or you're going to find yourself walking down the aisle with Charles Robertson before you have time to blink an eye. Now I know you're adamant that you won't do it, but I think in this matter Bradford has the upper hand."

"I know I would lose everything. But wouldn't that be better than a life with Charles?" Storm inhaled a deep breath.

"Do you want to live in poverty?"

"No, but the Duchess or Ravyn would take me in."

"You wouldn't have your horses," Ella countered.

"Better than having Charles for a husband. I've got some serious thinking on my plate. So what if I did talk to the elusive Mr. Johnston? And he agreed. What then? That still isn't going to solve the problem of paying Henry back. We would still lose the stables, so what's the point?"

Ella paused for a moment, looking a bit sheepish, then said, "I think after a woman gets married, her debts become her husband's responsibility. So Mr. Johnston would probably be legally bound to pay Mr. Robertson."

"Ella!" Storm was stunned by her friend's despicable plan. "That's horrid. I can't believe you'd think this let alone suggest it. I would never do that to Hadden Johnston. I don't even know the man, except from doing business with him, and he's never been anything but honest and polite with me. I couldn't possibly deceive him like that."

Ella waved a dismissive hand. "Nonsense. We'd figure out some way to pay him back."

"How?"

"I don't know. Let him have your best racing stallion and all of that horse's colts to do with as he pleases. He could keep them for himself to ride or he could train them to race."

Storm's eyes narrowed as she thought about all of the possibilities. "You might be on to something. I don't think he'd want to ride. I've heard he doesn't like horses, but racing them. If the horse wins, I could have the debt paid off in no time, and I wouldn't lose the stables and my beloved horses either."

"Right," Ella nodded excitedly. "Everybody wins. You get to keep the stables and you're safe from Charles Robertson, and Hadden Johnston saves a fortune. And, you can also use the shipping contract he has with the Graham brewery to further cement the deal."

"Well, in the first place he hasn't lost anything. So that brings me back to the beginning. Why don't I just go to Mr. Johnston with the proposition that he pay off my debt and receive the winnings from the races and the colts that are sired and see what he says? If he accepts, there is no reason for marriage."

"Because that won't save you from Charles," Ella countered. "You know what that man is like. He's crazy-insane. If Henry thinks Charles wants you, he won't give up. What you need is protection only a man like Hadden Johnston can give you. No, you need to marry Mr. Johnston."

"Well, I still don't think Mr. Johnston will agree to something quite so preposterous. How on earth would I go about approaching him?"

"Play on his sympathies. You just said the two of you have a good business relationship, which means he likes you. Tell him about the deal you're willing to offer him, and if he argues, confess you're being threatened by Charles and your father. But don't call your father, Bradford. That will not do at all. Hadden despises Charles, so he'll most likely take pity on you."

"Why does Mr. Johnston hate Charles?"

"Ah, a couple of years ago a cousin of his came to visit and there was some trouble between Mr. Hadden and Charles over her."

"Indeed, Charles asked her to go buggy riding. Hadden allowed her to go, but something must have happened, because afterward, Mr. Johnston challenged Charles to a duel. Of course that's no longer legal, but Charles agreed then turned and fired at Mr. Johnston before the count of ten. Charles missed and Mr. Johnston was gentleman enough to shoot him in the arm when he could have killed him."

"I remember. Did the Robertson's press charges?"

"And have Charles' cowardice come to light? No, they didn't. But there were enough people in attendance that the truth could not be hidden for long."

"Knowing what I know now, I hate to think what Charles might have said or done during that buggy ride," Ella said.

"Anyway, knowing how he feels about Charles, if you tell him you're being forced into marriage with him, he just might agree to help."

"Or he could kick me out."

"You have nothing to lose. The worst he can do is say no."

"If he told me no, I would just be back where I am now. I really don't want to leave my home and my friends or my sisters. What if he laughs in my face?"

"He won't." Ella pushed away from the counter and gave Storm a reassuring hug. "After all, he can't be all bad. He did challenge Charles to a duel, and he didn't kill him when he had the chance."

Chapter Two

"Who's that?"

Hadden Johnston looked up from the golf ball he was about to hit then tipped back his cap. He frowned, staring down the fairway, unable to tell who was walking toward them. Her long legs showcased in the riding trousers she wore. The golf club she carried appeared to be more of a weapon than a piece of sporting equipment.

"I don't know, Garret. Can't tell from this far away." Hadden shielded his eyes with his hand in hopes of rectifying the mystery.

"Who ever she is, it looks as if the girl means business." His ball boy Garrett pointed out.

"Storm Graham?" Hadden's surprise was apparent. "What is she doing out here?"

"Does she want to play golf with you? I'm not carrying her bag," Garret said with an indignant air about him.

"She doesn't seem to have one—a bag." Hadden laughed, amused by Garret's assessment of the tomboyish and impulsive Miss Storm. "We'll have to ask her why she's here. Despite the fact she's carrying a club, I doubt if golf is the reason."

With a nod, the pair waited for Storm to catch up to them.

"Whew that was quite a long ways to walk." Storm wiped her forehead with the back of her hand. A few moments later, she inhaled a long and deep breath of air then smiled at the men.

Impressed by her smile and her fortitude, Hadden motioned to the ball that was still sitting on the ground, giving her a cheeky grin. "You're supposed to play the course not just walk it."

"Oh I know that, but I don't know how to play. I thought I should carry a club in case anyone questioned me. I could always pretend I know what I'm doing." She laughed and it sounded like a breath of fresh air.

"Women don't belong on the fairway," Garret said, seeming rather annoyed with her. "They're supposed to be at home, cooking and cleaning."

"What?" Hadden was astounded by Garret's assessment.

Storm drew in a sharp breath as she gazed up at Hadden. Although she'd met him before, his size and amazing good looks never failed to awe her. He didn't fall short of the mark now.

Bronzed. That's the only word she could think of to describe him. Bronzed skin, bronzed hair, bronzed eyes and a body so large and muscular that even the most contented of wives secretly speculated about what he would look like with his shirt off. No man should look that good in buckskins and a white shirt. Her eyes roved his frame. What on earth was she doing on this fairway about to ask this perfect male specimen to marry her?

She coughed to gain a moment's time and maybe some courage too, not at all sure this was such a good idea. Second, third and fourth thoughts assailed her, knowing she should have turned and run without causing herself more humiliation and that was exactly what she should have done.

All he can do is tell me no.

Fiacre had loved the wild ride to the golf course. When she'd entered the stables, he'd known he was about to get some much-needed exercise. And when she'd saddled him, he'd pranced and shook his head in anticipation. Before she'd tied him to the hitching post, she'd walked him around the yard. The time she'd spent with her favorite horse had been as much fun for her as it was for him.

Days had passed since her conversation with Ella before she'd summoned the courage to meet with Mr. Johnston, and when she'd first made her way to the docks and inquired about him, his men had told her he wasn't on board the ship then they'd quietly gone back to work.

She'd had to persevere and demand someone tell her where he was. After fifteen minutes of question and answer, one sailor took pity on her and gave her directions to find him.

Now she stood in front of Mr. Johnston without the privacy she needed for this delicate venture. And she still wasn't sure she could go through with the crazy plan her friend had come up with.

"What brings you here, Miss Graham?" He squinted into the bright summer sunshine as he nonchalantly leaned on his golf club. "Seems a strange place to find a lady such as yourself."

"Well, yes, you've got that right." She pushed an escaped lock of hair behind her ear, mesmerized by the way the sun danced highlights on his thick dark hair. She cocked her head sideways, and he stared at her.

"What can I do for you?" he persisted.

His whiskey-colored eyes and deep, rich voice made her feel as if she couldn't draw a steady breath. "I need to talk to you about something. Something very important and private." She slanted Garret a look she hoped would tell him he should leave them alone.

Hadden nodded, but when Storm looked away unable to string together two coherent words let alone a few sentences, his expression became more inquiring."

Hadden looked down the fairway before glancing at Storm. "Is something wrong at the brewery?"

"No." Why was he bringing up the brewery? She frowned at Garret when he wouldn't take her less than subtle hint. "Could we have some privacy? I know this isn't what you had in mind when you came here to play." She spread her arms and gestured. "But this is important, and I won't take much time."

Hadden sent a dubious look Garret's way. The man shrugged before sauntering toward the trees on the left side of the fairway. "All right then, we can talk here for a minute."

That was another trouble. She didn't think this would take a minute. "Thank you, Mr. Johnston. You don't know how much I appreciate having a moment of your valuable time."

Turning, he headed to the other side of the fairway and found a large rock to sit on. He gestured for her to do the same. "I feel a bit awkward not knowing why you would ride all the way out here to talk with me. Except for business we barely know each other."

Well she felt pretty awkward too. Storm perched on a rock so she faced him and waited for him to say something else. When he didn't speak, she smoothed the fabric of the riding pants she wore.

"Okay," he grinned. "What do you want to discuss?"

Marry me. Don't ask why. Just say you'll do it.

"I have a business proposal to present to you. One I think could benefit both of us."

Hadden's eyebrows rose a fraction, looking a bit perplexed. "I don't know what I expected you to say, but now you've got me guessing. I think I'm intrigued. So, I'm listening."

Storm drew a deep breath, praying she wouldn't faint or throw up before she managed to say what she'd come to say. "I'm here to offer you my finest racing horse and all his offspring to do with as you please. You could sell them for a profit or hire a trainer and a rider, either way you'd make a clean profit."

A long silence ensued then he stood, walking around a bit then turned back to her, frowning. "Go on."

"That's all, really." Storm was so relieved he hadn't laughed at her that she didn't realize she hadn't stated her terms.

Hadden continued to gaze at her with a wary look in his eyes. "The offer is extremely generous. You understand I don't ride except in cases of emergency. Don't like horses. Care to tell me why you're willing to do this for me. Do I have to kill someone?"

"What? Oh, no, nothing like that. I guess you would like to know why I'm proposing this." The palms of her hands were sweaty so she wiped them on her pants and tried for the courage to finish.

Hadden nodded. "Yes I do."

"Well, I guess, this isn't easy but I need something from you in return." She grimaced while her heart did flip-flops.

"That's not surprising." Hadden smiled. "And what is it you want from me? My first born?"

Storm turned her head, suddenly unable to meet his bronzed gaze. "I need for you to marry me." There, she'd said it, and now he'd say no.

Now she would have to find a way to flee and make her way to London. She knew the Duchess would protect her even if her father would sell her to the highest bidder.

"I don't think I heard right." He shook his head and pretended to clean out his ears.

She looked back, forcing herself to meet his gaze. "I said...I need for you to marry me."

Hadden did the expected. He burst out laughing. When he finished, he said, "Well, Miss Graham, who put you up to this prank? Was it Garret over there? Or my first mate, Perkins? Or perhaps my entire crew?"

When she turned to look, Garret was fiddling with something in the ball bag and didn't seem interested in their conversation.

"Mr. Johnston, I am speaking from the heart. I..."

"It's all right, you can drop the act. I knew Garret was going to do something to get back at me for telling the Widow Brown he was sweet on her, but I never gave him credit for being so original."

"Mr. Johnston," Storm interrupted, dismayed he did not take this matter in a serious light.

"Tell me, Miss Graham, how did Garret ever convince you to go through with this crazy drama?"

"Mr. Johnston, please, I don't know Garret."

Hadden's broad grin faded while he scratched his head for a moment. "This isn't a joke?"

"No, in no way would I think of this lightly." Storm felt the ensuing anger rising from the pit of her stomach. "I assure you. I'm serious. My offer stands if you will marry me. The arrangement could be advantageous for both of us."

"I think I'm going insane. I don't believe this is happening, and I'm willing to forget this conversation if you are." Hadden rose from the rock, looking as uncertain as she felt.

"You're not crazy and I'm dead serious." What could she say to win him to her side? God, she searched her brain for the words but they weren't there.

"Your proposition is ludicrous."

Storm's expression registered a combination of embarrassment and defeat at Hadden's blunt assessment of her offer.

"I'm sorry you feel that way." Giving up, she turned to march down the fairway back to her stables where she could hide. "I'll not take up any more of your time."

"Just a minute."

She stopped midstride, wanting to turn and look at him, afraid to acknowledge he might have second thoughts.

"We could talk. I didn't mean to embarrass you or hurt you. You must have a reason, and I'd like to understand why."

Storm hesitated, knowing he had given her another chance. Slowly she turned, drinking in the air around her as if it were her only lifeline.

With hands clasped tightly together, she made her way back to her rock and sat down.

"All right then, why don't you tell me what this is about."

"There's nothing to tell." Embarrassment settling in the pit of her stomach, Storm suddenly found it impossible to confess the real reason she was trying to bargain with him.

"Really? Now why don't I believe you?" Hadden countered. "So, you're trying to tell me you came up with this harebrained idea just to turn around and tell me it was nothing. Miss Graham, I'm finding contradictions in everything you are saying."

"Yes. I know. But there are extenuating circumstances I don't want to admit to."

"Oh, come on. Do you really expect me to believe that? We don't even know each other. It hardly seems conceivable that you just unexpectedly developed an overwhelming longing for my affection."

This last eloquent statement made Storm look at him in surprise. Well he was right about those two things; they didn't know each other, and she didn't have an overwhelming need for his affection or any one else's.

"Of course you're right. I don't long for your affection." She agreed with him wholeheartedly.

Hadden frowned at her a moment while he rubbed his chin. "I understand now. You're in the family way, aren't you?" His voice had fallen to a soft barely audible level.

"No!" Storm's eyes widened in horror at his outrageous assumption. The skin on the back of her neck prickled, and she felt an urgent need to run.

"And you need a husband quick."

"No. I'm not and I don't. But I do. Oh, bloody hell." She didn't know what to say and knew all her thoughts had turned into gibberish. "Why, in order to be in that condition, a woman has to...and I never would...I never have... Mr. Johnston, that is preposterous. How dare you." Now her hands were fisted. If she were a man she'd hit something, maybe him.

"I'm sorry, Miss Graham. I didn't mean to offend. Look, why don't we stop playing games. This proposition might be easier for me to understand if you tell me the reasons behind it. You've denied being in love with me and in being in the family way. So what is it? Something made you approach me."

Storm gathered in a lungful of air, realizing this was now or never. He was giving her a chance, and once again she reminded herself all he could do was say no. She tried to figure out how much of this sordid tale she should confide. She couldn't tell him about the debt her father owed. No, she thought better of that and decided just to tell him about Charles and the forced marriage.

"All right, I'll tell you why I'm here."

"That would be nice." Hadden directed his full attention to her, his cheeky grin returning.

She licked her lips and swallowed, trying to force moisture into her throat. "I need your protection. For reasons which I am not at liberty to discuss, my father contracted with Henry Robertson to marry me to his son, Charles. It's signed and I have no recourse but to honor it. But I loathe the man and don't want to marry him."

Hearing the sound of Hadden's sharply indrawn breath, Storm

knew she'd hit a nerve. "I don't want to marry him," she repeated.

"I can certainly understand that. But what do I have to do with all this?"

Storm cleared her parched throat then forced her gaze upward until she looked directly at him. "The contract my father signed is binding, and the only way I can think to escape it is to marry someone else before Charles returns from his hunting trip."

"So you decided I'm the one? How did you come up with me?"

Storm nodded, not wanting to answer his second question.

"How?" he persisted.

"Because I didn't think you wanted to get married, and neither do I. I thought you and I could come to an agreement where we would be married in name only. I would be free of Charles, and you would turn a profit by being able to earn the winnings from my horses. I can assure you there won't be any...entanglements."

"You're wrong, Miss Graham. There are always entanglements."

"I promise you, there won't be. Besides, think of the benefits. This plan could make you very rich."

"I'm already damn rich, Miss Graham. But you're right about one thing. I don't want to get married. In name only or any other way."

Storm's heart sank. "So you won't consider my offer?"

"I'm sorry, but it's out of the question. I'm flattered you thought of me, though."

"Well don't be," she retorted so angry she saw red flashes in front of her. "The only reason I thought of you is that you're the one man in town powerful enough to intimidate the Robertsons. So if you're entertaining the misconception that I came to you because I was attracted to you, you're deluding yourself."

Hadden's face reddened and for the longest time he stared at her. She saw his hands clasp into tight fists then suddenly he was relaxed as if no emotion had just swept through him. "I think we've said everything that needed saying. Good day, Miss Graham."

Her nerves sizzling with anger and humiliation, Storm bolted from the rock and fled down the fairway.

~ * ~

"He told you no? How dare he?" They sat in Ella's kitchen.

"Yes." Storm nodded, wondering what she would do next. She'd counted out the money she'd hid in the barn. One thousand pounds would take her to London and the Duchess, but she didn't want to leave. And she couldn't stay, not if it meant marrying Charles. What if Charles came after her?"

Ella sighed, taking a sip from her tea then setting the cup on the table. "I'm sorry, Storm. I feel guilty for suggesting you talk to him. He's made it clear to everyone he doesn't want a wife. Yet I did think he might look kindly on your proposition."

Storm let out a squeaky laugh. "He didn't. Just wanted to get back to his golf game. Words of marriage put a horrified look on his face. I don't think he likes women."

"That's odd. He was engaged once."

"He was? When?"

"Five or six years ago. You never heard? Well, maybe you didn't listen to gossip. All you've ever cared about were your horses."

"He was really engaged. That must have been something. What was her name?"

"Elizabeth...don't remember her last name. They broke it off one month before the wedding, but he never told anyone why. She left and went to London. I haven't seen her since."

"You really don't know why?" Storm found her curiosity was growing.

"Nope. But it must have been pretty serious. He'd fallen so head over heels in love with her that he was building a house for her. When she left, he just quit so it's half built and some say an eyesore. While others say it's a testament that men shouldn't get married let alone engaged."

"That half-built house a quarter mile out of town? It's gorgeous and the small lake nearby is a favorite swimming hole."

"Yes. And don't you get caught swimming there."

"If he never goes to the house, he'll never see me swimming. I don't even think he'd care."

"Well, as I said, something terrible must have happened between him and Elizabeth, and after what you said about his reaction to your proposal, it seems as if he isn't over it yet."

Storm shrugged her shoulders, staring pensively out the window. "So what do I do next?"

"I don't know, honey, but I'm sure if we put our heads together we can come up with another plan."

"What would happen if I just said no? A woman can still do that. I don't have to walk down the aisle if I don't want to."

"You would lose the stables and your favorite horses."

"I know it's worth the price. If I have to pay it, I will, I just wish there was another way out."

"You could always tell Charles you can't get married because you have to take care of your father."

"What? He doesn't need anyone to take care of him. Besides, that's the last thing I would do, and everyone who knows me knows that for the truth."

"Honey, is it the truth? He is still your father no matter what you think of him. And you have a good heart. At the very least the ploy would give you time to think of an alternative."

"If only Hadden had agreed."

"You know, you almost sound as if you'd enjoy being his wife."

"Oh, Ella, don't be absurd. Simply put, he is convenient. Nothing else." But somehow the thought seemed to grow sweeter with every second. He was bewitchingly handsome.

"Of course," Ella grinned, "convenient, and drop dead gorgeous, and rich as Midas."

"And most assuredly not in the market for a wife."

"Do you think you might be giving up to quickly? Maybe all you need to do is think of another way to approach him. Perhaps you could give him a bit more incentive. Bring up something about the shipping contracts the Graham's have with him."

"Why?" Storm threw her hands out in exasperation. "What would you have me do?" Trick him, threaten him, blackmail him? I keep the books for the brewery, but I don't have authority to do anything."

"Of course not, but there has to be another way to convince him to agree. Every man has his weakness. We just have to discover Mr. Johnston's."

Chapter Three

"I think someone should teach her a few manners. Didn't her father ever tell her she shouldn't be so brazen?" Hadden slammed his glass on the wooden table in front of him. His anger simmered deep inside. He liked the girl but, bloody hell, he didn't understand why she felt she had to ask him to marry her.

Perkins, his first mate, let out a belly roll of laughter. "If I weren't married to the sea, I might take her up on her offer myself. She's a pretty little thing, delicate as a flower, and I bet she smells sweet as one."

Hadden snorted and downed a shot of whiskey before pouring both of them another. "I tell you, I do feel a bit sorry for her. No one should be forced to wed Charles Robertson. But she's not going to find the answer to her predicament with me."

Hadden knew what kind of person Charles was, and he knew Charles had played a hand in Ella's shame. But he didn't want to marry anyone he didn't love. He couldn't go through that shit again. Well he hadn't been married, but he'd fallen in love. Bloody hell, he'd been so damn stupid. He didn't believe in love, only shackles and chains. Nothing she could say or do would force him into a loveless marriage.

"Then step up and do the right thing. She's helpless in a man's world. If you don't help her, I'll bet Robertson has her with child the night they wed. And he'll probably be knocking at her door the night after she gives birth." Perkins sipped the whiskey, eyeing Hadden over the rim of the glass.

"From what I've heard it wouldn't be much different than what her father did to her mother." Hadden had never cared for Bradford Graham. He was a pompous ass, thinking he was better than anyone else.

In London he'd run into many men just like Bradford.

"I don't think you have a choice, man." Perkins downed his drink.

"There's a choice in everything. It's just that this one isn't simple. I'm damned if I say yes, and she's damned if I tell her no." Perkins was right. She was beautiful, her long dark hair begged for a man's hands, and her lips, God but her lips were full and looked so soft.

"You already told her no," Perkins reminded him while he poured another shot.

"If I needed to avoid her, I could always change my plans and leave port when the *Wind Star* sails." He loved the sea, always had. The endless miles of rolling blue-grey water had a way of easing his mind and calming his nerves. He'd been fifteen years old when he'd first sailed. The merchant vessel had gone to India and he'd never felt more alive when the ship dipped in the swells and picked up speed when the sails caught the wind. On that first voyage he'd vowed he'd own a fleet of ships. And now he did.

"You're not the type to run and hide. Why would you flee a tiny little slip of a girl who's the prettiest little lass in this village?"

"Because I don't want to marry anyone." Hadden ran his hands across his face and closed his eyes. He couldn't stop thinking about Storm and the look she gave him when he'd thoroughly humiliated her.

Perkins grinned. "Have a good day at golf?"

"What? Oh, no..."

"That's what I heard. Worst score of your life. Thinking about wedded bliss can do that to a good game of golf. Well, we're sailing on the morning tide, and I need my beauty sleep. You best be off the ship when the tide rolls in or you won't have a choice."

Hadden nodded at his friend before downing another drink. He knew he wasn't going to like waking up tomorrow morning. "Going home then. Don't need to escape yet."

Sitting back in his chair, hands folded across his lap, he thought back. His fiancée was beautiful but that was about the only good thing he could say about Elizabeth. She'd flirted with him, winked and blushed, pulling him into her web of deceit and treachery. Remembering those first

27

days of their courtship, he admitted he'd been easy prey.

They'd taken a trip to Edinburgh. He'd found the best cafes, and she'd spent money as if it grew on trees, purchasing dresses and bonnets as if they were free. She had a reason for every purchase, telling him how much she needed it and how she had to be presentable when she became Mrs. Hadden Johnston.

At the time it didn't matter. He would have willingly given her just about everything she asked for if she'd loved him. But as he found out, she only loved herself and she was a selfish bitch. He thanked the lucky star he'd been born under that he'd found out before they'd wed.

One of the sailors poked his head inside the cabin. "Perkins told me to look out for you. Doesn't think you want to be sailin' with us. Time for you to go home, Captain."

"Thanks." Hadden downed the shot of whiskey that had been sitting on the table since his first mate had left. "What time is it?"

"'Bout 2 AM."

"Guess I should be going home." Hadden rose on shaky legs, steadying himself on the table. "Guess I had more to drink than I thought."

"Want me to walk you home, boss?"

"Like a little girl?" Hadden grimaced. "No, I haven't had that much, and I don't have very far to go." He didn't want a nursemaid walking him home because he couldn't hold his liquor. He steadied himself on the chair then stepped forward. The room whirled in a blur. He closed his eyes and waited for the sensation to pass. When he opened them, the floor seemed calmer.

The sailor stared at him as if he'd lost his mind. "All right then, see ya when we get back." The man ducked from the doorway, and Hadden was alone with his reminiscing.

One more for the road—he looked at the bottle before he poured another drink. He knew he should quit drinking and walk the short distance to his little cottage near the docks. But he couldn't stop the wheels from turning in his brain.

Touching the tiny scar on the corner of his right eye, pain shot through him as well as the memories. The night had been cold, very cold, and sleet fell sideways to the earth. He'd pulled his coat closed and hurried down the streets. Taking a short cut through an alley, he'd run into a gang of men.

When he saw them, he'd turned but he didn't get away without a fight. Once they discovered he was poorer than they were, the men left him with a gash on his face but alive. That was in the alleys of London and what seemed a lifetime ago.

There had been other times, some he remembered fondly. He'd been a daredevil and hot blooded. He'd spent his youth on board ship, and he found a girl in every port. Wisely he'd stayed away from the brothels, but he knew he'd left many broken hearts behind. He wasn't proud of those moments in his life, and he'd prayed he hadn't left a child as well.

He knew what it was like to grow up without a parent. After his mother died, his father led a hollow life. Hadden guessed William, his dad, must have loved her very much because he never recovered from Sara's death. When he gazed at his son, he looked at him with vacant eyes.

Hadden laughed. He'd really grown up without either parent. When he'd broached the subject of children with Elizabeth, she'd avoided the topic or changed the conversation to something about herself. Finally, she'd told him she didn't want children because it would ruin her figure.

Perkins poked his head through the door again. "Boss?"

"Yeah, I'm going." He rose from the chair not remembering when he'd sat down, and with a few strides was on the ship's deck. Wind blew in from the ocean, cold and fresh. Waves washed against the pilings while the ship rose and dipped with each new surge. Leaning against the railing, he stared at the sea and the emptiness to the east. Perhaps he could run from his past, hideaway and forget about living, really living.

He didn't want to let what happened between Elizabeth and himself mold the rest of his life. The parallel between this episode and how he reacted to it was too much like his father. He didn't want his jaded emotions to ruin his future happiness.

The thought shook him to the core. Bloody hell, he meant to change his life. He scruffed his hair away from his face as the night began to lighten. A star hung low in the sky, twinkling its last until night would descend again.

His men had started working, readying the ship to sail. He strode down the gangplank, making his way home. By the time he reached his cabin, it would be time to get up. He laughed again, feeling more tired than he'd ever felt before.

What had been the breaking point? He'd thought himself so in love with Elizabeth. Yet he didn't have to think on it very much. The fact she didn't want a family had been his breaking point. Yet without a wife, he was not going to have children anytime soon. And he wanted a whole passel of children to love and share his life with.

Even though he'd longed for a family, he knew he'd never survive a life with a woman as selfish as Elizabeth. He sometimes wondered what happened to her. She'd left the day after their breakup and never returned. He hadn't seen her in over five years.

He had wanted to get married. He longed for a real home, with a wife and children to love. It was a dream he had secretly held for a long time—and one Elizabeth had forever ended with her sneered epithets that the only reason any woman would want a man so crude as Hadden Johnston was his money.

Hadden pulled himself out of his melancholic reverie and slammed the door to his cabin. "The damn money," he growled. "It's more of a curse than a gift." He never thought of that possibility when he'd first set out to make his fortune. All he'd known then was having money had to be better than being poor.

He strode through the tiny living room and pulled back the curtain to his bedroom. Having drunk far more than was his usual habit, he sat down on the bed to pull his boots off. He didn't think he'd bother undressing, but he wanted his damn boots on the floor not on his feet.

With great effort, he finally managed to remove his shoes and with a sigh of relief he leaned back on the headboard. Closing his eyes seemed reasonable but sleep was elusive. While thoughts swirled and danced in his mind, he began to think a bit more clearly.

After several minutes of staring at the ceiling, he closed his eyes again and let his foggy mind drift back to this afternoon's tumultuous encounter with Storm Graham.

He recalled watching her cheeks redden with embarrassment as she hedged her way through their conversation until she finally spoke what was on her mind. Bloody hell but she was beautiful. So tiny and curvy, it made a man ache just to gaze on her. And that hair—that dark, soft, shiny hair. What would it feel like to thread his fingers through its silky thickness or bury his nose in its fragrant depths?

To Hadden's extreme annoyance, he felt his cock stir to life. With a grunt, he turned over on his side, giving his pillow an irritated punch. "You should never drink whiskey on an empty stomach, Johnston," he chastised. "It always makes you horny."

Desperately, he tried to concentrate on tomorrow's work. Not only was one of his ships leaving port, had left port, another should arrive on the evening tide and if not tonight then tomorrow. He needed to arrange the marketing of the goods as well as the unloading. After several minutes he gave up the struggle and rose to his feet. Unbuttoning his tight trousers, he pulled them off, releasing his stiff cock from their painful confines.

Looking down at his jutting arousal, he muttered, "Look at you, you damn fool. You're like a sixteen-year-old kid. This is exactly why you can't consider marrying her. Look what just thinking about her has done to you. Why with that face and that body, you'd be addicted to her so fast you'd never get any work done. Just forget her and let her marry Robertson, before you make yourself crazier than you already are."

With a determined jerk of his head, he lay down and slammed his eyes shut. But it was to no avail. The vision of Storm as she had looked that day with the light shining on her hair was like a fire in his blood, one he couldn't extinguish.

~ * ~

A torrid sun beat down on the tiny funeral party. Hadden swiped sweat from his brow, wondering if everyone else was as uncomfortable as he was. Everyone had thought Bradford Graham was wealthy and some said influential but he knew differently now that Storm had confronted him with the marriage proposal.

"Yea, though I walk through the valley of the shadow of death, I will fear no evil..."

He'd hated that psalm. It reminded him of his mother's funeral when he'd been a little boy. He'd missed her and cried copious tears not really understanding what had happened.

All he'd known then was what his father had told him. "Son, get used to it, you're never going to see her again."

His gaze drifted away from the coffin with the meager bouquet of flowers resting on it and settled on the small, black-clad figures of Storm Graham and her sisters Fayth and Larena. Ella and Lawrence Brummel stood nearby.

Fayth and Larena were openly weeping, dabbing at their eyes with small linen handkerchiefs and leaning on each other. Storm however, was stoic, her beautiful face set and emotionless, betraying none of the crushing grief that must surely be weighing her down.

Hadden kept his head down in respect to the solemn ceremony going on around him, but secretly he was watching Storm's every move. She looked so tiny, so fragile and alone, standing a little apart from her sisters.

What must she be thinking now that Bradford Graham has passed? Her father's death had been a shock, despite the fact everyone had known he suffered from a heart condition. For the past several years, he'd not been seen around town except on rare occasions and on those times it was usually at the track.

Hadden's furtive gaze fell on Charles Robertson, who was standing behind Storm. The thought of Storm marrying Charles sent a shiver snaking down his spine. In the month since Storm had approached him on the golf course with her request that he marry her, Hadden had heard many rumors concerning her impending nuptials. For the first several weeks after their confrontation, he had considered trying to intervene in some way, but as time passed and he had heard nothing more from her, her dilemma had slipped to the back of his mind.

For the past month he'd been completely immersed in business with little time for thought. Ships had come and gone almost weekly and the marketing and restocking of ships had consumed his time.

Now when he watched Charles hover over Storm, he regretted his self-absorption with his ventures. He could have checked on her, seen how she was holding up, maybe even intervened and helped her work out the details of the contract to her benefit.

"Ashes to ashes, dust to dust" and a shovel full of dirt hit the lowered coffin. Suddenly the immediacy of her plight again came to the forefront of his mind.

At some point he'd heard rumors that the marriage to Charles had been postponed since Storm had the responsibility of her father's care. He'd also heard she'd refused to marry Charles, vowing steadfastly that she'd rather die. But Bradford was dead now, and she had no one's protection.

She asked for my protection.

He thumped himself in the head, reminding himself it wasn't his business. "She's a grown woman who can take care of herself." Still, as he glanced at her forlorn figure, he couldn't deny the feelings of sympathy that welled up inside. The thought of her in bed with Charles brought bile to his throat.

His attention was drawn back to the here and now as the minister closed his prayer book and said, "Will you please join me now in the Lord's Prayer?"

When the prayer was completed, the cleric added, "You are all invited to attend a reception at the Bradford home when our service here concludes."

As Hadden started to leave, he noticed Charles had stepped forward and solicitously offered Storm his arm, which, after a slight hesitation, she reluctantly accepted. Hadden's eyebrows rose in reaction to her obvious aversion to Robertson's possessive gesture, and for a brief second he thought about stepping forward to join them. He changed his mind, telling himself it wasn't his place. The last thing he needed to do was give Storm the idea he wished to become involved. With a slight shrug, he turned away and strode from the cemetery.

"Mr. Johnston?"

Hadden turned to see Ella Brummel racing after him with her skirts hiked. Turning and walking towards her, he said, "Mrs. Brummel?"

"Are you coming to the reception? I'm sure Miss Graham would love to have you there."

"I had not thought to attend. I have business to take care of and..."

"Please, I would appreciate it, and I'm sure Storm would also. It would mean a great deal to everyone. And you can always take care of business later. What's more important?"

"All right." He wasn't entirely sure why Ella Brummel would make a point of singling him out, but she was right, business could wait. "I can stop by for a little while and pay my respects."

"Thank you so much." She cast him a wan smile then turned away and stepped into the waiting carriage. After seating herself, she looked out the window. "See you there, Mr. Johnston."

"Yes," Hadden nodded, cursing the fact he was now going to give up the latter part of his afternoon. He hated funerals and the following receptions. But Ella's request had been so heartfelt that he couldn't bring himself to say no.

Turning to look back at the departing people, he paused to watch Charles Robertson assist Storm into his plush carriage. The look of distaste on Storm's face gave Hadden one more reason to attend the reception.

A few minutes later, Hadden entered the large Graham home. The size of the crowd who had gathered was not indicative of the man's position in town but more suitable to the man's condescending demeanor. Not many of the residents of this small town liked Graham Bradford. Rumors about Graham and how he'd treated his wife had run rampant after Ada's death. Again this wasn't his business, and it had happened a long time ago.

Thoughts of his mother's funeral assailed him and filled his mind. He remembered the pain and the sorrow and how his father had abandoned him that day. The scene had been so different. He remembered all the people who had crowded into his family's lavish London townhouse. His mother and his father had been loved and respected by their family, friends and business associates. They had all been intent on offering condolences.

It seemed possible some people found comfort in this public outpouring of grief. But he knew from firsthand experience, all he wanted after laying his mother to rest was to curl up in a little ball and cry himself to sleep. He didn't want to talk to anyone or have them pat him on the head or pinch his cheek telling him everything would be all right.

Nothing had been all right for a very long time.

Ten minutes, he told himself, as he took off the jacket he'd worn to the funeral. Right, he'd stay just long enough to shake hands, have a cup of tea and eat a cookie. Then he would get out of here, change his clothes, grab his clubs and play a few holes. Business could wait until the sun went down because he needed to calm his ragged nerves and come to terms with his thoughts about Storm Graham.

Hadden greeted everyone as he walked down the hall to the parlor. He knew most of the townspeople who had attended the funeral. It took almost ten minutes for him to talk to everyone who stopped him. He was used to small talk and greeting people. But most of the time he stayed away from social gatherings, preferring his few friends and the time he spent alone. Hadden glanced around trying to find Storm. He spotted her, standing a little to the right of her sisters and listening with a strained expression to something Charles was saying.

Frowning, Hadden sidled closer to where they stood, hoping to overhear the conversation.

Standing by the refreshments, he tried to listen but their muffled voices allowed him to catch only a few words. And what Charles said had him clenching his fists with suppressed anger.

"No, no, I can't see a single reason...want to marry...need to get started on an heir...as soon as possible."

Storm said nothing to Charles' conversation. Her expression continued to become more vacant and depressed, and her body more rigid. He noticed the tight clasping of her fingers and glazed look in her eyes.

To his surprise, he had the sudden need to step forward and rescue her and protect her from any and all harm. But he reminded himself this was not his concern. Yet he set down his cup of punch and wove his way through the people standing in front of him until he stood next to Storm.

"I'll stop by tomorrow, and we can start making plans," he heard Robertson saying.

"No, no, I need some time. Not tomorrow. Not next week. I'm in mourning. Have to wait a year."

"Nonsense. Mourning for Bradford? I've heard the stories. You are probably glad he's dead. Now I won't wait any longer." Charles' expression hardened. "There isn't a person in this room who would fault you for taking a husband this soon. After what your father did, you're penniless unless you find a wealthy husband."

"I have the revenue from the stables," Storm told him.

Hadden's fists clenched and the tick at his jaw intensified. The man's high-pressure tactics enraged him. He stepped forward. "Miss Graham," he said, alarmed by Storm's exhausted, drab expression, "please allow me to offer my condolences."

Storm turned, her moisture-filled eyes widening. She looked at him as if she'd never seen him before. "Thank you." Her gaze slid back to Charles, whose ruddy complexion grew darker as the man glared at him. "I appreciate your appearance here today, Mr. Johnston. I didn't know you knew Bradford."

"I did some business with him a few years back and of course I ship the Graham Scotch all over the world." Hadden's eyes narrowed as he returned Robertson's icy stare.

Storm's brows drew together as she looked at Hadden, seemingly confused. In the days since Bradford passed away, she had functioned as if in a dream. The shock was deep, her grief unexpected as she and her sisters planned the funeral and reception afterwards. None of what she was doing registered. Even Charles' constant reminders that she needed to plan the wedding didn't sink into her head. She should have told him a resounding, no, and damn the consequences but even that one word didn't form in her mind. It was as if she'd donned a protective cloak around her, and nothing could penetrate.

Hadden's appearance at the funeral and now at the reception was unexpected. She couldn't explain the sensation of his hard-calloused hand holding hers that gave her a sense of confidence and security. For the first time since she'd left her father's deathbed, she noticed what was going on around her. She gazed around the family parlor amazed that anyone, even this handful of people had come to pay their respects. More than anybody she understood Bradford's reputation. As with his family, the people of the town disliked him.

She withdrew her hand from Hadden's, understanding that at this time the gesture, while comforting, was far from appropriate. When she looked at him, she wondered at the feelings coursing through her. This man should have made her uneasy, instead he'd given her a sense of purpose and a renewal of life.

Understanding why was not something she had the time or energy to contemplate. But knowing he'd intimidated Charles gave her another surge of confidence that perhaps her life would not end with a marriage to Charles Robertson. She was also relieved that her first encounter with him since the mortifying day he had turned down her marriage proposal had not caused her the embarrassment she'd expected. He seemed at ease in her home, and his nonchalance allowed her to salvage some small bit of her devastated pride.

"Good day, Miss Storm. I hope everything goes well." With that said, Hadden turned and walked to the other side of the room where he leaned against the wall, continuing to focus his gaze on her.

Charles was assailing Storm with another torrent of verbosity. For a moment Hadden cursed himself for walking away from Storm, but it had been so unsettling to hold her hand that he needed to distance himself from the feelings surging through him, feelings he'd not felt since before his engagement to Elizabeth.

"Why the hell doesn't the bastard leave her alone, at least until the body is cold?" His lips thinned into a hard line. He stood staring at them for a moment longer. Then he came to a decision. Pushing away from the wall, he walked to the sisters who were standing together on the opposite side of the room.

"Girls?" He wasn't sure how to address them. They were younger than Storm but had no one else to protect them.

Larena and Fayth looked at him with a curious expression on both their young faces.

"Mr. Johnston?" Fayth said, questioning.

"I'd like a word with both of you, when you have the time."

"We have time now, Mr. Johnston." Fayth responded, looking a bit flustered at his request.

"Good, good then." He swallowed hard, understanding he was about to do something that would affect his entire life and Storm's.

"You want to speak to us about what exactly?"

He cast a glance in the direction of Storm and Charles. "I wonder if there is someplace we could go where we could talk privately for a moment?"

Fayth looked to Larena, a confused expression on her face, but she nodded and inclined her head toward the library. When the door was closed, she drew a deep breath and smiled. "Will this do?"

"Yes. First of all let me express my sympathies for your loss. While my mother died when I was very young, I understand what a difficult time this is for you. I recall her funeral as if it was yesterday."

"Thank you." Fayth nodded.

"I'm sorry for your loss," Larena said. "What is it you want to discuss?"

"I'm not sure if you know that I'm aware of your sister's predicament."

"Predicament?" Fayth asked, at a loss for a second as to what he was referring.

"Yes, regarding Charles Robertson."

"Oh, she did speak of it after Father passed. She was clearly distraught. But there wasn't anything either of us could do to help her," Larena pointed out.

Hadden shifted his weight from one foot to the other. "I want to help her."

Fayth's eyes widened. "You do?"

"I do." He cleared his throat. "And I wonder if you might tell her that if it's convenient, I'd like to call on her tomorrow afternoon at three to discuss her situation and what I can do to help."

"Tomorrow afternoon at three," Larena parroted. "Yes of course I'll tell her."

"If that's not a good time, have her send a message to my office at the docks, and let me know what would be."

"I'm sure three o'clock will be fine," Fayth responded, the tone of her voice suddenly changing.

Hadden looked at her in confusion, wondering what was causing her sudden agitation. "Are you all right, Miss Graham?"

"I'm fine." Fayth waved her hand in the air to cool her face. "It's hot in here that's all. We'll make sure we tell Storm."

Hadden nodded and turned to open the library door, gesturing the girls through in front of him. "I have to leave, but again, please accept my condolences."

"Thank you so much," the girls said in unison then Larena added, "For everything. You're very kind."

Hadden shook his head, brushing off her compliment. "I just don't like to see anyone forced into a situation they don't want to be in." Then, with a quick smile, he headed toward the parlor and the front door.

The girls sped across the room to where Storm stood with Charles. "Excuse me Mr. Robertson," Fayth said breathlessly, "but we need to talk with our sister." Fayth tugged on Storm's arm. "Now."

Storm tossed her sisters a look of grateful relief at finally being rescued. She excused herself with a murmured apology and followed her sisters to the library. When they were alone, Fayth and Larena turned toward her.

"Thank you for the rescue but what is it?" Storm asked, amazed and confused at her sisters' excitement.

To her further bafflement, the girls burst into peals of girlish laughter. "You better sit down because you are not going to believe what just happened."

"Mr. Johnston is going to help you, and we all know the only way that can happen is if he agrees to your proposal." Fayth sat down and looked at Storm with shining eyes.

"Did he say the words? I want to marry Storm."

Chapter Four

He didn't say he would marry me. What he did say was he'd help me. The sleepless night, the death of Bradford, and Charles' constant nagging at the funeral had left her exhausted. Now she stared at the grandfather clock in the parlor, listening to the steady tick, tick, tick. Time didn't seem to move as she waited for Hadden to free her from Charles Robertson's odious plans.

Would he come to her rescue? Why should he? She wasn't anything to him.

But marriage to Mr. Johnston would be her only way out of the contract Bradford had made with Henry Robertson. She smoothed the nonexistent wrinkles from her black day dress. The clock chimed twice. Storm inhaled a long deep breath, closing her eyes and wishing for this meeting to be finished.

For what seemed like the millionth time, she looked out the window in the parlor. This time she was met with the sight of Hadden Johnston walking up the brick path, leading to the front door. Dressed in buckskins and a white shirt, he was as handsome as ever.

What do I say to him?" Her nerves raced with anticipation. Even as she held her breath, forgetting to breathe she watched his long easy strides travel the length of her walkway. "Calm yourself. He has your interests in mind. He wants to help you." Holding her hands on her chest, she willed her thundering heart to slow. Still, when his sharp knock on the door sounded, she jumped.

"Take a deep breath and wipe your sweaty hands on something before you answer the door. You don't want him to think you're too eager." *You are eager, you ninny.* She inhaled and found a clean napkin that hadn't been picked up from the reception and dried her hands before she walked around the corner and opened the door.

Hadden was dressed in his usual buckskins and boots sporting a white shirt that set off his bronzed skin and chiseled features to perfection. He appeared so fetching that for a moment Storm gaped at him in awe.

"Hello, I hope I'm not too late. I had a meeting that lasted a little bit longer than I'd anticipated. Business doesn't always pay attention to the clock. You look very nice today." He grinned.

She melted inside. "Oh, thank you and no, no, it's only a few minutes passed the hour. Come in." As her gaze swept over him, she was amazed by his sheer size. Somehow, she mused, when he was out in the open, he didn't seem so large. But when he stood in a normal-sized room with normal-sized people, he seemed to fill up all of the space. She reminded herself of a schoolgirl about to swoon and made a mental note to act like a mature young woman.

Hadden looked at her for a few minutes before gesturing to a small table near the door. "May I put my hat here?"

"Oh, my goodness. I'm sorry. I'm not usually so rude. Of course you can. Here let me take it for you." She reached for the hat just as he set it on the table then awkwardly drew her hand back when their fingers touched. "So sorry," she blurted.

"You don't need to be nervous. Perhaps we could sit down somewhere to talk," he said with a tentative smile and a cock of his head.

Storm jerked and closed the front door with a bang. "We can go in the parlor." Nervous? He had no idea how every nerve ending she possessed was racing through her body.

Hadden nodded and followed her across the foyer.

Hearing the steady clomp of his steps as they walked, Storm wondered what he must think. Yesterday, he'd been in her home but the room had been filled with people and refreshments. They'd had a few servants there to keep the food on the table, but it had been an expense they couldn't cover.

She looked at the worn carpet and the blank spaces on the walls where paintings had once hung. *He must think we are paupers.* Well, except for the money Ravyn's husband Aric had sent them, they would have never been able to afford the food let alone the help for the funeral. Just by looking at the room, he could surmise why Bradford had sold her to Charles. Still, she'd never condone his selfishness.

Storm gestured toward a rose-colored velvet settee. "Please sit and make yourself comfortable, Mr. Johnston." She wasn't too sure what to do next. The awkward silence seemed to engulf her. She fiddled with the fabric of her dress and tried to look at him without him noticing.

Hadden sat down, his gaze focused on her as he ran a finger around the inside of his collar.

"Well," Storm smiled, sinking onto a settee opposite his and clasping her hands in her lap. "You said you wanted to see me about something." Anticipation of a proposal left her breathless, and she tried to calm herself and breathe deeply.

"I did." Hadden nodded, his gaze moving away from her to the door then back. "I feel sorry for the situation you have found yourself in. And..."

Storm waited for him to continue but it didn't seem as if he knew what to say next, and she wondered if he was as nervous as she was. Silence stretched for what seemed an eternity. Finally when she could stand the quiet no longer, she said, "Would you like some tea? Or some brandy? I made fresh bread and it's still warm from the oven."

Hadden cleared his throat, looking relieved. "Some brandy please. I'm not hungry."

With a smile, she rose from the settee and walked over to a carved sideboard upon which rested a crystal decanter and four snifters. Pulling the stopper out of the decanter, she poured a quarter of an inch of brandy into one of the glasses and carried it to Hadden.

"Here you go." She had no idea how much to pour. When she drank with Ella, they filled the snifter. At this moment she didn't want to appear brazen.

His eyes sparkled when he looked at the glass of brandy, but he accepted the liquor. "Thank you, Miss Graham."

"Why don't you call me Storm?" she asked, returning to her seat across from him and folding her hands in her lap.

Hadden swirled the brandy around the bottom of the glass. "Only if you'll call me Hadden."

Storm nodded and smiled. "Of course, Hadden. Do you like the brandy?" The question seemed innocuous, and she wished she could take it back. When had she become so tongue-tied?

Silence invaded the room again, and the grandfather clock ticked the seconds away. Storm heard the frogs croaking outside her window. Looking at her fingers, she clasped and unclasped them. Finally when they did speak, it was at the same time.

"I really appreciate your offering..."

"Maybe we should talk about..."

Just as they both started, they stopped in unison. Gazing at him, she cleared her throat and planted her lips together. But she needed to hear the words from him not her sisters.

"Please feel free to talk first. I don't understand why you wanted to see me, so perhaps that should be the first order of business." Good lord but he was handsome, and every time she looked at him, nerves or no nerves, he stole her breath.

"Well, when I spoke to your sisters yesterday, I did say I'd like to help you with your problem." He sipped the brandy then set the snifter on the table. Rubbing his legs with his hands, he stared at her as if he had no idea what he was going to say next.

"That's what they told me, and I do thank you. How do you think you can help?" She went straight to the point, praying for a proposal of marriage so she could relax.

Hadden picked up his glass and swallowed a tiny bit of the brandy she'd poured. "I don't know what the circumstances are surrounding your father's contract with Henry Robertson, but I hate to see anyone forced into doing something because of an agreement someone else has made. This situation you've found yourself in seems entirely unfair."

She stiffened her back, straightening. Those were her sentiments but short of fleeing the country she no longer had any ideas of how not to be forced. "I agree with you but that doesn't help." She didn't want to bring up her dire financial straights because she couldn't guilt Hadden into paying her debt.

"I'd like to propose, a, er... I'd like to propose..."

Misunderstanding where Hadden was going with this, Storm smiled. "Contractual legalities won't mean much once we are married. Of course it will be a marriage in name only. You shouldn't be forced any more than I should. We need to go about this quickly however. I'm sure if Charles or Henry hears about our intentions, he will do everything in his power to put a stop to the proceedings."

Storm paused for a quick intake of air. "I don't care what kind of wedding we have. We can go to the justice of the peace. Gretna Green is too far to travel, and I'm sure Henry would send the bloodhounds after us if he discovered the plot. What would you like?"

"Storm."

"Speaking of the marriage, we should draw up an agreement pertaining to the terms of our union. Things like my stallion and the winnings you'll receive as well as Fiacre's offspring. Yes, I believe a contract would be just the thing." The relief that this was finally in the open filled her heart. She hadn't been this elated since—well she couldn't remember.

"Miss Graham."

"I'm sure it will be simple enough for you to have your lawyer draw up the legal papers. I'll tell my sisters and plan this for as soon as we can get a hold of the minister."

"Miss Graham!"

Storm stopped and stared at him, her mind racing with everything that needed to be done. "What?"

"I don't think you understand my intentions." Hadden rubbed his chin, staring at her with a strange expression.

"Of course I understand. You just proposed. I heard..." She paused in thought. Had she jumped to conclusions?

"I did not." Hadden wiped his hands down his pant legs again.

Storm felt her heart lodge in her throat. "I'm confused? I thought..."

"Yes, you've misunderstood my intentions and raced to an assumption that isn't true." Hadden rose and walked to the sideboard where he poured a liberal portion of brandy into his snifter. Without turning around, he said, "Did you think I came here to accept your marriage proposal?"

Storm swallowed the lump in her throat, her eyes closing for a moment in mortification at her sudden understanding. It seemed all her blood drained from her face. Embarrassment so strong, she wanted to race from the room, but she stiffened her spine, waiting for the final humiliating blow.

She watched as Hadden turned around and faced her, a grim expression on his face. "That's exactly what you thought. Wasn't it?"

Further mortified, Storm averted her gaze and tried to breathe. How could her sisters get this so wrong? Yet she understood. They had needed her to be happy and to find peace from the circumstances Bradford had handed to her.

Hadden walked to the settee where she sat and looked down at her. He placed one finger under her chin, lifting it. She didn't want to see him, couldn't talk to him. Her body trembled with shame.

"Miss Graham, I'm afraid you've misunderstood my intentions. Marriage never crossed my mind. I thought that if I better understood your situation, I could present a case for you in front of Henry Robertson— nothing more." He let go of her chin and stepped away from her.

Storm pressed her lips together, thinking about what he told her. "That won't rectify my situation, Mr. Johnston." Forcing herself to meet his gaze and seeing his fierce determination, she said, "Talking won't solve anything."

"It could."

"No, no it won't. Marriage to someone influential and powerful is the only thing that would prevent Henry and Charles from pursuing the contract. That's why I approached you with this ludicrous proposal. It was my only hope." The tension she'd lived with the past weeks left her weak and hopeless. Now, she would have to contact the Duchess for help.

"I understand, but I can only offer to speak with Henry. I'm sorry

I came to your home and got your hopes up. It was not my intention to deceive you. But I can't marry you."

"Why not?" Storm tossed back to him, determined to try every angle she could think of. "I've told you I don't really want you as a husband. I need the protection of your name. I promise you won't even know I'm around, and I won't ask anything from you."

He stepped back again, seeming to distance himself further from her, his brows furrowed as if in thought, yet his hands were tightly fisted at his sides. The muscle in his jaw ticked.

"Don't you see? You won't have to be a husband to me. I don't need that or want that. I understand you don't want to be married, and neither do I. That's why we are a perfect match. We can continue to live our lives anyway we want, and I won't ask any questions. The only difference is you have the potential to earn a great deal of money over the next years and even build a stable of racing horses for yourself. And I'll be saved from marriage to Charles Robertson. What can be wrong with that?" Pleased with her argument, she felt a tiny bit relieved. Yet she still had no way to pay the debt owed by her father.

"I'm astounded and left in complete disbelief. I'm trying to be patient but... But one of us might meet someone who we do want to marry. What would you do then? Would you want a divorce?"

"That won't happen. I'm never going fall in love or marry—not for real." She smiled at him, trying to hide her feelings.

"May I ask about your reasons? I'm suddenly curious."

Because," She was too distraught to come up with an answer to his question. "I won't, I can't, not after my mother. Bloody hell but I don't want to have baby after baby. I don't want to have to clean and cook for someone who doesn't appreciate me. I want freedom."

"Don't you like children?"

"Of course I like them. I adore Ella's children, and babies are so cute and cuddly. I just refuse to be at the beck and call of some man who wants an heir more than anything else." She stopped, realizing who stood in front of her and was listening to everything she had to say.

"I'm not sure I understand. So you like children, you just don't

47

want to have any of your own."

"Pretty much." Mortified, Storm wished she could take back everything she'd said. If she prayed maybe the floor would open up and swallow her. Yet why would she want to take back the truth? *Because you ninny, those words aren't the exact truth.*

"Well that's too bad, because I would love to have children when, of course, I fall in love with the right woman. In fact, I want a houseful of kids. This is another example of why I can't marry you, Miss Graham."

"I would rather not discuss this topic, Mr. Johnston. It doesn't seem appropriate." She adjusted her skirts, smoothing imaginary creases.

"Perhaps it isn't. But please believe me when I tell you that if there's anything I can do help you from your contract short of marrying you, let me know and I'll be there for you." His words were curt and pointed.

She'd made him angry, and that hadn't been her intention. "Nothing, there's nothing you can do for me, except perhaps help me flee without Charles discovering I've left. I'm sure the Duchess can call in some favors, and I can find a way to keep from marrying the hideous man. Of course he will have my beloved stable but it's a small price to pay." *And I hope the price tag on the stables will cover Bradford's debt.* "Whatever happens, I cannot stay here under these circumstances."

"I can provide a ship to take you to London. I assume that's where the Duchess resides."

"Thank you. I think it's time for you to leave."

"You're right. I'll be in touch." He set down his glass.

Silently they walked to the door. Storm reached it first and picking up his hat, she handed it to him then opened the door. "Good day, Mr. Johnston."

Hadden turned to her, his brows knitted together. "Miss Graham?"

"Good day, sir!"

~ * ~

"You're a bloody fool," Storm muttered beneath her breath. How had she thought he would ask her to marry him? *Because you had hoped and prayed for a miracle, and you'd gambled on Hadden Johnston.* "He made Fayth and Larena think he was going to propose to her and accept the terms she'd issued."

She paced the length of her bedroom and back. Then she turned and did it again. Tears ran down her cheeks in streams. "Think, think, he'd said he'd help you leave town." Picking up her cloak she raced to the stables.

Once inside she scanned the area and inhaled the aroma of horses and hay. This was her life. How could she leave everyone she held dear, the place where she grew up? If a ship didn't leave soon, she would have to depart in the night. At Fiacre's stall, she stopped and opened the gate.

"I'll miss you my fierce one," she murmured close to him, running her hands down his face. "I'll miss you so much." Tears clouded her eyes.

He nodded his head as if he understood what she was saying. "I could take you with me."

This time the stallion shook his head as if saying no.

"You're right. If I stole you, Charles would have one more reason to chase after me. But the Duchess would not let Charles into her townhouse let alone make me marry the horrid man. It would be a standoff. Duchess against Charles and Henry."

She leaned against the horse, hoping to gain strength and courage from him. Suddenly she stopped her moping and strode to the house then up the stairs to her room where she pulled out her trunk.

"I'll leave tomorrow and without his help. If the trunks are at the dock, he'll know I'm serious. I'll leave on the first ship. It doesn't make any difference its destination. I won't be a victim and I won't be forced into the same kind of life as my mother. Now what should I take with me."

~ * ~

Hadden's day had gone from hopeful to dreadful and the evening wasn't getting any better. Unable to erase the vision of Storm's distraught face when he'd told her he had no intention of marrying her, he thought to drown his emotions in a bottle of scotch. To his dismay the urge to protect her at all cost had risen inside him at an alarming pace.

"Bloody hell, how did she come to the conclusion I was going to ask her to marry me?" He sat at the small table inside his home, his hand clenched around the neck of his scotch bottle. "I don't want to get married. And to Storm Graham? She's beautiful and sweet, but she doesn't want kids. I can't live with that." Then he realized since the end of his engagement to Elizabeth he had withdrawn from the living. Until Storm barged into his life he hadn't thought about children or marriage.

Despite his musings, Hadden couldn't get images of her from his head. And overwhelming guilt ripped into him. "Trouble is," he hiccoughed, pouring himself another shot, "she's so damn sexy and when she blushes like she does, I want to pull her into my arms and kiss her. God, but I feel bad about turning her down." The thought of Charles touching her, making love to her, made him sick.

And if he admitted the truth, no amount of scotch could make him forget that she was gorgeous, and sweet, and sexy, and he wanted her.

~ * ~

"Captain, ya' gotta see this. There's two girls er ladies here to see ya. They say it's real important and can't wait."

"On my way." Hadden shuffled the papers he'd been looking at before he rose from his cluttered desk. "Did they say what this was about?"

"No." Perkins' brows snapped together. "Didn't ask 'em. Thought that was your job."

"Well, bloody hell. Couldn't you ask them what they wanted?" Frustration and anger pooled in his gut.

"Did. They said you was waitin' for them and the trunks; that you would keep them safe and out of sight until a ship left for London or the States. I gotta keep track of the crew not passengers ya might be bringin' aboard." Perkins shook his ahead again. "Ya didn't tell me there was gonna be passengers."

"Passengers? I haven't allowed space on this ship for anyone. It's going to India."

"I'm sorry, Captain. They said you'd understand about London. I'm just the messenger, and I don't know anything about this. I assumed they were passengers cause they got a trunk the size of small boat. Could be wrong."

"Let's hope you're wrong. Did you get a name?" Curiosity overcame his anger, he suddenly wanted to see what was happening.

"One was Fayth and the other Larena. Said the trunks were their sister's." Perkins wiped sweat from his brow and stared at Hadden.

"Bloody hell." He'd forgotten he'd told Storm he'd find a ship to take her to London. He'd thought she would have waited for him to come to her. But he knew she was in a panic and needed to get away. There wouldn't be a ship headed out of here for the other side of the island for a few weeks. "Didn't you tell the girls there weren't any ships for a while?"

"Sorry, didn't know you'd asked." Perkins turned away but spoke over his shoulder. "Want me to talk to the girls?"

"No, I'll take care of it."

"I didn't know she was looking to leave town. Kinda figured she'd be lookin' after personal business. There's got to be a lot to take care of. And who's goin' to look after her younger sisters if she leaves?"

"Good question. Maybe they're all leaving."

Perkins' eyebrows rose in surprise at this thought. "The house ain't up for sale."

"They don't have to sell the house to leave."

"I'll go if you want me to," he offered one last time, a knowing grin on his face.

"Forget it." Hadden strolled from his cabin and down the gangplank to the dock.

Neither Fayth nor Larena were waiting for him, he noticed, as he eyed the trunk sitting as if abandoned. "Where are the girls?" Hadden asked one of his men who was standing by the baggage, looking disturbed.

"Girls said they had things to do and expected me to keep this safe until it could be loaded on the next ship to London. They left in a wagon and didn't say when they'd be back." He wiped sweat from his forehead. "Didn't know we had a ship going to London any time soon."

"Can this day get any worse?"

~ * ~

Hadden stood outside the door of the Robertson estate, weighing his options. Against Storm's wishes, he'd pursued this line of attack. Any reasonable man would discuss this issue and come to a compromise. He'd just raised his hand to knock when the butler opened the door.

"That was fast." Hadden stepped inside and stared at the opulence of the foyer. All the décor was in reds and golds. The bannister leading to the upstairs was a dark brown.

"I was forewarned of your upcoming presence at noon. I have orders not to keep visitors waiting," the butler said stiffly. "Follow me." He turned and led the way through the parlor through another door then to the library.

Floor to ceiling books on three of the walls, showcased Henry Robertson's collection. Heavy red drapes framed a lone window that appeared to look toward a garden. Henry rose to greet Hadden when he entered the room, but Charles remained seated, a glare on his face.

"Good afternoon. May I ask why you're calling on us? Your letter said little as to the reason of your visit. In any case, we are delighted." Henry sat down then nodded to Hadden. "Would you like a drink? And sit please."

"No thank you." Hadden remained standing, disliking the smirk on Charles Robertson's face. "This is about Miss Storm Graham. I understand you have a contract with her father."

"True, so true." Henry leaned back, resting his clasped hands on his opulent stomach. "Charles, would you pour me a drink. I think I can use a good whiskey. What does this have to do with your visit? The contract is binding."

Charles rose, walking to the sideboard where he poured two drinks before he returned with them. He handed one to his father then returned to his place on the settee with the second drink.

"I told Miss Graham I would talk with you and see if we could reach an amicable decision about her situation and the contract. She doesn't want to marry Charles. I would like to have our lawyers meet. Perhaps there is a solution we can both agree on."

Henry bolted upright, his relaxed demeanor vanishing. "The only way out of this contract is for Storm to pay Bradford's debt by marrying Charles." His voice was tight, menacing—today. "She has no funds. She is dirt poor. We are doing her a favor by offering marriage to the wealthiest man in these parts."

Hadden stiffened. "She has a stable full of the finest racing horse flesh in the British Isles. Marriage to Charles or the Robertsons acquiring the stables was the bargain she made. Am I correct?" Hadden paused but hearing no response continued. "She is not the wastrel her father was." Hadden had never liked Charles Robertson, and he'd never had any dealings with Henry. But now, he was beginning to understand Storm's fear. A growing dislike of both Robertsons became a danger signal in his head, determined to find a practical way out of this devil's bargain.

"No, no, that part of the bargain is no longer acceptable. Charles wants Storm, and their marriage is the only way the debt can be repaid." Henry had relaxed again and was sipping the whiskey his son had poured. "It's already been many years since I loaned Bradford the money. At the moment, I'm not asking for interest. And I won't give her anymore time." A smile formed on Henry's face. "I wanted heirs yesterday."

Hadden had the urge to punch him and watch the old man's gloating fade. "That's highly unfair. Miss Graham has just learned of the debt and with her father's funeral, she's had no time to pull her resources together." Bloody hell, they only wanted her as a brood mare.

"The Graham's have had more than enough time. That's all I heard from her wastrel of a father. Time, I need more time. And what became of that, I ask you? Nothing, no compensation. Not only did

Bradford not pay me back, he continued to gamble away the funds I loaned him." He slammed his fist on the desk in front of him. "I will have the stables now or she will wed my son."

"Storm doesn't want to marry your son. This is not a time when anyone can force a marriage on a young woman. You cannot make her marry Charles." Hadden's fists tightened. A strange determination to help Storm anyway he could surged within. "You will take the stables in exchange for payment of the debt or nothing."

Henry leaned back, a smile on his face. "Charles no longer sees the acquisition of the Graham horses as acceptable. As I told you before, he wants Storm, and if that's what my son wants then who am I to stand in his way? We don't need the money or the aggravation of another business."

"She has offered the stables as you had requested earlier." Hadden was determined to help Storm, his protective nature sweeping through him. For some reason Storm's plight, despite his own reluctance to wed, made his need to solve all of her problems.

From behind, Hadden Charles spoke. "I want Storm and I will not barter away my chosen bride. I don't want the stables unless they come with Storm."

Hadden swiveled to meet Charles' gaze, anger flaring. "You really want to marry someone who despises you?"

Pure evil slashed across the younger Robertson's face as he sneered at Hadden. "It doesn't matter to me how she feels about the marriage. I will have her, and she will be pregnant as many times as needs be until she gives me an heir."

"You would force yourself on her?"

"I would do whatever is necessary." Charles' grin was smug and defiant. "I'm a man of great wealth and authority. She will bend to my will and she will do everything I say."

Hadden's gut churned as he realized Storm's fear of Charles was nothing compared to what it should be. No way in hell would he allow her to marry Charles. He knew an abusive man when he saw one. While he didn't love Storm, he found he liked her, and he didn't want to see her hurt—or raped because he knew beyond a doubt if she wed Charles, he would rape her.

"Is there nothing I can do to change your mind?" He looked to Henry first then to Charles, his fury growing.

"Nothing save bringing Storm here and getting hold of the good reverend so they can say their vows," Henry said, drumming his fingers on the shot glass.

"That, will never happen unless it is what Storm chooses, and I know she will not. She's made it damn clear the last man on this earth she wishes to wed is your son."

Henry cocked his head to one side, his smug grin vanishing and in a moment of bravado, he said. "One shouldn't visit on another's behalf unless they know all of the facts. Good day."

With that, the butler was at the door. "I will see you out Mr. Johnston."

~ * ~

"Hadden Johnston is here to see you, Miss Graham."

Storm's head jerked up from the horse she'd been grooming. "He is?" She cleared her throat as she tried to cover the tremor in her voice.

"Yes, ma'am," came from the stable hand.

"Did he say why he's here?" Her hands shook as she continued to brush the horse. At the sound of his name, she wanted to melt into the shadows.

"Something about a ship and it isn't going to London any time soon and the trunk your sisters left on the dock."

"Tell him I don't want to see him." She felt the sting of humiliation from his last visit.

"But... Miss Graham—"

"You heard me Terry, tell him I don't want to see him." Storm gripped the handle of the brush as if it were her lifeline while energy drained from her body. She couldn't see him, she just couldn't.

"I understand why you don't want to talk to me, but this is important." Hadden stood framed in the doorway.

The stable hand whirled around and gaped at Hadden, seemingly amazed the man had followed him into the stables.

"It's always important with you, and it's never anything I want to hear. What is it this time?" she snapped the question then felt guilt wash over her. "Unless you can help me, I don't see any reason for you to be here."

"I know you're busy, Miss Graham, but I don't know what to do with the baggage your sisters left on the dock. There is no ship going to London for a number of weeks, and I have no place to put it. You have to send your sisters back to get the trunk before someone steals the damn thing."

"I have to get out of town. You told me you'd help me. If you can't do that, then I just don't want to see you or talk to you. I'll tell Fayth she needs to retrieve it." Storm closed her eyes, inhaling a breath of courage. What was she going to do now? She'd thought she was leaving on the morning tide and now...well now she'd have to hire a carriage, and Charles was sure to learn of her imminent adventure. She was positive Hadden had told her a ship would be leaving in a day or two. But then her head had been so muddled she didn't know what was true and what was false.

"I will help. But you need to wait until I send word." Hadden's face darkened and his brows closed together. "I haven't decided what I'm going to do yet. But I'm making plans to..." he stopped short of finishing his sentence.

Storm's brush hit the floor with a muted thud, and her lips thinned as she stiffened her back. "Please excuse us." Storm spoke to her helper, flicking her gaze toward the door in a gesture that should tell the boy she expected him to vacate the premises and give her privacy.

The boy's bewildered gaze traveled between the two combatants. "But Miss Storm, I've work to do."

"The lady said to leave!"

The boy took a startled step backward then with a quick nod, turned on his heel and fled the stables.

"Now listen here, Mr. Johnston," Storm began, trying for a calm she didn't feel. Nervous energy centered in the pit of her stomach.

"No, you listen to me, Miss Graham. Just because you're mad that I turned down your crazy scheme of getting married, I still have to get you to London, and I mean to help you, but you can't leave your stuff on the docks."

"I told you I'd send Fayth to retrieve it."

Crazy scheme, Storm's mind screamed. How dare he call her cry for help a crazy scheme? At least a thousand stinging responses swept through her head.

"Oh no you don't, sir."

"What are you talking about?"

"It's a miracle you can do business with anyone. You don't seem to know where any of your ships are." When Hadden had first walked into the stables, Storm had had no inkling what she was going to say to him, but his last words had inspired the seed of an idea, and despite her need for honesty in dealing with Mr. Johnston, and before she could talk herself out of the notion, she seized the opportunity.

She leaned against the stall, and in a voice as calm as if they were discussing the weather, said, "As of today, the Grahams will no longer send shipments with you or receive them from you. We will do our business down the coast at Berwick-upon-Tweed."

For a moment Hadden's mouth dropped open then he smiled. "Really? I'm sure I don't understand how you could have that much authority with your uncles."

Taken a back for a second, she paused to regroup her thought then continued, "You well know the Grahams are your main business and I can. If I go to my family and tell them how underhanded and mean you are, they will send their business elsewhere." She tossed him a fake smile. Her heart nearly stopping from her blatant audacity, she picked up the brush she'd dropped earlier and returned to groom the stallion. "My family is no longer going to do business with your company, which means you are going to have to find yourself more merchants. It's as simple as that."

"You're being absurd," Hadden said, calmly stepping toward her. "I understand how desperate you are, but you do understand I would lose a great deal of profits if the Grahams boycotted my ships."

"Precisely."

An endless moment passed as Storm brushed Fiacre and thought how ridiculous her words had been. She had little to no influence over the other Grahams. Bradford's actions had managed to separate the family.

Hadden inhaled a deep breath and said, "All right, I understand your feelings are hurt and you want to punish me because I won't marry you, but let's get serious, Miss Graham. Do you really believe your uncles will want to transport their goods overland when they can bring them to the docks?"

Storm looked over her shoulder and graced him with a serene smile. "The majority live closer to Berwick. You've always given them a fair price, but I understand the price went up recently." Bloody hell but her heart raced, and she could barely breathe. This was ludicrous what she was attempting. She should back down this instant.

"I bought more ships."

"That's not my problem."

"Perhaps it will be." He stepped closer to her. "Perhaps I've come to my own conclusions about certain things."

Storm had thought this out, and she had not intended to coerce anyone. She'd already made plans to leave town, but her wayward mind had forged ahead, and she spoke without thinking anything out. She wasn't at all sure the rest of the Graham clan would go along with her. If pressed, they would probably stand behind Mr. Johnston because they'd disliked Bradford almost as much as she had.

All she'd meant to do was humiliate Hadden into begging her the way she'd been forced to beg him. But now that he had offered her the solution to all her problems, she grabbed at it. Formulating her words so as not to betray her, she said, "Exactly." She paused, trying to recall his exact words. "What things?"

"This is an outrageous game you're playing Miss Graham. But I do understand how loathsome marrying Charles would be. I wouldn't wish it on my best friend and for some reason I've a need to protect you."

Storm pursed her lips with distaste, praying he wouldn't see through her ruse. "I'm not your best friend, Mr. Johnston, although I desperately need your protection."

"But you could be. Why don't we negotiate this business plan of yours?"

Storm sighed with extra drama. "What is there to negotiate? Until I see a wedding ring on my finger, your ships will be minus seventy percent of your cargo."

Hadden stared at Storm, his eyes twinkling as if he didn't understand the magnitude of what she'd just been saying to him. "You can't make me marry you. I don't love you, but I might be willing under the right circumstances. And understand this, Miss Graham, your innocent attempt to blackmail me won't work. I'm a man who makes his own decisions."

Storm pushed a wayward lock of hair from her face. "You're right, of course. I-I didn't mean to blackmail." Tears flowed from her eyes. "I'm lost and desperate..."

"I understand and my heart goes out to you. My ships will be full. The Grahams, each and every one of them, signed a contract with me for this year's shipments, which states that the Graham merchants guarantee Johnston shipping to carry five million crates."

She stiffened but this time she understood she'd lost. Instead of recouping her losses, she blustered on and said, "My Berwick Grahams were at the funeral. When they noticed you'd taken an interest in me, they spoke of their contract with you. Very proud at the time that business had been good, very good this year. Bradford's oldest brother even bragged about the number of barrels of scotch they'd sent to the United States, South America, India and more." She tapped a finger to her chin. "If my memory serves me right, the number was close to that five million mark. I think he said four million nine hundred ninety-five thousand. That leaves five thousand barrels. And I think they have a shipment meant to leave on tomorrow's tide. Am I right? How many barrels do you think will show up?"

Hadden leaned on the side of the door, his arms crossed in front of him. He appeared to not have a care in the world. With a lazy grin, he said, "You damn well know the answer to that question."

"Well then," Storm said calmly, setting her brush down, and folding her hands in front of her, "I'm afraid they will be sending the scotch to Dunworthy's shipping company in Berwick."

Hadden stepped forward, his grin still smug. "No they won't. You didn't read the entire contract. There is a codicil to it that states, if by any chance they produce more scotch than the specified amount then I have first right of refusal. Which means it is my choice whether I take their cargo, not theirs."

"I don't understand." Storm felt the earth ripped from under her feet.

"Funny thing is, neither do I. I'm feeling things I don't want to feel."

"What do you mean by that statement? What is it you don't want to feel?" All her bravado had vanished and once again she was resigned to fleeing. London and life with the duchess was looking better with each passing second.

"I don't love you, Miss Graham, but the last thing I can do is to stand by and watch you marry a man as despicable as Charles Robertson. I haven't been able to figure a way out of your predicament, although God knows I've tried. I don't even understand why I care so damn much but for some reason I do." Hadden scraped his fingers through his brown hair.

The brunt of his words made Storm's nerves reverberate down her spine, sending tremors throughout her body, but her expression remained impassive. "Even at your worst, you are better than Charles. I—I thank you for your concern. You've even humiliated me a number of times, maybe you're doing the same right now." Storm didn't know where her words had come from. She didn't want to make Hadden's life miserable, but this time she meant to think about herself.

"I'm sorry I humiliated you; that was never my intention. I wish there was another way."

"I think we both know I have to marry someone."

"Well, then, can you find someone else to wed? There are hundreds of men in these parts who would love to be your husband."

"That's not true," Storm answered, shaking her head, "No one else will do. You know how powerful the Robertsons are. They would just buy off...or kill... whomever I married, and I'd be right back where I started."

"Do you truly believe Henry Robertson would have someone killed just because you broke a contract?"

"Oh, it's not me the Robertsons want," Storm said, shaking her head and spreading her hand across her chest. "I mean, I'm sure that he would be delighted to have me around as a breeder for his heir..."

Hadden's eyebrows rose.

"...but what he really wants are the stables and Fiacre especially."

"I've spoken with Henry. He doesn't care about the stables. The Robertsons know they have the means to find their own horses and build a stable of their own, if it's so damned important to them. God knows they own enough land around here."

"It would take years for them to have a stable of racers as good as mine. My horses are the finest in England and Ireland. When they finish their racing careers, I keep the best as breeders and sell the others. In order to develop racers as good as mine, they would have to buy from me. And I would not sell the best to them. They know it."

Hadden paused for a moment then closed his eyes. "I'm going to try one more time to help you understand my feelings about your proposal. I have told you before and I will tell you again—I am not going to marry you. I don't want a wife, especially one I don't love and one who doesn't want children," he persisted, yet he didn't sound sincere.

"All right." She sighed. "As you wish." She walked around him and to the stable doors. Leaning out, she looked for her stable hand. "Jonathan, grab a horse and go see Henry Robertson. Tell him in payment of my father's debt, he has the stables today if he wishes."

"Yes, ma'am." Jonathan hurried into the stables to saddle a horse.

"Just a minute." Hadden lunged toward her and grabbed her arm. "You don't want to do that..."

"That's not your concern." Storm stared pointedly at his fingers until he released his grip.

Silence seemed to stretch into infinity. Storm held her breath, wondering how she would live her life without her beloved horses.

Jonathan was mounted now. Sunlight filtering through the door rested on the boy and the horse. Jonathon paused as if reluctant to continue. "What do you want me to do, ma'am?"

Storm looked at Hadden for an answer as if he could solve her problem, but she knew he wouldn't. She'd played her last card and lost. "Wait... I..." This was her life but what else could she do?

Hadden's eyes narrowed to glittering sparks and a hard knot of muscle jumped in his jaw.

"Eleven o'clock, Saturday morning. Methodist Church."

"What did you say?" Relief swept through Storm, and she stopped holding her breath. She couldn't believe her sudden good fortune and didn't understand his change of heart, but she didn't want to give him one second to change his mind. She wiped the tears from her eyes. "I guess you can forgo that ride, Jonathan." Then she turned to Hadden. "Eleven o'clock will be fine."

Jonathan nodded, dismounting and leading the horse to his stall.

"We will probably both regret this." Hadden's voice was soft and she couldn't tell what he was thinking.

"Perhaps." Storm swallowed the breath she'd been holding. "But no one could be worse than Charles Robertson."

"And, Miss Graham, I don't know what the bloody hell happened just now, but I will honor this agreement."

Chapter Five

"My God, Captain, what are you thinkin'? It's your wedding day. You can't go to the church drunk."

Hadden looked down at his faded trousers and wrinkled shirt then shrugged. "Why not? I'm just celebrating hell before the ceremony rather than afterward. She didn't even give me a chance to propose. I meant to do it right, but she got me so damn mad I couldn't think." He didn't want to get married, but he'd agreed, and he would have asked her because he didn't want her to marry Charles.

But she never gave him the chance to ask. It all happened so fast, he felt as if the wind had been knocked out of his sails.

Perkins frowned and glanced out the window of the ship. He knew his captain had spent the evening sitting in the cabin drinking scotch. "Despite what you did or didn't do the other day, you should have a little bit of respect for your future wife. It's not everyday a man gets married. And referring to this ceremony as hell, is not going to make the day go well."

"You're impertinent. I could fire you. I didn't plan this, and I sure as hell didn't want it. So why should I show up, looking as if I proposed because I love the woman? Besides as soon as this thing is official I've got work to do." The bitterness he felt didn't become him, and he reminded himself she wasn't forcing him, no one could force Hadden Johnston to do anything he didn't want to do.

So...do I really want to marry Storm Graham?

It was a question Hadden didn't have an answer for.

"Work! That's one fine pickle you've got yourself into. You need to make the best of this and see where it might go. Take her somewhere.

A honeymoon would be in order and just the thing unless you want to make it a marriage in name only. Would it be so wrong to try and get to know your bride? And I can remind you, arranged marriages have been successful marriages for hundreds of years. Why..."

Hadden threw his hand in the air. "That's what she wants. And if she has her way, it won't be a real marriage. She wants to let me see other women as long as I'm discreet."

"What the devil are you talking about?" Perkins tossed him a fierce glare. "You're not going to let her get away with that. I see now why you're calling it a marriage made in hell. How could you live with that pretty little thing and not take her to bed?"

"Stop and think, my friend. When a person agrees to a name-only marriage, they're going to have to take a lot of cold baths. Once the ring is on the pretty little thing's finger, I'm gone, going to sail with the next ship out of this little village. I don't think I could live in that house of hers and not do something she might regret."

"That's not for another month. What are ya goin' to do until then? Does the little gal know your plans?"

"Haven't seen her since we agreed to the wedding, so no she doesn't. I doubt if she expects anything from the marriage. She told me there would be no demands. I could take anybody I wanted to as long as it wasn't her. The deal is that if I marry her, she won't have to marry Charles Robertson but she will have to hand over the stables. Now Henry is telling me he doesn't want the stables. Bloody hell, I've jumped out of the frying pan and into the fire."

"I don't understand."

"Neither do I. If Charles isn't going to get Storm then why the hell doesn't Henry want the stables?"

"Well then, if it's a marriage in name only then I guess it doesn't matter what you wear or if you're hung over. But if Henry guesses the marriage isn't consummated then he can sue to have Storm turned over to Charles."

"I'm going to do what I need to do for Storm's sake," Hadden agreed, wondering why he felt so protective of Miss Graham. "Now let's go to the church and get this circus over with."

With a sigh, Perkins picked up Hadden's hat and handed it to him, walking out the door with him and down the gangplank. They reached the docks and Hadden kept walking.

"Where's the carriage?" Perkins asked.

"There isn't one."

"How are you going to bring Storm home? Are you going to make her walk?"

Hadden shrugged. "Guess that's her problem. My guess is she'll have a carriage take her to the church so she'll have one to go home."

Perkins put his hand on Hadden's shoulder. "I know I'm your first mate and nothing more. But I've been through a lot with you, and I've never seen you act like this. You can't abandon her at the church."

"Of course I can." Hadden was still angry and this discussion had brought him to a place he'd never wanted to be. He wanted her for a real wife not a name-only wife but the deal he'd made with her wouldn't allow him to touch her. His insides burned with the need to have a real marriage.

Without a word, Hadden picked up his pace and left Perkins to his own endeavors. He didn't care if the first mate followed or not. And he sure as hell didn't want to listen to anything more Perkins might have on his mind. But he did hear some parting words from Perkins.

"Captain you're going to regret this to your dying day. This is a horrible, horrible mistake."

~ * ~

"I'm so excited. Do I look alright?" Storm swirled in her dress, the smile in her heart when she looked at her sisters and her cousin Aidan.

Storm had sent out invitations to all of her cousins but hadn't expected any of them to come. This had all happened so quickly. But Aidan and her ever-present bodyguard, Blade, had arrived late yesterday evening. Aidan had helped her pick out a dress, and next she was going to work on her hair.

"You're beautiful," Aidan told her. "Exquisite."

"My only wish would be for you to have a real wedding dress. This color is so depressing. Gray was never meant to be worn at weddings."

"You would have been beautiful in pink." Aidan stepped back folding her hands in front of her.

"Really," Fayth countered, "red is her favorite color."

"Either would have been better than gray," Larena chimed in.

"If the truth be told, I don't feel right wearing this." Storm smoothed the folds of the dress.

"Nonsense," Aidan entered into the discussion, her blue eyes sparkling. "We all know what kind of man Bradford was. The fact you can mourn him at all astounds me."

"Leave it to Aidan to be brutally honest," Fayth said with a little laugh.

Larena frowned and sat down on the settee. "I hope you're doing the right thing, Storm. I'm just not sure that beginning a marriage by saying it's a marriage in name only to the soon-to-be husband is starting off on the right foot."

Storm felt a shiver of apprehension slither down her spine. The mood had darkened, and she knew what Larena said had a ring of truth. "I did what I had to do. I can't imagine a life without all of you, or one with Charles coming to my bed, and Hadden told me he didn't want a wife. I don't want a husband so we should be compatible."

"That's pretty convoluted. But what's going to happen? Do you think there will be repercussions?" Fayth asked.

"Probably. He was furious when he left."

"Do you think he will show up? You said he left angry." Aidan pointed out while she brushed Storm's hair. "I found some of your mother's pearls. We can weave them in your hair. They'll look stunning."

"If nothing else Mr. Johnston is a man of his word. He will show up but what happens after that is a big question." From the view in the mirror, Storm watched as Aiden finished her hair. It was bittersweet to see the pearls her mother had once worn adorning her hair. She had so wished her younger sister could have had more time with their mother.

"Well I'm worried, Storm. I know you understand what goes on between a man and a woman in the privacy of their bedroom, but..." Larena said.

Storm looked at her sister with a smile. "But...?"

"Well, if a man doesn't, well if he isn't gentle...well it might not be pleasant and..."

"Okay, you don 't have to worry. You see I made it clear to Mr. Johnston I didn't want to have anything to do with the marriage bed. We have an understanding."

"You have what?" Aidan gasped.

"You heard me before. That's part of our agreement. No intimacy and we're both free to come and go as we please."

Aidan's eyes widened. "And your Mr. Johnston didn't have any problem with that?"

"He didn't exactly agree," Storm admitted, "but that's only because we never had a chance to discuss it. He raced from the stables as if he couldn't get away from me fast enough."

"Storm," Aidan's voice took on a distinct warning tone, "I believe your naivety is showing. No matter what, Mr. Johnston is a man and he's going to want to claim what is his. Maybe not on the wedding night but sooner than later."

"No, Aidan," Storm said, "he isn't any more interested in me than I am in him. When I first spoke to him, I assured him I'd make no demands on him and that there'd be no entanglements—except, of course, for putting on the pretense of a happy marriage for Charles' sake. Other than that, his life and mine will go just as they always have."

"How did he respond to that?" Fayth asked.

"Well, he said something about there always being problems, but I know he's wrong."

"Bloody hell," Aidan spoke up, "I do hope this doesn't backfire."

Storm looked at herself in the mirror. "Of course it won't. I know it won't."

~ * ~

"Bloody hell, you'd think she could be on time for her own damn wedding." Hadden stared down the street from where he stood in front of the church.

Blade, Aidan's self-proclaimed bodyguard, stood by Hadden's side. They'd met a couple of years ago at the Graham residence. "Give her time, it's only a couple of minutes after eleven, and I'm sure Aidan has everything to do with her late arrival. Aidan is late to everything."

"Don't feel like giving her a bloody minute."

"Hadden..."

"I'll give her five more minutes. If she isn't here by then, I'm off and she can find herself another damn fool who wants to be married in name only."

"That's not going to help her out of her predicament with Charles Robertson. You must care for her a little to have agreed to the wedding," Blade reminded him.

"You have a way of making a man feel ashamed of himself." Hadden shuddered, and he was ashamed of what he was doing, but he didn't have time to change anything, and he wasn't sure if he would do anything different if he had another day, week, month or even a year. He wanted to protect her, had feelings for her he didn't understand and that made it damn uncomfortable.

"Oh," Blade grinned as he looked down the street, "here comes the bride. Happy to see Aidan was with them, never know where she's going to get herself off to."

With a disgusted snort, Hadden turned to watch the oncoming carriage. "Didn't need a carriage for her..."

"You ready for this?"

They waited for the vehicle to stop and the girls to disembark.

"Storm, he looks furious," Larena whispered to her sister. "You sure you want to go through with this. You could call it all off right now."

Storm peered out the window, and her nerves ricocheted, sending sparks of fear down her spine. But she wasn't about to let on how terrified she was, and looking at Hadden now, she knew she had every right to be terrified.

These last few days she'd been afraid she'd see him at her front door, and he would tell her the deal was off. Then as that didn't happen, she'd been afraid he'd stand her up at the church just to humiliate her.

"He doesn't look furious, Larena. He looks smug."

"What does he have to be smug about?" Aidan questioned as they began their walk to the church and the waiting bridegroom.

"He means to jilt me—right here in front of everybody. I just know it."

"No he won't," Fayth said. "He's an honorable man. He'd never do something so despicable."

Storm inhaled a deep breath, praying for the courage to go through with this public humiliation. "If he doesn't have some plan to destroy me, why does he look like he's hung over and that he slept in his clothes?"

Fayth hesitated for a moment. "I couldn't possibly understand. Your arrangement with this man is nothing like anything I've ever heard of, and I suspect he's not too happy with this devil's bargain the two of you made."

"You're right the devil must have had a hand in this, but I don't regret anything unless he denounces me right here, right now." With a resigned sigh, she gathered up her skirts and walked the remaining distance to meet Hadden Johnston.

"Good morning, Mr. Johnston. It's a beautiful day isn't it?" She tried to sound normal, tried to keep the quivering she felt from echoing in her voice.

Hadden's gaze swept over her long-sleeved, high-necked dress with a visible indifference. "A bit hot for that concealing dress, don't you think?"

"It is, but since my father's death, I have certain restrictions on what I can wear. But it's more appropriate than what you are wearing and your condition."

"Why? I just had a little pre-marriage fun last night. A few us single men out on the town to celebrate my last night of freedom. Didn't have time to change." Then pointedly, he added, "I didn't want to be late."

Blade jumped into the conversation. "Why don't we go inside? I'm sure the reverend is waiting for us."

"Go inside?" Storm waited for Hadden to tell her he'd changed his mind.

But Hadden remained silent. Instead he looked at her as if he thought she was the stupidest woman he'd ever met. "Did you think the ceremony would take place outside?"

She pushed her lips together in concentration before she answered. "No, but I didn't think, well..." she decided she'd better stop while she was ahead. And with a quick nod, she pasted a smile on her face.

Hadden gestured for her to go in front and when she passed him, he fell in behind.

Once inside, Hadden greeted Reverend McCloud.

"What an unexpected pleasure," the reverend beamed, trying unsuccessfully to hide his astonishment at Hadden's choice of apparel and his swollen red eyes.

Turning quickly toward Storm, he added, "Is everyone here or do we still need to wait for more guests?"

"We're all here," Hadden answered. "Do you think we could get this over with? I've work to do and other commitments."

The good reverend tried unsuccessfully to hide his surprised expression. Then with a quick nod, he gestured to the tiny group to move to the front of the church. "Groom right here, Bride here," he directed as they gathered near the altar. "Maid of honor beside the bride, best man by the groom."

He looked over the unusual party as they assumed their rightful places, then flipped open his bible and started. "Dearly beloved, we are gathered here..."

For the first time since entering into this bargain, Storm began to have self-doubts. So lost in thought, she absorbed the words without hearing them. All she was aware of was Hadden's indifferent presence next to her. It seemed his disgust radiated outward to encompass her.

It wasn't until the reverend posed the unavoidable question that would bind them together for life that Storm began to listen to his words.

"Do you, Hadden Johnston, take Storm Graham to be your lawfully wedded wife?"

Storm held her breath and listened to the thundering of her heart until Hadden finally answered, "I do," and the air she held inside shuddered from her lungs.

The reverend let out what sounded like a relieved sigh, and with a smile, turned to Storm. "And do you, Storm, take Hadden Johnston to be your lawfully wedded husband?"

"I do," she answered before she could think to change her mind, her words coming out in a garbled whisper.

Again the reverend sighed and quickly, before either half of this unusual group standing before him could change their minds, he finished the service. Clapping his bible shut with a bang, he grinned at Hadden and said, "You may kiss the bride."

"Not in this lifetime." Hadden turned on his heel and marched down the aisle then out the front doors of church, slamming them behind him.

"Really..." the reverend gasped at the little group still standing at the altar. "What on earth is wrong with that man?"

"Excuse me please." Storm whirled around before racing down the aisle in an effort to catch up with her new husband.

"Storm, wait!" Fayth called before she too rushed down the aisle after her sister.

~ * ~

By the time Storm reached the doors Hadden had just slammed shut and was able to open them, Hadden was several blocks away and headed toward the docks and the ship looming on the horizon.

"Mr. Johnston, wait. It's not legal yet."

His back turned to her, he started to jog, appearing as if he couldn't get away fast enough.

"Mr. Johnston."

He stopped and whirled. His hands fisted at his side then started a slow march back to the church. "What do you want now?"

He had stopped so fast that Storm, who was racing down the street after him was shocked to see him acknowledge her. She came to a sudden halt, losing her balance in the process and trying desperately to keep from falling. Hadden caught her and set her on her feet.

It took several minutes for Storm to regain her composure and distance herself from Hadden enough so she could stand by herself. Once she was away from her new husband, she smoothed her skirts and stared at him expectantly.

Squaring off, Hadden asked, "What do you want now? Haven't I given you everything already?"

"I just wondered...well...I was wondering what time you'll be home and if you would go back to the church and sign the papers?"

"Why would I come home?"

She was lost and alone, wondering how this conversation could get any worse. "For something to eat. Dinner? And the papers, they have to be signed."

Hadden stared at her, his eyes condemning and threatening. "You just don't understand, do you? But yes, I'll sign the papers."

"Understand?"

"You should understand that when we decided there would be no strings attached, I wouldn't be coming home ever. Not tonight. Not tomorrow night. Not ever. Let's just say, you got what you wanted, you don't have to marry Charles Robertson."

"But—?"

Hadden held a hand up to stop her comment. "Be quiet for a second so I can explain this in terms you will understand. We're married in name only and bloody hell, as long as that's what you want, you won't see me. Beyond our contract we have nothing. I don't want to see you, or talk to you. You can stay in your own bloody house, alone. Do you understand that?"

Storm stepped back, blood draining from her face so rapidly she thought she might faint. "Yes." She thrust out her chin in defiance. "I certainly don't want to spend any more time with you than necessary but

I thought at least I would be nice. I, we, still have to convince Charles."

They started back to the church, continuing their argument as they walked.

"I'm not going to spend my time trying to convince anyone of anything, madam. I've held my part of this bargain, and I expect you to hold yours. You promised you wouldn't make any demands on me, and you damn well better stick to your word. I don't want complications or entanglements."

Storm inhaled a long deep breath, and she blundered forward. "You have to make Charles believe we are married or he'll have this annulled."

Before she could sweep another breath of air into her lungs, Hadden stood in her space. She tried to step back but he stopped her. "Listen to me. I don't want to hurt you. God, but at one point I felt sorry for you. Now I don't know how I feel. Just stay away from me, and I'll stay away from you. If Charles gets some notion in his head that we haven't consummated the marriage, we can deal with him and his accusations later, but not right now. I have to think."

"No," she shot back, pushing him away from her. "We have to convince Charles and especially his father that you would protect me, that our marriage is not a farce. Otherwise, Henry will use his influence and find a lawyer who will have the marriage annulled. If it's annulled...I never thought no demands would mean not living together."

Hadden emitted a long sigh and gazed toward the ocean. "You've got guts," he admitted and after a long silence, he turned toward her, and with a smile, said, "seven o'clock."

"What?"

"Is that too late? Seven o' clock...that's when I figure I'll be done tonight."

Moisture welled in Storm's eyes. Relieved, she hastily pushed them back. "Really, then you'll pretend we love each other."

"I don't see I have a choice."

"No, I guess you don't."

Hadden shook his head and stared at the ground. When he finally looked up, Storm felt as if he'd hit her in the stomach. The laughter in his dark brown eyes sent her heart in a tailspin. "I've got to admit, I kind of like your determination. And, I'm glad I'm no longer your opponent."

"I beg your pardon?"

"I mean you've won this round, and I admire your audacity."

Relieved now that she knew she'd be protected from Charles Robertson, she didn't want to second-guess anything Hadden was saying to her. She'd already made too many assumptions about his intentions and was damn sure not going to make another one. "What would you like for dinner?"

"Hell, I don't know. I like just about anything. Surprise me."

"Then it's a surprise," she nodded, "seven o'clock then?"

"Goodbye." He nodded and turned to walk down the street.

"What about the papers?" They were at the front door to the church.

"Oh yeah." A few minutes later, everything was signed and they were outside the church. Hadden started toward the docks.

"Mr. Johnston, why don't you ever ride a horse? It would be a lot faster, going from here to there."

"Hate horses," he said.

~ * ~

Storm turned to walk back to the church. What she saw startled her. Ella was pacing, Larena and Fayth stood quietly near the doors, and Aiden with Blade beside her raced toward her, a look of concern on her face.

"Where is that man going?" Aiden asked when she reached her.

"I didn't ask."

"Did you talk about a reception or dinner after the wedding? Is he going to come back? He looked furious, no, beyond furious."

"I think everything might work out. He and I were discussing what he wanted for dinner. He wanted me to figure it out. But I don't know what he likes and what he doesn't like." It occurred to Storm she didn't know anything at all about Hadden except he hadn't wanted to marry her and he liked to play golf.

Aiden put both hands on Storm's shoulders and stared at her as if she was insane. "Dinner? You two were discussing dinner?"

"Yes. Is that so strange? We are married. What do married couples talk about?"

"Well, I certainly don't know the answer to that question. Maybe you had better ask Ella. So what did you decide to fix?"

"I don't know. Do you have any suggestions?"

"He might like fish. You could pick up a fresh catch by the docks, or chicken. Most people like chicken, and potatoes are always a safe idea."

"Chicken it is then. I'll have to go to the market."

Aiden stepped back and studied Storm's face. "Why Storm, if I didn't know better, I'd think you were trying to please that man."

Storm tossed her cousin a smile. "Maybe I'd like to please him, but that doesn't mean I'm eager to embrace marriage in the truest sense of the word. I need him if I'm going to keep Charles and his father at bay."

"Of course you do, Storm. Why would I think otherwise?"

Chapter Six

Seven o'clock had come and gone. The roasted chicken was drying and the potatoes were starting to crack around the edges. Everything was cold. Storm wiped her hands on the apron she wore and leaning on the kitchen sink, peered out the window. The sun had set and the tide seemed to be coming in, while the ships at the dock rocked with the waves.

"Seven-forty," Storm muttered, pulling back the lace curtain so she could peer down the street. "Well, punctuality is not his strong suit."

With a huff of indignation, Storm moved away from the door and paced the hallway to the kitchen then back. It was a short distance, and she soon grew bored. "I know it doesn't make a difference and remembering the way he acted at the church, I shouldn't care if he ever gets here." But even as she said those words, she stopped in front of a little oval mirror to pinch her cheeks and touch up her hair.

Moving a couple of steps back, she smoothed the apron then cocked her head to one side and thought about the red apron she liked to wear. "You're in mourning. The red apron is not appropriate."

Striding down the hallway to the kitchen, Storm pushed through the double doors. "You shouldn't care what he thinks. He doesn't even have the good manners to show up on time. And you've spent all afternoon cooking and cleaning for him. Good God you've become Ella. Well at least I don't have to worry about children."

She picked up a wooden spoon then set it down, not knowing why she'd picked it up in the first place. Everything was cooked and was now cooling and would probably be a congealed mess in another few minutes. But why did she care if he didn't?

She pulled open the door to the oven to stare at the chicken. It still looked the same, but she knew it was drying out and all her work would be futile. She wasn't sure how it would taste. And despite all her wayward thoughts, she had wanted to please Hadden.

At least the dessert would taste good as she glanced at the windowsill where the lemon meringue pie was cooling. "I always wanted to eat dessert first."

Time did not stand still. The clock continued to tick away, and Hadden Johnston had not arrived. Storm rechecked the chicken then the potatoes. The vegetables had turned to mush. Trying for some way to spruce them up, she added salt and pepper, stirred the pot then added more.

For several moments, she continued to mix the pot with the wooden spoon until she was startled out of her musings by a sharp rap at the front door. *Good God he's here.* Returning the salt and pepper to the dinner table, she headed for the door. "Stay calm, he's not going to bite. Stay calm, take a deep breath."

When she saw him, she inhaled a sharp breath of air, surprised by his appearance. Instead of the buckskins and worn white shirt he'd dressed in this morning, he no longer looked as if he'd been keel hauled. He was dressed in black trousers and a white shirt that had been pressed. His eyes were no longer red rimmed and his hair was clean and brushed. He didn't even have unshaved stubble on his jaw.

As Storm's gaze shifted past his broad shoulders to his chiseled face and his sparkling brown eyes, she realized how handsome Hadden Johnston was. And tonight, standing in the soft glow of her porch lamp, he surpassed all of her wildest dreams. Hadden Johnston looked like the bronzed predator he was so often compared to. Storm didn't know what it was that set him apart from other men, but whatever that element was, it sent a shiver of anticipation down her spine.

"Come in, come in." Storm stepped back and pulled the door wide, feeling the heat of embarrassment all the way to her toes.

"I'm sorry I'm late." He didn't look at her as he stepped inside and set his hat on the little end table beside the door.

Storm, with her hands clasped in front of her, stared at him, waiting for him to continue with an apology but it didn't come. "I'm sorry I'm late," she realized was as close as she was going to get. No remorse, no polite plea for forgiveness, just and acknowledgement of the fact.

"Dinner is ready." *Past ready.* She decided to ignore his tardiness and not dwell on the fact he didn't really apologize. "You can go into the dining room. I'll bring dinner." She started for the kitchen, but was brought up short by the sound of his deep voice.

"Storm?"

"What?" She turned, her cheeks suddenly heating.

"Where is the dining room?"

Nervous laughter escaped her. "Oh, I'm sorry, I... Down the hall first door."

Hadden nodded. "Can I help you with anything?" He stepped forward and stopped her with a hand on her shoulder. "You don't need to be nervous."

"I'm not...well not too anxious. I need to get to the kitchen." How did he know she was uneasy? She tried to breathe but the air didn't want to enter her lungs.

"Please," he gestured then turned to make his way to the dining room.

When she pushed open the door to the dining room, he was staring at the table as if it baffled him in some way. She set the platter filled with chicken and potatoes and the bowl of vegetables on the table.

"Is everything all right?" She cocked her head to one side, eyeing him curiously.

"The table, you didn't have to go to such lengths for me." He pulled out a chair for her.

"I thought you would like it. I brought up a bottle of wine from the cellar. Could you open it?" Her hand shook as she handed it to him, and she prayed he wouldn't notice.

Hadden nodded and inserted and twisted the corkscrew she'd handed him. Popping the cork out, he smelled the wine then poured a small amount into each glass. "The flowers, the candles, it's all nice. But you didn't..."

"I wanted to make this first meal with you nice." Storm felt a bit of moisture pool in her eyes. She didn't want to cry, and she was sure he was going to tell her there was no reason to have a romantic dinner. What the bloody hell had she been thinking?

"To our first meal together. Thank you." He raised his glass then sipped before setting it on the table.

"To friendship." She did the same and cleared her throat. "I know we've started out on the rocky side, but I hope to have smooth sailing ahead."

For a second, she didn't think Hadden was going to join in her toast, but with a shrug, he picked up his glass. Storm tipped hers toward his, but he ignored the gesture and drank, avoiding the customary clink of crystal. Putting his glass down, he reached for the platter, stabbing a large piece of chicken and asking, "Precisely what do you think is going to happen now?"

Storm gulped, setting down her glass with shaking hands. "First we will announce our marriage. Tomorrow during Sunday service seems like a good time. We will have to go together. Presenting a united caring front is the only way to proceed. We have to convince Charles and his father that we are taking our marriage vows to heart."

Sermon."

Storm barged ahead. "Will you go with me, please? People will talk if you're not there and I don't know what I would tell them."

"I don't know why. I never go to the services. Why should I start now? It seems if I show up in places where I don't normally go, that's when people will talk."

"When a couple are married they do things together." Now her voice shook as well as her hands.

"We're not really married."

"But we are." She would argue this until she turned blue in the face. And she would find a way to change his mind.

"What happens after church?"

"That's up to you." Annoyed by his endless questions, she said, "I would guess people would like to congratulate us and perhaps have a party for us. You know a celebration."

"Nothing to celebrate." Hadden popped a piece of chicken into his mouth. "No parties. I'm not a hypocrite."

"But Hadden—"

"Absolutely not. Pass the vegetables, please. The chicken is a little dry. Did you overcook it?"

"Really," Storm bit down on the words she was about to exchange with him. *Hypocrite indeed.* If he'd been on time the chicken wouldn't be dry.

Hadden spooned out a large portion. "These look a little mushy."

Perhaps if..." Once again she stopped mid-sentence. But the moisture pooling in her eyes would not go unnoticed if she didn't stop the eminent flow of tears. She rose to go to the kitchen. A little privacy was what she needed. Pushing through the doubled doors, she leaned on the sink and sucked in air then she wiped the tears from her eyes. *Don't cry. Don't let him make me cry. He doesn't know anything.*

Suddenly the doors were flung open, and Hadden was at the sink. He pushed on the handle to get water then he gulped it down.

Perplexed, she stepped back and watched. "What happened?"

"What happened? You smothered the vegetables with pepper. I thought my throat was on fire. That's what happened."

"For heaven's sake, I only peppered them once." But when she thought back, she really didn't know what she'd done. He'd been so late, and she didn't know what to do. She remembered stirring and salting, then stirring and using the pepper grinder.

"That, sweet lady, was more than once."

"Perhaps it was. For politeness sake, you could have pretended to like them." She wanted to yell at him that this was his fault but she stopped herself. She could have paid more attention to what she was doing, admitting her mind was not on cooking.

Hadden began to laugh, a rich, rumbling sound that surprised Storm. "You are truly incredible. Is there nothing you can't turn to your advantage?"

Storm didn't know what to say. "Is that what I'm doing?"

I'm in my kitchen wishing for privacy, and I've somehow turned something to my advantage. I don't know what he's talking about.

"I'm going to be honest. I didn't want to like you, but I'm finding that not only do I enjoy your company, but I find your resilience in the face of difficulties is intriguing. And I promise you that tomorrow I won't be late."

Tomorrow? Storm's heart leaped into her throat. He was talking about a tomorrow. What more could she want? That could only mean he was agreeable to moving into her house and carrying out the marriage charade. *Now don't get ahead of yourself. You know you have a way of doing just that very thing.*

But then this wasn't a charade and never would be. They were married in the eyes of man and God. That thought sent a shiver down her spine. He could expect his husbandly rights.

Hadden took her hands in his, sweeping his thumb across her knuckles. "Now, I think it's time I went home. It's late, we're both tired, and I have a long walk ahead of me."

"But," Storm protested, "you can't go. What about church tomorrow? And anyway, I thought we agreed you'd move in here." She was begging again. Just let him go and hope he changes his mind.

Whatever happens between us, I have to stop pleading with him.

Storm watched Hadden's mouth tighten into what appeared to be an angry line. "We didn't agree on anything of the sort. You demanded I move in, and I decided not to have another argument so I didn't speak my intentions of remaining in my home."

"But you can't do that, go to your house." She was hard pressed this time to keep the tears at bay. She'd been successful several times this evening but this was the last thing she wanted to hear. "If you don't stay, Charles Robertson won't believe we are really married, and he'll make me..."

"Bloody hell, don't cry. I can't stand tears." Hadden placed his hand on the side of her face and with his thumb, wiped away the tears. "I'll take you to church tomorrow morning. I promise, and I won't be late this time. Just stop crying."

She shook away from his tenderness not wanting to feel more than she already did. "That's just not good enough. If you spend the night somewhere else, people are going to think we don't have a real marriage. I don't understand why you don't want to live here."

"How did the dinner go?" Larena waltzed into the kitchen, Larena, Aidan and Blade behind her.

Hadden gave them each a pointed look then turned his attention back to Storm. "I believe you have a full house. So, with that said, I will see you in the morning." He turned on his heel and hurried to the front door, Storm following behind him, wishing she could think of something to say that would make him change his mind.

"Hadden?"

"What?"

"Please don't hate me."

~ * ~

Hadden didn't understand what had happened. "Bloody hell, I'm going to church with my not-so-much a wife. How did I get myself in this predicament?" At this moment he wasn't sure how he felt. For some strange reason he wasn't angry, but he bloody well should be furious. He wanted to protect Storm at all cost, but he resented what had happened. He'd lost control of his life, and he didn't know where it was going.

He brushed his hair back and adjusted his cravat, then with a handkerchief, wiped the speck of blood off his chin. He didn't shave on Sunday mornings either. Now he was doing a whole lot of things for Storm Graham, no Storm Johnston, and he couldn't think of one good reason why.

He felt as if some strange being had infiltrated his body and his mind. That strange being came in the form of a beautiful woman who he couldn't tell no. A half hour and he needed to be at Storm's house. Maybe he'd go for a long walk first, and perhaps the walk would work the kinks out of his shoulder muscles. He circled his neck, hearing the vertebrae crack.

With one last look at himself, he strode through the door. The day was beautiful and in the early morning, birds sang and frogs croaked. Redolent with spring flowers, a smile formed on Hadden's face. He whistled as he strode in the sunlit day to the Graham home.

Almost hating to admit it, he was beginning to like Storm. She had a way of changing everything he said and reforming the words so the situation went her way. He had to keep his wits when he talked to her. It seemed she was always at least two steps ahead of him.

Storm Graham was a challenge in every conceivable way. Suddenly he stood in front of her door and lifting his hand to knock, he was surprised to find the door opening.

"You're on time?" She smiled at him and pulled the door wider. "And dressed rather nicely."

"What? Did you expect me to show up in my work clothes?" Bloody hell, but he'd done that very thing yesterday when they were married. No wonder she'd had such a strange expression on her face when she opened the door.

"Well, where you are concerned, I'm never too sure."

Hadden pulled out his pocket watch and looked at it. "It's time to go. Let's get this over with."

Storm nodded and swept past him, picking up a bonnet she'd set on the table near the door and tying the ribbons beneath her chin. Hadden liked the way the hat framed her face and accentuated her stunning violet-blue eyes. He gave thanks for one thing, she was easy to look at, beautiful.

Whistling through his teeth, he closed his eyes for a brief second, determined to make the best of this church thing she was so determined to pursue. What was it about this woman who set his well-ordered world into upheaval? He needed balance in his life. He'd always thought of himself as a reasonable and calm man but Storm had a way of infuriating him like no other. And how could that be? He was always objective—known as the mediator—the solver of problems. In this instance he couldn't solve his own problems.

What was it then, about Storm Graham that could so quickly bring him to a furious rage? No other woman had ever had such an effect on him. Not even Elizabeth had been able to make him angry. He'd dealt with his one-time fiancée with a tranquility that had surprised not only himself but his friends too. But then he acknowledged he'd never before had a wife.

So what was this marriage of convenience going to be like? Would every discussion between them end with an argument? If it did, he'd take to the sea or pursue his lifelong passion of creating a home for orphaned children. The house he'd started for Elizabeth could serve this very purpose—an annex from the widow Stewart's home. He employed Adele Stewart to watch over and take care of several orphaned children.

Bottom line, he didn't want a marriage with no love or sex. This was damn inconvenient. Hell, at this point they weren't even friends, and he didn't like the idea of living with her little sisters.

Now looking at Storms smiling and animated face as they neared the church, he felt a surge of hopefulness he hadn't known before. He wondered what her expectations were. She seemed to surprise him at every turn. And he hadn't been the easiest person to deal with, but she'd persevered and except for the incident with the vegetables, she'd pretty much kept a smiling face.

When they entered the church, he noticed the many curious looks being tossed their way by the members of the congregation. He heard the murmurs all around him and inwardly cringed, wishing this was over and done.

"Please take my arm," Storm whispered as the stunned looks intensified.

He was such a dolt. Why did she have to suggest things he should have thought of for himself? "Sorry, didn't think of it." With that said, he felt a bit inadequate. He was a gentleman, and he wasn't born in a barn, but she had an uncanny way of making him feel as if he had been.

He offered her his arm, and they continued down the aisle. The church wasn't full. He guided her into a pew near the back of the church. Larena and Fayth, who had joined them on their way to the services, continued up the aisle to the front.

"Why are we sitting back here all by ourselves?"

"Because," he cleared his throat, "when the good reverend announces our marriage yesterday, only the rude people will turn around and stare at us."

Storm nodded. "I guess that's a good idea. I never thought of that. But, if we sat in the front, they would have been staring at our backs, and we would not have seen them."

"I would have felt the stares."

The announcement didn't come until the end of the sermon and the last blessing. Then with a broad and unexpected smile from the serious Reverend McCloud, he walked to the middle of the dais and clasping his hands in front of him, he said, "I have an important and happy announcement today, Hadden Johnston married Storm Graham yesterday morning in a private ceremony that included only family and close friends. I'm sure all of you will want to stay for the social hour afterwards and congratulate them on their good fortune of finding each other. And my wonderful wife has made a cake to celebrate the occasion."

A stunned silence ensued as the people sitting in the little church absorbed the information they were given. Then, as if someone was directing a play, all the heads in front of them turned to look at Hadden and Storm.

Hadden ran a finger underneath his collar and held his breath. "Guess I made a mistake sitting in the back," he whispered.

"Guess you did," Storm agreed, raising her voice to be heard over the loud applause and the chattering voices.

"And the social hour is going to be hell." Hadden wanted to proclaim he wouldn't go, but he knew he'd been less than civil to her, and he wanted to behave in a more gentlemanly fashion.

"What? I'd expected you to state unequivocally that we wouldn't go. Thank you." She smiled at him.

And for the first time he was glad he'd seen her smile. It softened the lines in her face and while she was always a beautiful woman, the smile made her radiant.

Clasping Storm's hand in his, he raised them briefly in a gesture of unity. "I just want to make you happy."

The instant the reverend had finished speaking, Hadden grabbed Storm's hand and raced out the church doors.

"Whoa, stop what? Where?" she asked breathlessly as he bolted down the steps to the pathway below, dragging her along with him.

"Nowhere, I guess." He came to an abrupt halt. "I had to get out of there. I was getting claustrophobic, and I just couldn't stand and watch everyone stare as they filed past us. This way we can avoid as many well-wishers as possible."

Storm cocked her head to one side as she looked at him. "You really hate this, don't you? I'm sorry for that. It will all be over soon."

"Yeah, what did you think?" His tone was on the belligerent side. "I really do. It's a lie, and I hate lies."

"I'm sorry, why don't you go ahead and leave. I'll make excuses and stay for the social hour. I really don't want to make you feel uncomfortable. And if you are angry, it won't look so good. Couples are supposed to be happy."

Hadden looked down for a second then blew out a long frustrated breath. "No, I'm a big boy. I can stay and support you. It can't be easy for you either." To Hadden's surprise, he meant every word. Storm didn't want to be married any more than he did. For her, marriage was the lesser of two evils.

"You really don't have to stay. I understand, and my sisters are here. I'm sure the congregation will understand."

"I won't leave your side. It's the right thing to do. And if we were really married and I mean really married, I'd be eager to show you off as my new wife."

Out of nowhere the reverend's wife hustled across the lawn toward them. Her grin was infectious. Her bright red curls bobbed around her face as she made her way to greet them.

"Oh, there are the new lovebirds," she trilled, her plump cheeks pink from excitement and the exertion of running. "I'm so glad I found you. Now, just come over here, under these trees. I've set up a table for you to cut the cake, and I want to have both of you in position to receive the rest of the congregation." She tossed a distracted look over her shoulder, and seeing the crowd start to exit the church added, "Hurry, now! Everyone will be here in a second. This is just so much fun."

With a resigned shrug, Hadden looped Storm's arm through his and trudged after the reverend's wife, taking up a position next to a wooden table where he saw a large cake and several bowls of what appeared to be punch.

"You didn't have to do this but thank you." Storm smiled.

"Oh, I was so happy to do it. Why I remember the day I was married as if it happened yesterday."

Hadden glanced at the rickety table covered by the inexpensive and worn muslin tablecloth and felt a surge of affection for the reverend's wife. "This was a very nice gesture. Thank you."

"Oh, you are just the nicest man," she cooed. "I'm so glad you approve."

"Where do you want us to stand?" Storm asked.

"Why over here," she pointed in a general direction. "Just make sure it's a place where people can shake your hand and wish you well. When that's done you can move behind the table to cut the cake."

Storm nodded and stepped away from Hadden.

"Oh, and Mr. Johnston, remember now, you need to feed the first piece of cake to your beautiful wife."

Hadden's grin widened. "I'll be more than happy to feed the first piece to my wife." He had every intention of feeding a slice of wedding cake to Storm. She'd look cute with frosting on her face, and it might relieve some of the tension and nerves that seemed to spiral out of control.

The reverend's wife clapped her hands together and stared at them. "This is so much fun."

Hadden watched her move the crowd of well-wisher's. She was smiling and chatting with all her friends. All he could do was shake his head and greet the people as they formed a line.

Storm looked at him, a frown creasing her brows. "Don't you dare do what I think your thinking."

Hadden titled his head back and laughed. "And what is it that I'm thinking?"

"If you're not thinking it, I don't want to put any ideas into your head. But please don't embarrass me."

"Or you'll do what?"

"I don't have a plan yet." Storm turned and whispered to him as she greeted an older lady. "Maybe I could steal all of your golf clubs."

"Well, I won't then, but it did cross my mind that it would be great fun to see you with icing on your face."

"You're horrible. Maybe I'll smear it on your nose."

"If you do, be assured I will retaliate."

"Oh you are terrible. To think I once thought you were a gentleman."

"And I thought you were a lady."

It seemed as if the line would never end, but eventually it thinned and the last of the parishioners greeted them.

"Thank you for putting up with all of this." Storm told him for the hundredth time.

"I didn't do it for you but for myself."

"Well, I still thank you."

"You're welcome, then."

As was the habit, the town's people were grouped together by age and chatted happily while they caught up on gossip. Hadden was pretty sure their hasty marriage was at the top of the list. And he wondered what reasons they would think up for the wedding. He didn't like the idea that they might jump to the wrong conclusion. After all when Storm had first come to him with this hair-brained idea, he'd immediately thought she was pregnant.

"I hope they aren't talking about us." Storm turned her attention back to Hadden.

"You could probably bet on the fact they are. Every time someone laughs they look our way. All I know is the sooner we cut the cake the sooner we can get out of here."

"What could they possibly be talking about to keep the laughter flowing?"

"I truly doubt you want to know."

Time seemed to stand still while they waited for the reverend's wife to gather everyone around the table. Finally, the woman spoke up and gestured to the congregation. "Let's get this cake cut."

The chattering group of people gathered around the table. Hadden looked at them and smiled. Taking Storm's hand in his, he picked up the knife and sliced the first piece.

Hadden grinned and fed the delicate confection to Storm then she did the same. He made the huge mistake of slipping his fingers through her lips.

Storm gasped when his fingers made contact with the inside of her mouth.

But at the first contact with the warm, wet interior of Storm's mouth, a surge of desire swept through him that was so sweet and so intense it caught him as if he'd just received a blow to the gut.

Before he ignited any more flames with such intimate contact, he withdrew his fingers and stepped backward, gaping at Storm in stunned confusion.

"Kiss her, Hadden," a man in the back of crowd yelled. Then to his dislike a chant began.

"Kiss her...kiss her...kiss her!"

Bloody hell, if he kissed her, he didn't know how his body would respond. The last thing he needed in this tenuous marriage would be sex with his wife. Yet he understood the congregation would not stop until he did their bidding.

Leaning forward, he grasped Storm by the shoulders and planted a quick and very chaste kiss on her lips.

"You can do better than that, Johnston." The man who'd started the chant yelled. "Let's see a real kiss."

Hadden looked at Storm with the resignation they would not get out of here without a real kiss. He placed his hands behind her head and slowly drew her to him and lowered his lips to hers.

She leaned into him as if his presence gave her strength. Beneath his assault her lips softened, and he heard a tiny sigh of surrender as she threaded her fingers through the hair at the nape of his neck.

It was Hadden who ended the kiss. Reluctantly raising his head, he stared at Storm, not understanding the sensations rushing through him.

"That was a kiss," a man yelled.

"Better take her home before this goes farther than you'd want it to go—in public that is."

Hadden knew he should respond to the lusty and sexually driven comments being tossed their way. It was expected, and he remembered many an occasion when he done the same thing to a newly wedded couple. Yet at this moment he couldn't think of anything to say. He watched Storm, her moist swollen lips beckoning for more. He cleared his throat.

"Don't do that again," he whispered, "or you might get what you're asking for."

Turning to the laughing crowd, he grinned and yelled, "I know you'll excuse us if we leave."

More shrieks of laughter and catcalls followed his outrageous statement. Hadden needed no more encouragement to leave the unwanted festivities. Grabbing Storm's hand, he pulled her toward the reverend and his wife.

"Thank you so much for everything." Hadden held his hand out to shake the reverend's hand. "And to you for the cake and your thoughtfulness."

"Thank you," Storm followed suit.

Walking across the lawn to the road, Hadden stopped and pulled Storm against him.

"What are you doing? Aren't we leaving?"

"Not yet." He stared down the road.

He heard Storm draw in a sharp breath. Galloping down the road, his face a mask of fury, was Charles Robertson and behind him, his father Henry.

Chapter Seven

"You've got something that's mine, and I want it back." Charles jumped from his horse. Hands fisted at his sides, he strode toward Hadden and Storm.

Hadden moved Storm behind him. "And what is that?"

Spittle flying from his lips, Charles shook his fist at Hadden. "I've a contract. She's mine."

"Last time I heard one can't buy or sell women." His blood pounded in his temples, and he felt the enraged tick at his jaw. There were few men who could bring him to anger this quickly and Charles was one of them. He inhaled a deep breath, not wanting to lose his composure in front of Storm and the entire congregation.

Henry waved a piece of paper in the air. "It's signed by Bradford Graham. It's legal and binding. She will marry me." He stabbed himself in the chest with a finger.

"May I see?" Hadden reached out to take the paper.

"Don't play games with me you son of a bitch." Robertson folded the paper and stuck it inside his coat pocket. "Not going to let you rip it up. My father has retained a lawyer. You will be hearing from him."

Hadden stiffened, his intentions clear at this point. "Do you really want to discuss this matter in front of all these people?" With a tilt of his head, he gestured toward the lawn and the gawking flock of parishioners.

"I don't care who the hell hears what I have to say." Charles stepped closer to Hadden. "The more people who learn exactly what you're capable of, the better. You think because you have more money than anyone else in this part of England you can do whatever you want. Well, I'm here to tell you that you can't. I'm going to hold you and your so-called bride responsible. Storm will marry me."

The crowd had gathered closer to Hadden and Storm as Charles and Henry continued their rant. In the background he heard several audible gasps then Storm's sisters and cousin trying to shoo the crowd away from them, but to no avail. Nothing like good gossip to bring people together.

"You may have a contract but you're not going to marry Storm because I already have. Perhaps the other terms will be more agreeable to us. She is ready to hand over the stables, to pay off the debt owed by Bradford. I believe that was also in the contract."

Charles seemed to ignore Hadden's question while his face grew redder with each passing second. "We both know this marriage is fake, and I don't want the stables, I want Storm."

"Fake?" Hadden smiled. "No it's not but if you want proof, ask the reverend and his wife. He performed the service yesterday, and his wife was a witness along with Storm's sisters, her cousin and Blade."

"I did." The reverend stepped forward seemingly ready to defend Storm and Hadden. "They were married and it's legal and binding."

"We were also there." Aiden gestured toward Larena and Fayth.

"As was I." The reverend's wife stepped through the crowd.

"The words might have been said, but I know for a fact that was all that happened yesterday," Henry said.

"I don't understand." The reverend looked from Hadden to Storm then back again, rubbing his jaw.

"What I mean is that Mr. Johnston did not sleep with his new bride. He was on board his ship and in the captain's cabin—alone. The happy bridegroom spent the night at the docks downing whiskey as if it was water."

Chatter swept through the crowd behind them.

"I don't see this is any of your business. Where I sleep is a private matter between my wife and myself. Were you spying on me?" Hadden wasn't feeling anything but frustration. His usual calm façade in the face of adversity was rapidly vanishing.

"Hadden please." Storm's face had turned crimson. "Let's go

home."

Hadden looked at her then turned back to Charles and Henry. "You're embarrassing my new wife, and I won't stand for that to happen. Please excuse us. We're leaving."

He turned to Storm and offered her his arm, which she promptly took. A look of profound relief etched across her face.

"You're going to regret the day you crossed me." Charles put his face close to Hadden's. "Damn sorry."

"Don't threaten me, Robertson." With a last controlling look at both men, Hadden guided Storm past them and down the street. "Come on, honey. Let's put the rumors of a chaste marriage to bed."

At his comment, Storm stumbled and had to hang more tightly onto his arm. He squeezed her fingers, trying to encourage her to put on a bold front. But he wasn't too sure she could handle any more of this conversation. A good time to get to her home and shut the doors.

"Why did you embarrass her in front of everyone?" Aiden caught up to them. "Can't you see how much you've hurt her?"

"Would all of you rather have everyone know what Charles said is the truth? Our marriage is for the sole purpose of breaking the contract." Hadden grit his teeth.

"No, but couldn't you have thought of something different to say?" Aiden took hold of her cousin's hand.

"I wanted to leave them with no doubts about our marriage." Hadden glanced at her red cheeks and grinned, thinking how beautiful she was and how much he wanted to protect her from the likes of men like the Robertsons.

"I suppose you have a point. Still..." Storm looked into his face. "I don't think he's going to stop."

"Neither do I." He tightened his hand on her fingers. "We are going to have to do something about this."

"What can we do?" Her voice was agitated, and the frown creasing her brows sent a surge of remorse through him.

"I don't know."

"Oh, Hadden, he scares me. I don't want to be married to him. Can he really have our marriage annulled?"

"Not if it's consummated." Hadden was blunt.

"How would anyone know if it's consummated or not? We're not going to let anyone into the bedroom."

"I suppose the only way is if you were to get pregnant. So, I'm moving in with you."

~ * ~

"Well it's about time." Aiden's hands were on her hips while her foot tapped a rapid staccato on the kitchen floor.

Storm lifted a steaming kettle of water from the stove and poured the water into a teapot.

"He was adorable when he defended you and the marriage." Aiden sat down and handed her cup to Storm.

"Hadden's dreamy," Fayth said.

Storm's mind kept going back to the words consummate and marriage. But from everything they'd discussed, he had no more desire to consummate this marriage than she had. But what if...

What if it's the only way to get Charles and Henry off their backs?

"Sweety, what are you going to do?" Aiden asked as she sipped her tea. "I know how you feel, but for your own sake you have to find a way to work through this. He is your husband."

Did Aiden know how she felt when she wasn't sure herself? And how was Hadden feeling now? He'd gone to his cabin to retrieve clothes and personal items so he could move in with her.

"We're going to have to share a bedroom." Her words came out in a monotone as she put voice to her thoughts.

"And a bed," Larena chimed in to the conversation.

Storm felt the color drain from her face. Hadden had made it damn clear he wasn't interested in her in any sense. He didn't love her, and she didn't think he even liked her. And despite what he'd said on the way home from church, she didn't believe for one second he was serious about consummating the marriage.

"He doesn't want to make love to me." Storm twisted the cloth napkin in front of her, looking at the table as she spoke. "And I don't want children. So where does that leave me, us?"

"After what happened to our mother, I know having children frightens you. But Bradford was a bad, evil man who hated women. Hadden doesn't hate women," Larena offered with a shrug of her shoulders.

"No, just me." Storm said with a tiny wince. "I've forced him into marrying me simply because he understood the alternative, wedding Charles, was no alternative at all, and now I must deal with the fallout."

"Wasn't there a second part to the contract?" Fayth asked. "Can't you pay him back the debt?"

"He didn't mention money only the horses, Fiacre in particular. I don't think repayment is factoring into this, although I believe Hadden might consider payment instead of consummation if Charles and Henry will accept that course of action." A slight glimmer of hope brightened her dark thoughts. But the only way she could pay the debt was to give Henry the stables, and now he said he wouldn't accept them. In addition, she didn't want Hadden to feel obligated to pay whatever sum Bradford owed for her.

"I don't think Charles or Henry will agree to payment," Aiden said, biting into a scone. "He wants you. The horrible man has made up his mind, and he's not going to change it. When he says your name, he looks crazed."

"There is only one solution. I'm going to have to get pregnant. It would be a miracle if I could seduce him into my bed."

"And you know how much about seducing a man?" Aiden nibbled on a scone and thoughtfully stared at her.

"Absolutely nothing." Storm clenched her shaking hands in frustration. Could she bring herself to be intimate with Hadden? She touched a finger to her lip remembering the touch of his mouth on hers when he'd kissed her only a few hours ago. She closed her eyes, seeing the look of shock and tension on his face when he'd finally lifted his head. Had he felt the same way she had?

"You could ask Ella," Aiden offered. "She could tell you how to seduce your man."

Storm tapped her fingers on the table. "I suppose but I don't know when I'm going to see her. This is all so confusing. I'm not in love with him, but I can't stop thinking about the kiss." The infamous kiss. She had no desire to become intimate with the man, and yet the thought of how his muscles had felt beneath her fingers sent her nerves spinning and her heart racing.

"Or you could just ask him to take you to bed." Aiden's smile dared her to do that very thing.

Her body felt flushed and when she tried to lift her teacup, the water nearly spilled over the top. "Yes, I'm going to walk up to him and say, 'Hadden would you make love to me until you get me pregnant?' " The sarcasm in her voice left her cringing inside.

"You could. But didn't you tell him you didn't want children? That's a bit unexpected and a huge turn around even for you." Aiden dusted the crumbs from her hands and slanted Storm an Aiden sized grin.

"Is there any other way I can convince Charles this is a real marriage?" She sighed and gave up on drinking her tea.

~ * ~

Blade strode beside Hadden as they made their way to his cabin located in the woods above the docks. Everything had happened so fast, Hadden didn't know what to think.

"You going to move in with your wife?" Blade asked.

Hadden glared at Aiden's so called bodyguard. He wasn't sure why the man followed Storm's cousin around as if he were her protector. Aiden always did seem a bit uncontrollable but this was civilized here. He threw open the door to his home and marched to his bedroom. Pulling a valise from a top shelf in his closet, he threw clothes into it. "I am and I don't need any help. Why did you follow me?"

"To make sure you returned. I wouldn't want Aiden's cousin disappointed in you or anything you did. After you married her, you should have moved in last night. Then Charles couldn't assume you didn't have sex with his so-called-property."

It was close to a warning, no, his words sounded more like a threat. "In hindsight I have to agree with you. But I didn't have that privilege last night, and I had no idea Charles would react the way he did."

"Storm didn't lie to you, did she?" Blade's eyebrows lifted.

Hadden paused and turned to look at Blade in surprise. "No, she didn't. I should have taken her more seriously. After I visited Charles..." His voice trailed off as he thought about that encounter.

"You going to take this seriously now?"

"Still threatening me? You know, I hate everything about this sham of a marriage. Charles had that much right. But I'm in it and I'm going to protect Storm. Short of murder, I don't see any way out."

Blade rocked back on his heels, hands in his pockets. "A man like you doesn't get forced into anything, and he doesn't do anything he doesn't want to do. I think you protest a little too much."

"You don't know anything." Hadden went back to tossing items into the suitcase. Then pulled down a second. "As long as I have you with me, might as well put you to work."

"You planning on consummation?"

"Bloody hell, what does that have to do with anything? Not that it's any of your business." The man didn't give up, and he was damn tired of explaining his actions and his thoughts.

Blade laughed. "I'm making this my business since Storm's father is dead. If you're not sleeping with her then you're not really married, and they can get the marriage annulled if they wish. I hope that isn't what you want."

"Or what?" Hadden turned to look at Blade, his hands fisted at his sides. He was ready for a fight even if it was a fight with a friend not a foe. "I'm staying in this until the end and unless someone is in our bedroom, they won't know if we're sleeping together or not."

"You do have a point, but if she doesn't get pregnant there will be questions. So tell me, how are you going to get her with child if you don't take her to bed? A puzzle to be solved." Blade laughed.

Hadden fisted his hands, wishing he could take out some of his anger on Blade. "I'm working on it. So far we've agreed on a marriage in name only. The advantage for her is she'll have my protection."

"And for you? What do you get out of this little marriage for Storm's convenience?"

"For me? I will no longer be asked to every party, dance and recital held in this town and the neighboring ones. Mamas won't parade their daughters in front of me in hopes of a proposal."

"You going to share the same bedroom?"

He really hadn't thought on that too much. But now that Blade brought it up, he didn't think there was a spare bedroom, and he didn't think it polite to ask Larena and Fayth to move in together. "Yup."

"Really?" Blade asked, his question filled with the sound of sarcasm.

"You're not going to let this go are you?"

"Nope," Blade responded cheerfully.

Hadden swiped his hair back, astounded at Blade's boldness and even more amazed at himself when he realized he'd been having this discussion with someone he barely knew. "Even if we share the same bedroom and the same bed, I'm not going to touch her."

"Good luck with that," Blade countered with a hearty chuckle following.

"I'm not going to need luck. What the hell do you mean by that?"

"You're not really that naïve are you?"

This wasn't going the way he needed it to go. "If I slept with her, things would be a thousand times more complicated than they already are. Simply put, sleeping with her is not something I would ever consider."

"She's your wife now for better or worse until death do you part. Do you mean to stay celibate for the rest of your life, or are you going to take a mistress? I know I wouldn't stay celibate."

"Well, I'm not you." Hadden snapped the valise shut then turned his attention to the second one.

"You're reputation with the ladies precedes you. I heard enough from the church ladies to tell me you're not a man to stay away from the women."

"I've had enough, Blade." Hadden pointed to one valise and lifted the other from his bed. "Time you made yourself useful."

Chapter Eight

Blade opened the door then poked his head inside. "We're back."

Aiden stepped through the kitchen door, wiping her hands on a dishtowel. "Good but, Blade, don't get too comfortable. The girls, Fayth and Larena are leaving with us. We packed while you were gone with Hadden. If we leave within the hour, we can be at McLellan castle just after dark."

"You don't have to leave on my account," Hadden said with a cocky grin. "This is your house."

Blade shrugged, still sporting the grin. "Aiden thinks you and Storm need space. Newlyweds and all."

Storm pushed through the double doors smiling, liking the feelings that swept through her when she looked at her new husband; tall, broad shouldered with vibrant brown eyes.

"Where can I put my things?" Hadden looked toward the stairway.

"Up the stairs second door on the right. Do you need help? She smoothed her dress, wishing she knew what to say.

"I'll go with him," Blade said, "then I'll help the girls with their bags."

"Aiden, you really don't have to do this." Storm knew she was losing a shoulder to cry on and someone to confide her darkest fears. Yet she had Ella too and it seemed selfish to keep Aidan here any longer.

"I feel blessed. I came for a funeral and ended up staying for a wedding. I really hope everything works out for the two of you." Aidan hugged Storm, a sweet smile on her face.

When everyone left she'd be here alone with Hadden, and she had no clue what to expect. The grandfather clock in the hallway ticked and the ominous sound sent chills down Storm's spine. She rubbed her arms to chase away the goose bumps.

"When are you leaving?" The question sounded innocuous, but she didn't know what to say.

"As soon as possible. Don't worry, sweetie. It's going to be okay. You'll see. He is your husband, and you are going to have to learn to live with him."

"You sound so wise, Aidan. When are you going to tie the knot with Blade?"

"Turn this around to focus on me, all right. The thing is, I don't know. He doesn't want to marry, and I'm certainly not going to force him. I count my blessings he no longer thinks of me as a little girl, and I don't think he's seen anyone for almost a year. But I'm not holding my breath."

"Do you love him?" This was a stupid question. Anyone who had eyes could see the love shining in Aiden's when she looked at Blade.

"I love him very much."

The cousins hugged again. "Good luck then. I wish I knew what love felt like."

"You'll know, and I have a hunch it's going to be sooner than later."

"Ready to go?" Blade strode down the steps, arms piled high with various bags, Hadden behind him laden down the same way.

"Where are Larena and Fayth?" Blade asked.

"Saying a farewell to their horses. I told them it was only for a month or so, but they had to go see them."

The two couples walked outside to the carriage waiting for them. "Larena, Fayth," Storm called toward the stables.

The girls raced out, laughing and chatting. "We're here," Fayth said, breathless.

"Yeah, can hardly wait to go visit with your sisters Eveleen and Allura. Maybe we can finagle a trip to the island." Hugs and cheek kisses with Storm and they turned to go.

They loaded the carriage and piled inside. With heads sticking out the window, Storm watched as her sisters left for McClellan castle. A lone tear slipped down her cheek. She would miss them so much.

She turned to Hadden, unsure of what to say. He brushed the tear from her cheek.

"I guess it's just the two of us now," Hadden said. "What do you want to do?"

She shivered and tried to smile. "I don't have any idea. Did you get all your things moved into your room?" Knowing that if he still needed some help she could do that. Needing to keep busy was paramount on her mind. It wasn't time to start dinner, and she didn't feel right, sitting down and knitting.

"Yup." He rocked back on his heels. "Decided I didn't like the guest room."

"What?" she asked surprised. "What's wrong with it?"

"Because I like the master better."

"You can't have that room, it's my room."

"True."

"Excuse me but...you don't expect me to move out." She instantly regretted the statement because if he moved in she would have no choice but to move out." Her breath caught in her throat, and she knew she had to sit down before she fainted.

"Isn't the room you're occupying the master suite? Or am I wrong?"

"Of course it is."

He shrugged and grinned at her. "Well then?"

"But..."

"Go on."

"But I'm sleeping in that room." She repeated, dumbfounded by what he was telling her.

Hadden looked at her for a moment and a glint of amusement sprang to his eyes. "And..."

"It's not appropriate, and we'd have to share the bed because there is only one and..."

"Think about what you're saying. I'm your husband, and you're my wife. There is nothing inappropriate about a husband and a wife sharing a bed."

"Well in most cases you're correct. But we don't have that kind of marriage." But if she wanted to get pregnant, well, some bed sharing would be necessary.

"I'm not sleeping in the guest room, Storm. Either I take up residence in the master chamber and your bed, or I pack my bags again and go home. You decide." The sparkle in his eyes intrigued her but didn't ease her nerves.

She wanted to throw herself on her bed and cry the tears she'd been holding back since Bradford had told her about the insufferable contract. Now one bad thing after another seemed to fall on her shoulders.

"Very well, I'll move into the guest room." She wasn't sure why she'd caved into his demands. But her fear of intimacy eclipsed all her thoughts, even though a few hours ago she was asking Aidan if she knew how to seduce a man. This was exactly what she should want him to do.

"No you won't."

"What? Well, okay. If that's what you want." He'd caught her by surprise and right now her head was in such a jumbled state, she didn't know what to think or say.

"I'm astonished at your sudden acceptance of this proposition," he told her bluntly. "But I'm glad you see it my way."

Storm's nerves splintered at the roots. She rubbed her sweaty hands down her dress, hoping that would ease her mind. But it didn't. "I don't care where you sleep," she told him then swallowed back her fear of the unknown marriage bed. Even if they slept in the same bed, it was huge, and she didn't believe he'd force her.

But you need to seduce him, and how are you going to do that if you jump every time he makes a move or talks?

"Good, then I'll go up stairs and finish unpacking."

~ * ~

Hadden slipped from the makeshift bed where he'd spent the night. Stretching to rid himself of the kinks in his back and shoulders, he stood. Despite his adamant behavior and the acknowledgement the night before that he share the bed with Storm, he couldn't bring himself to interrupt her sleep. When he'd finally walked up the steps to the bedroom, he'd seen her on the bed, curled up in a tight ball. He knew she was innocent, and he shouldn't take advantage of her.

Hell, he'd provoked her and taunted her then she'd shocked him by agreeing. He'd expected another round of sidestepping and hedging coming from her. But she acquiesced.

He hadn't been ready for that turn of events.

It was still early, the sun had not risen, but he needed to get to the docks. There was a ship arriving from India, and he had to oversee the unloading. The same ship would be sailing to Baltimore with barrels of the Graham scotch.

Hadden was shrugging into his jacket when he looked up and saw Storm's bare feet at the top of the staircase. He paused, unable to take his gaze from her figure and watched the provocative way the bottom of her robe gapped open, displaying her shapely calves and thighs through the gauzy fabric of her nightgown. His focus swept upward, taking in her disheveled hair and transparent, sleepy eyes. A sudden and too familiar tightening of his body surged through him.

No woman should look that beautiful at this time of the morning. Her thick brown hair begged to be unbraided and the sleepy expression in her dark eyes was enough to set an inferno boiling in a man.

"Why are you up so early?" Her voice beckoned to him and seduced even with her innocence.

He shrugged and smiled up at her. "I have to go to work. Ships coming in today, and one going out tomorrow."

"Would you like me to make breakfast for you?" She started down the steps, one hand on the railing the other holding up her nightdress, revealing more of her slim ankles and legs.

Hell, the last thing he needed was to watch her glide around the kitchen making his breakfast in that filmy little nothing. "I had bread and made myself a cup of tea. Go back to bed. It's too early to be up and around."

"I wish you'd let me help. I would have been up if you'd told me."

"Don't worry about it. I'm not helpless. Been living alone for a long time. I've learned a few things about survival in the early morning." If he stayed here and watched her, he wouldn't make it to the docks. Just the sound of her voice saying his name caused the erection he was fighting to grow, and he was afraid if he didn't get out of here real fast, he was going to do something he'd regret.

"Time to go." With that said he hurried to the front door.

"Will you be home tonight?" Her voice was low and soft. And reminded him of the bedroom.

He paused, careful to not look at her. "Not tonight. Too much happening but if everything goes well, I'll be home for dinner tomorrow."

"Would you like me to make you dinner and bring it to you?"

He closed his eyes for a moment, lost in thought. Trying to control his breathing and his need to bury himself deep inside her, he cleared his throat. "No need for that. Perkins is an excellent cook."

"Are you sure?"

"I'll see you tomorrow night." He jerked the door open and raced from the house. He couldn't get out of there fast enough.

Hadden walked into the barn and closed the door behind him. He didn't like the way he'd talked to Storm. She deserved better. Breathing hard, he leaned against the wall and tried to adjust his cock to a more comfortable position. "Bloody hell, what was a man to do when presented with such an irresistible and beautiful woman in her nightgown?"

A few minutes later, not feeling much better, he walked from the barn and down the road to the docks. "Damn woman." Why in hell had she woken up and talked to him? He'd done everything he could to stay quiet and to keep her where she belonged, in bed. Another vision of Storm, in her sheer nightgown, flitted through his head, and he groaned. "Stop thinking about her. Think about the goods you're unloading and the scotch you're about to pack on board. The way I feel right now I'd like to drown myself in the scotch. Don't think about your curvy little wife parading down the stair case in her night clothes and bare feet."

But he couldn't help himself. Every image he had flitted through his head and teased him.

A shiver swept up his spine as he thought again about Storm standing barefoot at the top of the landing. She could seduce him with her bare feet and tousled hair.

What he needed was something to take the edge off. Maybe he could visit the widow Stewart down in Berwick. It had been too long since he'd seen the children. He imagined they must have grown in the last six months. He'd been so busy he hadn't been able to pay them the attention they deserved.

But he was a married man now, so the Widow was out of the question. No wonder all he could think about was bedding Storm. He hadn't had a woman since the last time he saw Adele.

Six months. Was it really six months since he'd been there? The children would be in need of new clothes and shoes. And Ned, his pants probably were up to his knees by now.

Maybe visiting the kids would get his mind off bedding his wife. "Hell, you wouldn't take her, even if she offered." He wished he could believe it. If he started a sexual relationship with Storm... Bloody hell, that was what he wanted, but he didn't know how to go about convincing Storm she wanted it too.

But why the hell shouldn't he try? Was he an idiot? She was his wife.

Far better to keep your mind on business and the children you helped Adele adopt. But he knew this task was going to be harder before it ever got easier.

Hadden sighed and rounded the corner to the docks. Lights on board the ship twinkled, and men were in the process of unloading the shipment of tea and exotic fabrics. Wagons waited at the base of gangplank.

Now all he had to do was figure out a way to make himself believe he could resist his beautiful wife.

~ * ~

With her sisters gone, she decided to ride to Ella's house. A good talk with her best friend might help her understand her new husband's churlish attitude this morning when she'd gone out of her way to be helpful and nice.

Storm accepted the cup of tea Ella handed her and idly poured cream and sugar into the brew. Stirring it, she stared at the swirls of cream blending with the darker tea.

"A penny for your thoughts." Ella set a plate of cookies on the table. "Are you still upset over the chaos Charles and Henry created at the church?"

"No, well yes, but there are other things that have piqued my curiosity and my patience. I don't understand my new husband. And I 'd love to know what he's thinking. He got up early this morning to go to work. All I wanted to do was make his breakfast, but he couldn't get out of the room fast enough." Storm paused for breath. "And yesterday Hadden insisted on moving into the master bedroom and sharing my bed, but instead he slept down the hall in the guest room.

Storm watched the smile grow on Ella's face. "What were you wearing?"

Storm blinked and sipped from her teacup. "What does that matter?"

"It could mean a lot."

"Well, I had my nightdress on and a bathrobe." A shiver swept through Storm's body. "I wasn't indecent."

"I've seen your filmy and very sheer nightclothes. And sometimes the hint of what's beneath the clothes has a more profound effect on a man than actually seeing the woman's naked body."

Storm set the teacup down and stared at Ella with open-mouthed astonishment. "What are you talking about?"

"I'm talking about the subtle art of seduction. When I want to get Lawrence aroused, I put on the most gauzy nightgown I own and he goes crazy."

Ella's words were a lot to digest. If what Ella said were true, she'd unwittingly seduced Hadden. Another shiver swept through her and heat flushed her face.

"Is that what I did? Seduce him?"

"Yes, honey. I think so. Is that what you want?" Ella rose to take the bubbling teakettle off the stove then make more tea.

"Yes, I believe so. This all goes back to Charles and his father, doesn't it. They won't give up easily. A real marriage is what I need, isn't it?"

"You could just ask Hadden for the money to pay your father's debt then it would all be over."

"Nothing is that easy. Hadden believes it's the horses, or me. He doesn't know there is a dollar amount attached to the debt. And I want to keep it that way. If he doesn't know he won't feel obligated to pay my father's IOU." Storm sighed then inhaled a deep breath. She knew what she had to do but the question was could she do it.

"Well, are you going to ask him?" Ella persisted. "Now that you're married it has to be paid."

Storm shook her head, a resigned frown on her face. "I can't do that. Ella, I just can't. It's not fair and it's not right. He's married to me against his will. Messing up his life was not what I ever wanted to do. If I set up a payment schedule, I should be able to pay it off in no time."

"You realize if you don't ask him for the money, Charles will proceed to have your marriage annulled. And I think he has a good chance of succeeding. The contract your father made with him came before the marriage. Now, I don't know much about law but..."

Storm drummed her fingers on the table. Nervous energy coursed through her, and her mind seemed to act faster than it should. Her thoughts were always plausible in the beginning but when she acted on them, they never turned out as she'd planned. "Ella, I don't think there is a court in England who would declare my marriage invalid if..." She didn't know if she could say the words.

"If you what?"

"I could have a baby then..."

Ella gaped at her friend. "Your plan is to get pregnant?"

"I've gone over every possible scenario and that's the only viable one. I can't ask Hadden for the money and only other way to void that contract is to make a baby."

"Of course you're right. But I'm sure you will still have to make good on the debt. It's not as easy as you're making this out to be." Ella calmly sipped her tea before reaching for another scone. "A baby would do it. If there's anything that binds two people together for life, it's creating a child together."

"Oh damn, I never thought of that. I don't want to be bound to Hadden for life. But I am tied to him—for life—aren't I?"

Ella shrugged, a smile on her face. "Sometimes the best plans turn out to be the worst."

"My plans seem to backfire all of the time."

"As you just said. You don't have a choice. But don't worry. It won't be awful, and having a baby is the most wonderful thing in the world. You'll never regret it."

Storm sighed, wishing she could think of any other plan. "I never wanted children."

"Why not?"

"My mother died in childbirth. I remember that vividly. I also remember Ravyn crying, and that she had to take care of us after mother passed. Bradford hated all of us because we were girls. I think he made that contract out of spite."

At that moment chaos erupted in the street. Yelling people raced up and down the roadway.

"What's happening?"

"I don't know..." Storm raced from the little kitchen and out the door to Ella's front yard, Ella behind her.

The noise shattered the soft spring day. "Fire! Fire on the docks."

~ * ~

Henry sat back in his chair, hands folded on his lap, a worried feeling sweeping through him. He'd hit Johnston in the monetary gut with this. The fire had been Charles' idea, but he'd helped execute the plan, and now he had a few regrets.

Charles walked into the room, clapping his hands. "Well done, Father." Then he pulled up a chair.

"Do you have an alibi?" Henry asked.

"I was in the pub enjoying a glass of Irish whiskey. What about you?" Charles was pleased with the outcome of today's endeavor. He hoped the fire brigade didn't get to the ship in time to save the vessel.

"Working on the ledgers with my lawyer."

Charles strode to the window and pulling the curtain aside, gazed at the flames shooting from Johnston's ship. "Unfortunately the timing wasn't as good as it could have been. The ship had been unloaded."

"Damn, but I'll bet he loses this investment. The ship was supposed to sail with a new cargo."

"Do you think it would be prudent to join the town in fighting the fire?" Charles hated to get his hands dirty, but he knew without his father's answer that helping would be a good way to shift the focus from any foul play on his part.

"Of course, you should go. I'll join you later."

Chapter Nine

Storm froze, vivid memories of an earlier time, another fire. The scene in front of her whirled in a dizzy pattern of light and dark shapes. She saw horses, screaming and trying to get out of the stable. Her sister Ravyn had raced to the big double doors that were bolted shut. Even then Storm couldn't move. Her feet seemed tied to the ground, her body shuddering with terror.

"Grab a bucket. Hurry!" The call came from down the road.

"Fire! Fire on the docks! It's Johnston's ship! Hurry!" Cries erupted everywhere.

"Come on." Ella grabbed Storm's hand.

Staring down the street, her heart in her throat, Storm tried to respond. Her fear was tearing her apart. "Ella..."

"Storm, what's wrong? We have to help." Ella raced into the house and came back with four buckets.

By the time Ella returned, Storm had tamped down the horror from her memories. She inhaled a long deep breath. The air was smoke-filled. "I'm terrified of fire," she whispered.

"I know you are, but we have to go help put that out. It might be one of your husband's ships. You can do it."

Storm nodded her agreement. "I can do it." *I can do it. I can.* The thought of Hadden sent her flying down the street. She forgot the fear, and her mind turned to her new husband.

He could be hurt. Or worse...

"Get in the line," a man called out to them. "Stay away from the fire. Just dip the buckets in the water, and we'll pass them on to the men up front."

Storm and Ella found a place in the line and passed empty buckets along the line to be filled with more water. What seemed like hours passed. Storm's muscles ached from the effort. She pushed hair from her sweaty face, wishing she'd pinned it up or tied it back before she left her house this morning.

"Here, you two take a break." A woman handed them each a cup of water and took their place in the line.

For the first time since they'd joined the bucket line, she looked to the ship. Black smoke billowed from the deck. Sailors moved about the vessel, pulling down rigging and tossing black sails to the ocean below.

"Can you see him?" Ella stood beside her, one hand shielding her eyes from the afternoon sun.

"No, can you?" Storm's heart raced, thundering in her chest and her breaths were shallow. "Lord but it would be nice to see if he's alive." The thought of a second funeral swept through her head.

"What? The concerned bride? You play it very well, Storm." Charles Robertson placed a hand at the small of Storm's back.

The hair on the back of her neck prickled, and her skin felt as if vermin covered her body. She pulled away from him, stiffening her back. "Did you come to lend a hand? Or just to insult me?"

He pointed his cane towards the docks and Hadden's ship. "Just wanted to watch. It's so much fun to see people you hate have problems. This is going to cost Mr. Johnston a pretty penny." A smug look covered his face.

"Fun to watch?" Her body shook with rage. "How dare you show up here and with that attitude?" She studied his face. *He knows something about this.*

He nodded toward the crowds that had gathered around the dock. Many were watching and laughing. But most were helping put out the fire.

Henry stepped forward. "When are you going to pay the debt your father owes?"

"I don't know. I'll find a way. I've offered you the stables. I don't know what more I can do." She rubbed her hands up and down her arms.

They would never let any of this go. They didn't need the money. She looked at Charles, disgusted with his smug expression.

"Ask your rich husband. Or is he holding out for something better? Well either way it won't matter. I don't want the stables or the money, I want you." Charles' sneer sent a decided chill through her.

"I might." But Storm knew she'd never ask him for money.

"You could pay me in another way." Charles touched an embroidered handkerchief to his lips then put it back in his pocket.

"There isn't another possibility." The way this conversation was going was rather disconcerting.

"Oh, there is." He ran a finger down her neck. "You could sleep with me. It would have to be whenever I asked."

She jumped back, repulsed by his proposition. "I'm not a whore."

"You're not a proper wife either. Has your new husband taken you to his bed?"

"That is none of your business," she told him.

"I disagree. In lieu of the contract, if you don't sleep with him, I will have your marriage annulled. You see, Miss Graham, I don't take this situation lightly. And I always get what I want. I want you." He leaned close to her as if the gesture would give more emphasis to the point he tried to make.

Storm hesitated for a long time. She didn't know what to say to the arrogant man. *I don't want you.* The smoke emanating from Hadden's ship had all blown inland. Ashes covered her hair and dress. She needed a bath to wash away the soot and Charles' repulsive touch.

"I'll have you one way or the other." Charles turned her and lifted her chin. "Maybe I'll have a taste of you right now."

Storm tried to pull away, but his fingers tightened on her jaw. "No." Shoving his chest with more force than she'd expected, he stepped back.

"You should not have done that." He grabbed her shoulders, his fingers tightening.

"You going to force me like you did Ella?" Her body shook with rage, her nerves snapping. She couldn't think of any way to get away from him. Charles had manipulated Ella. Now he tried to do the same way with her walking her closer to the docks.

"That little slut, I didn't force her. She threw herself on me. Said she wanted to be married to a rich man." His words were smooth and evil.

"Liar." He'd let go of her chin. She should turn and run, but she wasn't a coward. She could fight every battle he challenged her with. "Ella is a sweet girl and she's never cared about monetary things."

"She didn't tell you that she asked me for a carriage ride. Aw, I remember the day fondly. The sun was shining and the birds were chirping. She asked me to take her to the lake."

"She did none of that."

He shrugged. "I didn't bodily pick her up and put her in the carriage. I didn't kidnap her."

"You coerced her into the carriage with the idea that you would take her home."

"Is that what she told you? Who is the person to believe? It is after all, my word against hers."

"I believe Ella."

Storm turned to walk away, her insides in turmoil, her blood boiling. Suddenly Charles stood in her way, blocking her escape. She turned again.

"You can't get away from me this easily."

"I'll scream." Continuing to turn away from him, she walked as fast as she could.

Charles grabbed her by the waist, pulling her close. "Go ahead, and I'll tell everyone you were trying to seduce me."

"I hate you—loathe you." Her forearms pushed against his chest, but he held tight.

"That will make this all the sweeter." He grinned. "Give me a kiss and I'll let you go."

"Never."

He lowered his head to take what she wouldn't give. Storm turned away. Suddenly Charles was on the ground, rubbing his cheek. Ella stood beside her, a worried frown on her face.

"Stay away from my wife if you know what's good for you." Hadden stood over Charles, his hands fisted, his feet planted firmly on the ground then he turned to Storm. "Are you all right?"

"No I'm not. He terrifies me, and he wouldn't let me go." Storm didn't want to start a fight between the men, but Hadden needed to hear the truth.

Charles sat in the dirt, staring at the couple. "She lies. She asked me to kiss her."

Hadden looked at Charles, his face void of emotion. "Really." His tone was dry.

"I didn't, Hadden, I told him I hated him."

"I know, honey, I know how you feel." Then he turned back to Charles who was standing now. "Heard tell you had something to do with the arson on board my ship."

Charles sputtered. "Lies, filthy lies. Why would I want to burn your ship?"

"Don't know, but I'm going to find out who is responsible, and they'll be held accountable."

Storm realized Charles had the means, motive and the opportunity to set the fire. He could have hired anyone to do it for him, setting up an alibi in the process. She knew his cruelty and the opportunity to kill Hadden might have been the reason. If Hadden died in the fire...

Then she would be at his mercy. Charles might try again. A sudden and violent wave of terror swept through her. This was all her fault and she didn't have any idea how to prevent the same thing from happening again.

"I was at the tavern, enjoying a tankard of ale. Ask anyone who was there," Charles said.

"I will and I'll ask more than those questions. Storm, Ella, come with me please." Hadden escorted the two women toward the docks where the excitement had vanished and the fire brigade had disbanded.

Storm accepted his arm when he offered it. His body, so different from Charles, gave her courage. She let the breeze from the ocean soothe her shattered nerves and sweep away the feel of Charles' touch. Thoughts of his hands on her sent shivers running up her spine.

Lawrence Brummell strode toward them. "Here, I'll take my wife home. Is everything going to be all right? Can your ship sail?"

Hadden put a possessive arm around Storm's waist. "With a few repairs the ship will sail a day late. My first mate Perkins smelled the smoke and made the call for all hands to attend to the fire. He sent one of the sailors to find me. The fire did little damage."

Storm leaned into Hadden, exhausted from her encounter with Charles. She wanted nothing more than to put that horrid experience to the back of her mind but the thoughts and his cloying scent loomed heavy. Closing her eyes she felt the play of Hadden's muscles. He smelled of smoke from the fire but it wasn't bad.

"Storm," Ella said. "Will you be okay, honey?"

She nodded, too tired to do more.

"I'll take her home then I'll have to come back to the docks. There's a lot of work if the Wind Walker is going to sail," Hadden spoke up, concern in his voice.

"Do you think it's a good idea to leave Storm at home, alone?" Ella asked. "Charles..."

It was disconcerting hearing everyone talking around her and about her. "Can I stay here at least until you finish for the night?" Storm turned to him. "I don't want to go home. I don't trust Charles, and he's so angry right now he might do anything."

Hadden nodded, brushing Storm's hair from her eyes, a protective light in his eyes. "If that's what you want, but it's going to be a long night. You can stay in the captain's cabin. Cook will make you dinner and if you're tired, you can lie on my bunk."

"I'd like that." She looked up and into his deep brown eyes. They were focused on her and she felt heat sizzle to the tips of her toes.

His hands were on either side of her face, and he lowered his mouth to hers. The kiss was sweet and gentle. His tongue traced the seam of her lips and moved with a slow steady purpose. She moistened her lips, and he caught her lower lip with his teeth and swept his tongue across it. Then he was inside her mouth, touching her tongue and teeth. Responding with a small sound, she reveled in the feel and taste of him. Her tongue danced with his as an inferno raced through her.

One of his hands roamed to the small of her back, pulling her closer. Against her stomach she felt the bulge of his arousal. Remembering conversations with her sister and cousins about their wedding night and other nights after that, left her breathless and with continuing thoughts of seduction.

He pulled back and stared at her, "Bloody hell, woman."

~ * ~

Hadden leaned on the railing of his ship *Wind Walker,* gazing out to sea. "You may own a fleet of ships, Johnston, but if you don't stop kissing the pretty little woman you married, pretty soon you're not going to own your own soul."

As it had a thousand times during the last hour, his mind drifted to the kiss he'd shared with Storm that afternoon. What the bloody hell was it about her that intrigued him so much? He'd had his share of women, tons of them—from chaste pecks on the lips when he was fourteen and thinking himself in love with Elizabeth to erotic feats with the beautiful Widow Stewart.

So what was it about this woman that made him feel as if he was about to explode every time he touched her?

Elizabeth had never made him feel that way. In fact there were times he didn't care if he kissed her or touched her. Hadn't he been in love with her? Now he wasn't too sure how love felt.

Well, damn, he didn't want to think about Elizabeth. Perhaps a trip to see Adele and the children would help ease his convoluted feelings. *I'm a married man. Maybe but I have needs and a body that can't control itself. But just around Storm Graham. No It's Johnston now.*

He'd thought to build a life with Elizabeth then everything went flat. And he was damn glad, he'd seen through her character before he'd committed himself for life to a shallow cold woman.

"Go see Adele and play with the kids, she'll talk to you and clear your head. She's always been a voice of reason," he muttered for the hundredth time and wondered why he'd never fallen in love with her. Adele was kind and caring. She'd given up a lot to help him achieve his dream. How many orphaned and abandoned children did she care for now? Was it eight or nine?

Perhaps it was past time he visited. He should check in and see if she needed anything. Perkins took a monthly check to her, and she never asked for anything from him. She seemed happy.

He smiled, thinking of the last tiny child he'd brought her. Mary had bright curly red hair and a splattering of freckles across her cheeks and nose. Her bright blue eyes seemed to take in the world.

One day in Berwick, he'd found her sitting on the curb and sobbing. When he'd sat down beside her, she'd scooted away but she didn't run from him. He'd offered her a candy he'd found in his pocket. Shying away from him, she stared at him as if she didn't quite know what to do.

He remembered his relief when she finally accepted the sweet. A few hours later, and after coaxing her to believe in him, he delivered her to the Widow Stewart's home. Now Mary was a happy contented child of five as were all of his children.

Sometimes, he thought, he shouldn't think of them as his but in so many ways they were. What would Storm think? He wanted her to love them as much as he did. Sometime soon he'd have to introduce them.

Damn but his thoughts sidetracked back to Elizabeth. Damn her for ruining everything.

But had she, really? Or had Elizabeth saved him heartache by revealing her true character before the wedding day. Perkins seemed to think so. He'd told him despite his feelings right now someday he'd be relieved and his broken heart would mend. The only tragedy would have occurred if he'd been trapped in a loveless marriage.

"So I've come a long way," Hadden muttered, lifting his face to the sun, "years later, trapped in a loveless marriage—and this time a sexless marriage."

His thoughts meandered back and forth. He just couldn't figure out why or how his life had turned upside down so fast and why he felt so protective and possessive when it came to Storm.

Hadden pushed away from the railing then found Perkins. "I'll be gone the rest of the day. Have something I've got to see about."

"Right, Captain. I'll finish up here. The loading is almost finished, and we'll be ready to sail with the morning tide."

"See you tomorrow." Hadden knew Perkins would be wondering what had spurred him to leave, and he was sure the first mate would think he was going to see his wife. But that would happen later.

Hadden hitched a horse to a wagon and set off down the street, stopping at the grocers to pick up a few items. He bought Adele's favorite tea then went to the drapers and bought fabric for Adele to sew new clothes for the children.

He hummed a tune as he went about his errands, enjoying the sun and the change of scenery. The drive to her home just outside Berwick seemed to fly. Before he knew it, he'd reached her two-story house on the hill he'd purchased several years back.

The children were outside playing and when they saw him, they raced to the wagon.

"Presents?" They all cheered.

"Of course." Hadden jumped from the bench he sat on and rummaged in the back of the wagon for the gifts and supplies he'd purchased. "But you have to wait until we go inside. I have a little something for each of you.

He picked up Mary and set her on top of his shoulders. "Hang on," he told her while he bent over and picked up the packages he'd set on the ground.

Her little fingers clung to his head, putting a smile in his heart. The rest of the children lined up behind him as if they were little ducklings following the mama duck.

Knocking on the door, then peeking inside, he called out, "Anybody home?"

"We're all inside." Adele walked from the kitchen, drying her hands on the apron she wore. "What brings you here today?" She gave him a hug, then helped Mary from his shoulders.

He shrugged. "Do I need a reason?"

"The presents," the children called out.

"Of course you don't, but I've heard rumors." She opened the bags and helped pass out the sweets to the children. "Fabric for clothes and my favorite tea," she beamed, opening the tin and holding it up to her nose, she inhaled the wonderful aroma.

"They grow so fast. I knew you would need to start on the next batch of garments."

"You're right. And most of the garments are worn so ragged they don't work as hand-me-downs." Adele looked through the bolts of fabric, fingering each piece and telling him which child would benefit from each one.

"I'll get started this evening." She turned to the children. "Now what do you tell Mr. Johnston?"

"Thank you," they chorused.

"Now go on and play. Stay close." Adele waved to them as they scurried out the door.

"Come in to the kitchen with me and sit down. I just pulled bread from the oven, and I have apple butter. Relax and tell me all about the rumors."

He watched as she poured hot water into a teapot and placed the tea inside. When the tea had brewed, she held the strainer and poured the hot liquid into the cups.

"Thank you," Hadden said. "This looks good."

"You're a married man?" she asked, her lips thinning perceptibly. "And it's not a real marriage. Any truth in that?"

Hadden let out a long slow breath of air. "Yeah, I married her to protect her from Charles Robertson."

"Wasn't there another way?" Adele sipped her tea then stared at him over the rim. "I didn't think you'd marry someone you didn't love."

"Charles and Henry were threatening her. I went to see the Robertson's to talk some reason into them but they didn't want to listen." He went on to explain the rest of the circumstances and the role Charles

Robertson played.

Adele set her cup on the table then pointed a finger at him, a stern look on her face. "Now I know you pretty well. Right?"

"Yup about ten years now. But who's counting?"

"And most of the time you've taken my advice or at least gave it credence." She turned her head sideways as she waited for a reply.

"What the hell are you getting at?" For the first time since he'd known Adele, he was angry with her. He didn't understand where she was going with her line of questioning, but it seemed to him that she didn't believe him.

"The man I know wouldn't let anyone force him. I think there is more to your feelings for Storm Graham than you're willing to admit even to yourself."

He sat back, crossing his arms against his chest. "She didn't give me a choice."

She smiled at him, shaking her head. "Of course you had a choice. There is always a choice. You're smitten and you either don't know it or you won't admit that you've fallen in love. Which is it?"

"I'm not in love with her." Yet Adele's words mirrored what Perkins had said. Why had he married her? Just as Adele told him, in the end he did have a choice and there was always a choice.

"Well as usual you've given me something to think about. With this marriage I'm safe from all the other marriage minded women in this part of England," he admitted to Adele.

"You've managed to hold them at bay for several years and quite successfully, I might add. And, you could have continued to do just that. So again, why marry now and why Storm?"

Deep down he knew none of the reasons he'd just spouted to Adele had any merit. Could he tell Adele that every time he looked at her or touched her he couldn't see straight, couldn't think, that his head swam and his cock hardened? "So why? Damned if I know."

"I think you've answered my question."

"Not really. I can admit I'm attracted to her. Hell, every time I close my eyes I see her as she appeared this morning at the top of the stairs, disheveled from sleep, bare toes peeking from beneath her nightdress. Just the memory of that vision makes my heart stop."

Her eyebrows rose as if she had a million thoughts racing through her head. "Do something about it."

"Storm is my wife and I've every right to do as you say. But she's made it clear she has no interest in me."

"Maybe bedding her is exactly what is needed."

"I'm not going to force her." Still, if Storm was half as sensual as he thought she was, it might be worth risking her displeasure to have one night with her.

"But you could seduce her."

Hadden snorted, disgusted by his lecherous thoughts. "Forget it. That is never going to happen."

~ * ~

Charles strode into a tavern in Berwick, thoughts of Storm paramount in his mind. He looked to one of the tavern girls and beckoned her to him. He needed, at least for the moment, to rid his head of the woman he wanted more than he'd ever wanted anyone. Hell, he was even willing to marry her.

"What's your name?" he wrapped his beefy arm around the girl.

"Delilah," she purred and put her hand on his chest. "What's yours?"

"Charles," he told her. "Want to go upstairs?"

"Can't, I'm working for another hour but if you want to wait, you can have a seat over there." She nodded toward a table in the back of the tavern. "I'll be your server."

Charles grinned and squeezed her arm. "I'll wait, Delilah."

"What would you like? Food? Wine? Ale?"

"You," he told her and winked. "But I'll take a bottle of wine and some roast beef and some roasted potatoes."

"Aww...so sweet. I'll bring you your meal." She sashayed to the kitchen, hips swaying provocatively.

He watched her rear, would have rather seen her from the front. Her ample bosom was made for his hands, and he couldn't wait to bury his cock deep inside her.

A few minutes later, she returned with the bottle of wine. He pulled her onto his lap, sliding his hand up her leg. "Join me?"

"You know I can't. Stop that." She told him, but she traced his jaw with a finger. "You got to wait."

She bounced off his lap before he could feel her breast, but he grinned. He'd found a woman ripe and lusty just for him. And she'd help keep his mind off Storm.

Chapter Ten

Storm stood outside the grocery store watching Hadden pick up various items, including tea. Her first thought was he was buying things for her but was soon dissuaded of that notion as she watched some strange items appear on the counter.

Not wanting her new husband to think she spied on him, she stepped around the corner of the building and into a shadow. Her heart beating a rapid staccato, she was surprised to see him leave the grocery and head for the drapers then the sweet shop.

Perplexed, she then watched as he headed out of town toward Berwick. What on earth was he doing, and should she ask him when he arrived home tonight? Was he coming home?

She saw Charles walking down the street. Her heart leapt into her throat and her body shook. She moved farther into the shadows, waiting for him to pass the little nook where she hid. A few minutes later, he entered the dockside tavern.

Breathing a bit easier, she left her hiding place and finished her errands. She'd planned to find Hadden and help him clean his ship *Wind Walker,* but now with Hadden headed out of town it could be a big surprise.

She hurried past the tavern and up the gangplank. Perkin's stood in the middle of the deck barking orders to the sailors who were repairing masts and scouring the deck.

Perhaps she couldn't do anything to help. And for the first time since she hatched her little plot, she felt unsure of herself. She stood behind the first mate, hands clasped in front of her, waiting for him to notice her.

When he finally realized there was someone behind him, he turned and grinned. "Now what can I do for you?"

Perkins' grin was infectious. His graying hair had been tied behind his head with a leather thong and his blue eyes twinkled merrily.

"I came to help clean up the *Wind Walker*. I hope that's ok." She held her breath, waiting for his answer.

"Does Mr. Johnston know what you're up to?" He stroked his chin in apparent thought.

Storm shook her head. "No, but I don't think he'd mind. I know he wants the ship to sail tomorrow and..."

"Most everything but the captain's cabin has been cleaned. There's not a whole lot of damage there, smoke damage mostly. Will take a bit of scrubbing before it's ready to be used."

Relief swept through her. "Well then, I'll get started there and it will free up the crew for other endeavors."

Perkins led Storm to the cabin. When she stepped inside, the reek of smoke emanated through the room. She opened the windows and inhaled the fresh scent of sea air then turning to Perkins, she asked, "Will you bring a tub and hot water?"

He nodded and hustled from the room. One sweep of the room told Storm this wasn't going to be an easy job. While she waited, she busied herself with tidying the cabin and shaking ashes from Hadden's belongings. She wondered if he was planning on sailing anytime soon. She knew he kept a cabin in all of his ships and she knew in years past he'd taken many trips. He might use this as an excuse to get away from her.

But not before she got pregnant.

"Here it is, Ma'am." Perkins appeared in the doorway with a group of sailors behind him. They marched in with the tub and others followed with the hot water and lye soap.

She spent the rest of the afternoon dusting ashes, sweeping, and scouring the cabin until the room gleamed from her efforts. She had left the bed until last. All the covers had to be washed, hanging the sheets and quilts up to dry on a makeshift line. She tackled that then scrubbed the bed from head to foot. Now, even though she was covered with a thick layer of grime, the room sparkled.

Pouring clean water into the washbasin, and looking at the mirror Hadden had hung behind it, Storm gazed at her reflection. She grinned at the black smudges on her cheeks and across her forehead. She was a mess, but she felt good about her accomplishment.

"You look like a chimney sweep." She laughed then turned to wash her face and hands.

Poking her head out the door, Storm looked for Perkins. As if by magic, he appeared in front of her. "Do you need anything else?"

"I'm done here and I'm going home but, someone needs to throw out the dirty water."

Perkins whistled, and two men strode to his side. Perkins gave the order, and the sailors disappeared through the doorway.

The sun was beginning to sink beneath the horizon. "I better get going."

"Thank you," Perkins told her politely. "Do you want someone to walk with you?"

For a moment, she gazed at the dockside tavern Charles had visited then back to the setting sun. "Yes, that would be nice."

Perkins called out to a nearby sailor, "Please escort, Mrs. Johnston home."

The man nodded and motioned for Storm to walk down the gangplank first. Relief swept through her as they passed the tavern and Charles didn't appear. She knew this man would defend her if necessary, but she prayed it wouldn't come to that. She didn't trust Charles.

They were almost to her front walk when the site of Hadden stole her breath. She stopped midstride, trying to decide if her husband had seen her or if she could race into the house and get cleaned up before he saw her. "I have the worst luck. Here he is all spiffy and clean, and I look as if I've been drug through the sewer."

"Storm, my God where have you been?"

The sailor escorting her home took this time to say, "I'm back to the *Wind Walker*."

"Uh, thank you," Storm told the man as she watched his back disappear down the street.

She turned to Hadden and with a sheepish feeling, she shrugged. "Oh dear, I must look a sight."

"I've seen you look better."

She smoothed her skirts and inhaled a deep breath before patting her hair into something different than dishevelment and in a prim voice, she said, "I'm sure you have."

Hadden stared at her several long seconds before he burst out laughing. "You went to the *Wind Walker*."

"Yes," she admitted, hoping he would understand her need to help.

Escorting Storm the rest of the way to the house and stepping into the foyer, Hadden laid his hat aside and took her by the shoulders, steering her to the oval mirror. "You're adorable but I probably can't convince you." He grinned as she gazed in at wide streaks of black painting her cheeks.

"But I washed my face." When she looked at her dress then her hands, she realized she must have picked up soot from her clothes and painted her face a second time.

Storm stiffened her back, refusing to believe Hadden would think less of her because she'd worked hard to help him.

"Not very well." He tapped her nose with a finger. "But thank you for helping me. I do appreciate your efforts on my behalf."

"You're welcome. You know then I was at the *Wind Walker*?"

"From your appearance I guessed. And I'm sure Perkins was delighted to see you. What did you clean?"

"Your cabin. It sparkles now and I think you'd be grateful." Her mind worked furiously as she tried to determine what really precipitated this early arrival. She hadn't expected him until eight o'clock and it was just six thirty. She should have had several hours to bathe and fix dinner.

"Thank you," he said with an easy nonchalance. "I'm sure the next occupant of the room will thank you too."

"Well, you answered one of my questions."

"Which is?"

"If anyone sleeps in the room if you don't sail." Storm wondered what it would be like to take a trip with him and lie in the bed she'd just cleaned—with him.

"It is the captain's cabin, and I rarely sail my ships any more. So the room will be occupied. What's your other question?"

She paused, not ready to divulge the fact she'd seen him leave town with purchases that weren't meant for her. "I forgot."

"When you think of it let me know and I'll answer." He moved farther inside the room. "Are you going to fix dinner? Or take a bath?"

She looked at her skirts. "Better take a bath first. If you're thirsty I have scotch. You know where and if you're hungry, you'll find bread on the counter. Help yourself." Storm dashed up the stairs and a little while later, after hauling water up the steps, she lowered herself into a steaming hot bath.

Laying her head on the back of the big brass tub, she closed her eyes. He hadn't seemed impressed or overly thankful for her efforts today but maybe he didn't show emotions.

Why had Hadden come home so early? She'd so wanted to impress him with a nice dinner, maybe by candlelight. No, she corrected herself, needed to impress him.

Storm opened her eyes and found the lavender scented soap she'd put out with her bath. Plucking a soft cloth from a table near her bath, she lathered it and began washing. "Well, you did make a lasting impression if not a good one."

Why had he shown up early? He'd seen her dirty and disheveled. Her heart sped, thinking about how handsome he'd looked sauntering up the pathway to meet her.

She couldn't remember when she'd been so tired. The morning and afternoon work had left every muscle in her body aching.

Storm sighed, stretching the exhausted muscles in her shoulders, and she didn't even know if he'd appreciate her efforts on his behalf. Men, she couldn't read their minds. What had he been thinking?

She didn't know what he wanted, a clean house, a good meal and what? Good sex? She wished she knew what would make her husband happy.

Storm's thoughts trailed off... What had he been doing in Berwick? Had he gone there for illicit purposes? He was a married man and wouldn't do that to her. But she couldn't help but think he just might because she wasn't giving him his good sex.

And she didn't have any idea how to seduce him.

Groaning with frustration, she raised an arm and scrubbed at a smear of soot that had caked in the bend of her elbow. What did she know about how a woman went about tempting a man?

Nothing. And that was the crux of the problem. She knew absolutely nothing.

She plunged the cloth into the sudsy water. *And you don't know a single person in this town who can tell you what to do.* Save Ella and she wasn't sure how to ask. *You're going to have to figure this out all by yourself.*

If only, her life circled around those words. If only she hadn't made him sign the agreement stating their marriage would be in name only, she could have gone to him and explained her fears about Charles Robertson in greater depth and asked for his cooperation.

But wasn't that exactly what he was doing? Cooperating? He'd shown up to rescue her from Charles this morning, and he'd kissed her. She touched her finger to her lips, remembering the rapid rise of heat and the compelling need to experience more than just a kiss.

For a brief moment, she closed her eyes, leaning her head on the rim of the tub and trying to calm her racing nerves. She breathed deeply and thought of riding her horse, the wind in her hair and feel of his gait beneath her.

Storm soaped her neck and chest then dipped the cloth beneath the surface of the water and raised it again to rinse. She looked down.

Breasts. She had breasts and men seemed to like them. At least that was what she'd heard. But she knew not to listen to gossip.

Storm gazed at the small round globes. What was it about this part of the female anatomy that men found so alluring? She'd always considered them an annoyance, especially hers. She was too small for most patterns and she had to alter everything she made. This was a thought provoking issue and she wondered how she would get to the reason.

She did, however, realize she had caught Hadden looking at hers. It must be some male peculiarity. But perhaps it was something she could use to her advantage. She pondered that thought for a while but realism loomed. In order for her to display that part of her anatomy she'd have to alter one of her dresses, something she didn't really want to do.

Giving up for the moment, she dropped the cloth into the cooling water and stood up, cupping water in her hands to rinse the soap off her legs. She'd just have to think of some other way to seduce her reluctant husband.

She stepped out of the tub, still unsure of any plan she might concoct. Picking up a linen towel, she dried herself, then walked over to her mirror. Holding the towel against her breasts, she lowered the edge until a tiny bit of her cleavage showed.

That's the right spot—right there. She focused on the expanse of bare, swelling flesh. Maybe she could lower the bodice of one dress. If she did, this would be the place. She didn't think she could possibly go any lower. She hoped this would tempt her husband without her looking like a whore.

"Hadden Johnston," she laughed, flinging the towel away and reaching for her underclothes, "you're not going to know what's happening to you."

Dinner the night before had gone fairly well. Storm had not been able to ask about Berwick and why he'd left town without telling her. Of course he didn't need to tell her anything. So, why did she expect him to do just that? Several times during the meal, she'd been on the verge of inquiring but something stopped her.

She was afraid of the answer.

Now, it was two days later, and Storm stood in front of her mirror in her bedroom, evaluating her image and frowning.

It had taken her more time than she wanted to admit, to redesign the dress Bradford had given her for Christmas two years ago. She'd never worn it, disliked it as much as she'd disliked her father and so, she'd chosen this one for the makeover. If she messed up and ruined the dress, it would make little difference to her. She'd never worn it anyway. Perhaps with this tiny change she could bring herself to put it on every once in a while.

The once high-necked garment now clung seductively to her shoulders. The new neckline revealed more skin than she'd ever meant to show. The fabric dipped daringly and left a line of cleavage at least two inches long. She gasped at the sight of the amount of flesh that was revealed.

She turned sideways then turned around before confronting her reflection once more. "Maybe I can do this." Assuming control of her life seemed right. So what if the neckline was too low. If the tavern girls could do this, so could she. Seducing her husband most important to her.

Storm pinched her cheeks and tugged the sagging bodice upward. Her nerves raced harder than a panicked horse. She inhaled a deep breath for courage, knowing her future with Hadden depended on what happened tonight.

"You have to do this," She gave her carefully arranged hair a shake. "Your life depends on it, so you will."

Self-consciously she pressed a hand against the upper curves of her breasts, trying to push the flesh into the bodice. But there wasn't enough bodice material even for her breasts.

"You better not take a breath or bend over," she muttered.

She glanced at the clock on the end table. He'd be here soon. "Courage, girl. Don't lose it now."

It was then the door opened and Hadden walked through. She whirled, her mouth falling open at the sight of him then dragging in a deep lungful of air. She felt her breasts swell and her lungs expanded and quickly looked down, horrified to see that her startled breath had accomplished what she'd been afraid of all along.

"You're on time, Hadden." She prayed the darkness in the hall would conceal her plunging neckline. Eating by candlelight had been a good idea.

"Yes, I am and eager to see my..." His gaze fell to her chest. "Wife."

"Oh, me too. I mean my husband. I didn't mean to imply..."

Their ridiculous conversation turned to a muted silence and seeing the path Hadden's eyes traveled, Storm clamped a hand across her chest and said, "Come in, let's sit down. Dinner is almost ready, so I hope you're hungry."

"Starved." He cleared his throat, shifting from one foot to the other as if uncomfortable.

Storm turned, walking to the parlor, Hadden following. They sat across from each other, backs stiff.

"So," Hadden began, "how was your day?"

"Fine, busy I guess. I'm getting the horses ready for a race coming up in a few weeks. The trainers were busy, and I spent most of my day at the stables."

Hadden nodded. "Mine was busy, too. The *Wind Walker* finally sailed, but a second ship arrived from the States carrying a load of tobacco. Spent the day unloading. Is that a new dress?"

Storm inhaled a swift breath, surprised at the unexpected change in conversation and a wave of heat surged to her cheeks. "No," she said. "I've had it for a couple of years."

"It...becomes you," he stammered. Turning away as if to look at something outside the front window, he bit down on his lower lip.

"Thank you. I think dinner should be ready. Would you like to move into the dining room?"

"Oh yes." Hadden jumped off the settee.

"Are you all right?" Storm asked, concerned with the strange way Hadden was acting.

"Yes. Just fine."

They walked into the dining room, and Hadden took a seat, while

Storm continued to the kitchen. As the door swung closed behind her, she gripped the edge of the sink and let out a long shaky breath.

Blazes, this wasn't working the way she had intended. Hadden wasn't interested in her indecent display; he was embarrassed. What had she done?

"Don't give up," she told herself. "After dinner see if he wants to go for a walk outside. It's warm enough. Maybe then you could try to get him to kiss you again." But now she needed to light the candles in the parlor. She grabbed her tinderbox and after taking a couple of deep calming breaths, she walked to the dining room, pulling up the bodice as she went.

"Here we are," she said, trying to force a note of gaiety into her voice. "I hope you like beef roast."

"I do." Hadden squirmed in his chair, pulling at his pants legs as if he was trying to adjust his clothing, which left Storm baffled at his actions.

"Would you like more water? You've emptied your glass."

"Yes."

Before Storm sat down, she poured him another glass, shaking her head and thinking he must have been very thirsty. The plates were heaped full and Storm's appetite had vanished. She picked at the food, thinking if she ate, she might lose it all.

Every time Storm looked up, Hadden's gaze was focused on her chest. She wished she hadn't been so stupid as to reconstruct the originally high-necked garment, which she felt confident wearing, into this revealing garment she felt insecure in.

Storm pushed her plate away.

"Aren't you hungry?" Hadden asked.

"Aren't you?" She gestured to his nearly untouched plate.

He shrugged. "Guess my mind is on other things. It's real good, though. Maybe you can wrap some of this up and I can have it for breakfast."

"Would you like to go for a walk outside, maybe down by the creek? It's still warm and light. I'd like some fresh air."

Hadden looked at her curiously. "I'd like that. Do you need a wrap?"

"I'll get one. If it's breezy it might be chilly on my bare arms."

"On your bare breasts..." he whispered.

"What?"

He frowned. "I didn't say anything." His face flushing, he scratched his neck and turned down the hall toward the foyer and the outside. "I'll wait for you."

With the shawl wrapped around her shoulders and covering her chest, she felt more herself—almost normal. "Ready?"

"Yes." He gave her his arm, and they strolled down the walkway toward the little creek behind her house.

"I love the feel of the wind on my face, and the scent of Daphne. " Storm turned to him, smiling, and he grinned back at her. Her uncertainty seemed to vanish with each step. Her hand rested on his arm, warmth emanating from him into her. For a moment, all her cares and worries about Charles disappeared. Even the silence between them comforted her.

"It is a nice evening." Hadden placed his hand on hers as they continued. "Where do you want to go?"

"Let's go to the creek. The sound of water rushing to the sea is soothing." Storm didn't want this idyllic moment to end. If she could preserve this incredible feeling forever, she would.

"Why Mrs. Johnston, you are a romantic." He slipped her hand from his arm before wrapping it around her shoulder.

She'd never felt this close to anyone. Maybe her little ploy of seduction was working. She shivered with warm thoughts, a bit frightened about what might come tonight, yet her heart felt suddenly lighter than it had for weeks.

He stopped at the edge of the creek and let her go. "Would you like to sit?" He pointed to a large rock.

She nodded as she sat down. "And you?"

"Perhaps in a minute." He bent over and picked up a flat rock before walking to a spot where the water slowed and pooled into a tiny pond. He skipped the stone across the water.

"You're very good at that," Storm said as she watched the rock bounce several times before sinking into the depths below.

"Had lots of practice." He picked up another pebble and did the same. This one jumped a few more times than the first.

"Can I try?" She leapt from the rock where she'd been sitting and found a rock. Mimicking Hadden, she let it fly, but it sank on the first contact with the water.

He laughed. "You have to find a flat stone and one that is not very big. Like this one." He handed it to her.

Storm smiled at him, tossed her hair and once again tried. The stone bounced three times before sinking. She stood with her hands on her hips disgusted with her efforts. "Think I'll watch you."

He obliged and tossed another rock.

"Why did you go out of town today and buy all those things?" Her question, abrupt and too soon, left her wondering where her head was and had Hadden gaping. She had not intended to introduce this topic yet.

"How do you know I left town?"

He didn't appear angry, just curious. "I saw you. I was in town running errands. I just thought it was odd you'd visit the drapers and buy cloth and the sweets? I didn't know what to think."

He was nodding then looking at the creek, walking to it and tossing another stone. Then with a huge breath, he turned toward her. Sitting down on the rock next to her, he picked up her hand. "Look at me." He waited while she turned her attention to him. He traced a line down her cheek with a calloused fingertip.

"Can I tell you a story?"

"Well, yes, if it's important to you." She closed her eyes for a moment and wondered where this was leading. She couldn't help but notice the scar by the corner of his right eye. Compelled, she touched it.

He smiled and took her hand in his. "When I was six, my mother died." He waited, watching her. "My father loved her beyond anything else, beyond his child, beyond even his own life. I think he died inside that day and he blamed himself."

"Why? What happened?" She squeezed his hand, hoping to give encouragement.

"It was an accident. He was showing off. He lost control of the horse he rode and it plowed into her. Mom was knocked down, and she never regained consciousness. She was in a coma for almost a week before she passed away."

"That's horrible. Is that why you are afraid of horses?" Hadden was finally giving her a glimpse of the real Hadden Johnston.

"Not afraid, just cautious. I spent most of my childhood alone and wandering the streets of London." He sighed looking back at that time as a growing experience. He'd become street smart, but he'd also developed compassion for the huge number of homeless and starving children.

"That's horrible. Even growing up in Bradford's home, I had company. I love my sisters, and there was always food on the table."

He shrugged. "I had food, but no love. My father had no love left inside of him to give anyone, including his only child."

She touched his chin. "I'm sorry. I wish I could have done something."

"What I learned and felt on those streets shaped my life. I never want to live in London again, and I'm glad you were not forced to live with the Duchess, although I'm sure life with her would have been better than my life on the streets."

She cocked her head to one side. "Does this have something to do with your trip to Berwick?"

"Yes, yes it does. I've a home for children near the village. The material I picked up was for the clothes."

"Really? Who takes care of them? I assume they are not yours." Storm's lipped thinned as if she was apprehensive.

"No they aren't. Even outside the cities one can find homeless children. When I encounter them, I want them to feel safe and loved. I take them to the Widow Stewart. She has a home near here."

"I see."

"You look confused." He wanted to know her feelings about this. "Would you like to meet them?"

"I would. I told you before I love children."

"Yes, you just don't want to have any of your own." A bit of anger surfaced. He'd married her because she intrigued him even though she'd said she didn't want children. He knew that now and understood no one could have forced him into a relationship he didn't want.

"I've changed my mind about having children." She told him, a strange smile on her beautiful face.

"Because it's the best way to seal the bargain you made with me, and negate the contract your father made with Henry?" His gut tightened.

"Yes," she told him bluntly.

"Then you would be giving me a gift made in the heavens above, a miracle to thank God for, and I would forever be in your debt." He meant every word. "But I don't want my child to have only one parent."

She pursed her lips together. "I would be a good parent. Parenting is not what I'm afraid of."

Having heard some of her family history, he had an idea but he needed to hear her say the words, and he needed to find some way to convince her he wasn't like her father. "What do you fear, tell me and I would chase it all away."

"My mother's life." She rose from the rock where she'd been sitting and walked to the creek. Her back was stiff but her shoulders trembled.

"Was it so bad?" His concern was heartfelt, and he didn't want her to regret her life or the fact that she'd married him. He wanted so much more than a marriage in name only.

She nodded. "I heard her cry herself to sleep every night. The sobs kept me awake almost as much as Ravyn's pacing."

He followed her and wrapped his arms around her, his chest against her back. He felt the shallow breaths and felt her pulse beat through her body. He pushed her hair away and kissed the back of her neck, felt the tiny shiver sweep through her body.

"Why did your mother weep?"

Storm turned in his arms. "Because my father forced himself on her. The only nights he left her alone were when she was pregnant. Rayvn told me the night after she delivered Fayth he made her come to his bed. Ravyn heard her screams."

"I'm surprised she told you." His fingers tightened around her waist. Easing her terrors, and he was beginning to think she had more than one, was paramount on his mind.

"It was an accident. A few years ago, before she left for London we talked. She wanted to warn me about men who might want only one thing."

"But she terrified you instead."

"Not really. I heard my mother weeping at night. I knew why."

He didn't know what to say, but he remembered the times he heard his father sobbing in the dark living room.

Sympathy, empathy or more, he needed to change the way she saw men. He could change her mind. Her eyes so blue, sparkled with moisture, while long cobalt lashes framed them. He lowered his mouth to hers. The kiss was gentle yet bittersweet. His tongue touched the seam of her mouth and traced the line.

For a moment he pulled back. "I will make sure you never sob in the night."

Chapter Eleven

Hadden swept Storm into his arms. She was light as a feather, her scent intoxicating. The steps to the house seemed to take forever. His pulse leapt and his body longed for the release he knew only she could give.

"I can walk," she murmured close to his ear.

"Not now."

With one hand, he awkwardly opened the front door then impatiently kicked it shut.

She kissed his neck, and he reveled in her initiative even while he hadn't expected it. He knew she'd redesigned the dress with the intent to seduce, but again, he was glad she had done just that. If she hadn't, they would probably still be exchanging awkward words.

"Where are you taking me?" She looked at him, her eyes sparkling with unspoken curiosity.

"Where I should have taken you on our wedding night." Without hesitating, he took the steps to the second floor two at a time, eager to learn more about his bride.

He set her on the bed then lit two candles nearby, needing to see Storm while he explored her secrets.

Silently she watched him as he loosened his neckcloth and tossed it to the floor. When he finished, he sat down beside her, placing her hands in his.

For a few seconds, he held his breath, praying she wouldn't change her mind. "Are you sure?"

"Sure of what?" she asked, a strange expression on her face. "Yes, I want you to kiss me."

"Did you or did you not set out to seduce me?" he queried, laughing a bit inside but relishing her innocence.

"Yes, yes I did," she told him.

Her honesty might just be his undoing. "What if I told you your plan was a success? Consider me thoroughly seduced and ready for your next plot."

"Oh, I don't have one." She lowered her lashes before looking back to him.

He bent over and kissed her, their lips melding together. *Take it slow. Don't scare her. You don't want her to tell you to stop.* He groaned, bloody hell that would be hard. For a moment, he wished she did have an agenda because he bloody well wasn't sure about his.

His tongue traced the seam of her lips, parting them slightly. They'd been down this road before, and he hoped she remembered the other kisses, sweet poignant kisses but innocent as hell.

Smiling when he heard a tiny moan of pleasure, he deepened the kiss. His hands around her waist, he pulled her closer, and the feel of her breasts against his chest sent a funnel cloud of heat coursing through him.

Sensations so deep he'd never felt anything like these flowed inside. Spreading his hand on her back, he waited for another response as his tongue reached inside her mouth, tasting her, exploring.

She ran her fingers through his hair then tugged his head closer before releasing him and their first contact.

"Is this how seduction feels?" Her warm breath feathered across his cheek.

When he looked down, he saw breasts and shadowed, titillating cleavage. Deep evocative sensations pulsed through him. He moved his hand from her waist across her bared shoulder, the contrast mercuric. The urge to dip his finger into the valley between her breasts overpowered common sense. She'd purposely designed the dress for him, for his touch. She was lush and ripe, and he realized she was not protesting as he had expected.

"Are you thirsty?" He rose, seeing the wine she must have set out and poured them both a glass.

She nodded. "A bit but I'm really more nervous than anything else."

"Don't be." When he handed the glass to her, she accepted and sipped, looking over the rim at him. The sight sent his heart racing faster. He sat down again and put his glass on the bedside table.

He ran his finger along the bodice of her dress, his knuckles brushing silken flesh. The warmth of her skin resonated on his own, her softness beckoning him, compelling him to sample more of her sweetness.

A fine wife and maybe a beginning they could both live with. He couldn't deny he liked who she was and what he saw—desired her in ways he couldn't comprehend. Lust was mercuric and all consuming at times.

"Drink." He nodded toward her. She hesitated a second before sipping the wine. She smiled at him and sipped again then moistened her lips with the tip of her tongue.

"Hadden," she sighed softly then put the glass down, "I'm feeling a bit fuzzy."

"No more then. I want you to remember tonight." He brought his finger to her chin and directed her to look at him. Their gazes met, and he stared into deep sapphire blue eyes, a face with delicate features, high cheekbones. He couldn't tear his gaze from hers. Her innate fears penetrated bone deep, right into his soul, and seemed to join with him. She'd been through so much heartache in her short life. He meant to change that for her, make her forget her father and what he did to her mother.

Lost for a moment in thought, he picked up his glass and downed its contents before returning his attention to his wife.

Storm touched her top lip with the tip of her tongue. Her slightly covered breasts brushed across his arm as she inhaled a deep breath of air. When a night owl cried out, she turned to look, her breasts swaying evocatively and her bodice slipping to give him a brief glimpse of a rosy nipple.

She didn't understand what she did to him, and he didn't know if he could wait much longer to sample her hidden beauty.

Then she smiled at him, an all-knowing smile as if she knew

exactly how she made him feel.

Hadden had no way to explain the rapid exhilaration of his heart or the hardening of his cock. Everything about Storm appealed to him. Her eyes held him spellbound and suggested an intimacy he could only guess at. How the devil did she learn that? He focused his attention back to the intriguing woman who was about to become his wife in more than name only. Her body was curved and soft. When she moved, the bodice of her dress stretched provocatively against her beautiful nipples that had tightened into hard little buds.

"I don't know how long I can wait, but I do know I want you. If you don't like what I do, tell me." He settled her on his lap, one hand resting on her waist, his fingers splayed upward, hoping to seduce her even more. He felt the weight of her breasts against the back of his hand.

"What are you going to do next?" She sighed softly.

He sure as hell didn't have an answer. He was going on gut instinct, and he needed to think, but his body's needs seemed to take over. At that moment, all he could think about was how she would feel when he was deep inside her. Her delicate feminine form intrigued him, thoughts of her hardening his body.

Even while she melted into him, her cheeks turned scarlet, giving her the appearance of an untried schoolgirl. But he didn't want her to feign innocence. He needed her to respond wantonly and fully. He wanted to see and feel her passion—Storm's passion.

He trailed his hand up her leg and beneath her skirt. She squirmed slightly. They both knew what the end of tonight would bring. She didn't protest, nor did she move his hand as he traced circles with his fingers.

It was his turn to seduce.

She looked up, and their eyes met for a second before his gaze drifted lower. She flushed, but at the same time she moistened her lips with her tongue. Passion flowered with his touch. Bloody hell he was as hard as granite.

"Hadden..." She lowered her head against his chest and for a moment, he thought she might have fallen asleep. He stroked her leg and she came alert, her fingers pressing just below his belt buckle. Nervous energy left his hand shaking. His experience with virgins was nonexistent.

"What?"

But she didn't answer.

The seduction of Storm and letting her passion free was all that interested him. Now was the time to bring this to its proper end, now when she was idly playing with his belt buckle and brushing his arousal with the backs of her long, sensuous fingers.

"Are we going to do it now?" her words were shaky, questioning and they pulled at his heart.

"Soon, my passion, soon." His hand moved upward, his thumb even higher. Lightly, and stroking one finger over the fabric of her dress, he traced a path around, then on her nipple, felt it harden with desire. This evening was looking more and more optimistic.

"Will I know?"

He chuckled softly, flicking his thumb across the swollen bud and watched her eyes turn dark and luminous. "I certainly hope so." *Passion should be her middle name.*

"I can't think when you touch me. Is that the way it's supposed to be? Hadden...I'm so hot and I feel strange."

He stood with her, holding her close, letting her body touch every hardened inch of his own. His fingers wound gently into her hair, pulling her back so he had full access to her mouth.

With his thumb, he touched her cheek, her lips, then he followed the caress of his fingers with his lips. The corner of her mouth, her nose, her eyes he kissed shut. Then he slanted his mouth across hers and traced the seam of her lips with his tongue, gently probing. Yet she didn't open for him.

Hadden..." she said, and his tongue found what he sought. The taste of honey, sweet nectar, met him. Like a wild man, he delved inside, tasting, exploring. His hands were everywhere.

~ * ~

"Storm," Hadden whispered her name, his voice husky and tender,

"Storm's passion, give it all to me." He breathed the words.

Once more his lips found hers, his tongue delved inside, and she opened for him. Her body, on fire everywhere, melted into his. Like quicksilver, he stole her senses, all her thoughts save one.

Storm wanted Hadden more than she'd ever wanted anything in her life. It was a new and unexpected feeling for her and one she didn't understand. His touch, mercuric and evocative, made her mind spin and her senses reel. The room swirled, and the candlelight danced and swayed with the rhythm he set. She wanted to crawl inside him and know all that made him the man he was—her husband.

"Hadden." Her breathless whisper sounded strange, and she wondered at her voice. She gazed at him, not understanding, but wanting to tell him how wonderful he was, to have him make her feel this way again. His name on her lips sounded more like a seductive caress than a plea for him to touch her. She had never felt anything so wonderful as the callused pads of his fingers tracing shivers the length of her spine.

She pressed closer, his hand, then his fingers spreading across the small of her back, compelling her hips against him. His powerful thigh moved intimately between her legs even as she allowed him to support her weight.

"We..." *Is this what I have to do to make a child?* She felt wanton and free, and she never wanted him to stop, never wanted this night to end nor his kiss. Could one kiss go on forever?

"Yes?" he answered her silent question with one of his own, subtle laughter in his voice, a sound that drew her farther into the seductive web he wove around her.

"You like my touch, my kiss?" he asked, but to Storm it didn't sound like a question.

He didn't wait for an answer. Nibbling on her lower lip, he bit it gently even while his hands moved expertly down her back, undoing all the buttons there. He stroked and caressed, sending a firestorm through her.

She ran her fingers through his hair, traced his broad shoulders, Her hands slipped inside the jacket he wore, then he shrugged it off. Cool air lapped against her back, then callused fingers explored, touching, arousing, seducing. She strained against him and toyed with the buttons on his shirt until they fell free and she could touch his chest.

"I've never known anyone like you." She ran her fingers across his torso.

Storm heard his laugh. It came from deep in his throat and seemed to pulse. "Thank God" was his answer.

"Oh..." she said in total agreement. This was what her fantasies were made from. Wild and erotic, something primal and alive, pumped through her. Red satin fell from her shoulders, then her hips, to pool languidly on the floor around her feet. She wore nothing but silk stockings, her corset, and high-heeled shoes. Embarrassment should have swept through her but it didn't.

Hadden moved back, his callused, work-worn fingers gently resting on her arms. He looked his fill, seeming to absorb all of her. Her hands fluttered upward to cover herself but he stopped them.

"Don't..." he said, "you're a man's dream come true."

I should tell him how I feel abut him. She tried to, but the words didn't form, or else she really didn't want to say them.

"You're beautiful," he told her. He brought her close and undid the strings of her corset, letting the garment fall to the floor. An instant later, he swept her off her feet and carried her to the bed. The power of Hadden's arms were a sweet promise and a reminder of how large and muscular he was and so incredibly handsome.

He leaned over her and found one of her breasts with his mouth. He licked and nibbled, then sucked tenderly. A shudder swept through her, and it seemed she could not form a coherent thought.

"Yes," she sighed into his mouth even while she answered his hungry kiss with one of her own. Eager and willing, she followed his example, stroked and caressed. She explored and seduced, delighting in the sensual feel of his flesh against hers.

What he taught her she committed to memory.

Pleasure spiraled higher and higher within Storm's body, drawing her so tight she thought she'd surely die. More pleasure exploded, drowning her in a liquid inferno. She made a soft mewling sound and shuddered, then softly begged, "More." Storm couldn't believe what she was letting him do, what she was aching for him to do, or the strange power he held over her.

Hadden laughed low in his throat and repeated the caress on her other nipple, gazing at her with a knowing grin.

Storm's hips rose from the bed then she arched, sending a nipple into his mouth. Wildly she pushed at his shirt, ripping a shoulder seam as she tried to wrench it from his body.

"Easy, my passionate one."

All thought was focused on the here and now, on the excitement Hadden evoked from her.

Hadden's free hands swept down her stomach and found a new resting spot between Storm's thighs. She stiffened, unsure of his touch in such an intimate place. Slowly his hand curved her softness. Long fingers explored in a gentle caress.

His fingers pressed deeply into Storm's core. Her body responded. Seductively, he compelled her and drew her closer, so close she was almost one with him.

His groan of desire awakened her to the sensual power she held over him. He wanted her as much as she needed him.

"Open for me, darling," Hadden whispered against her ear. "You're all sweet honey and liquid fire. Give me your pleasure and I'll satisfy you."

Storm hardly understood the demand. Mindless, in a sea of passion, she reacted to his knees pushing her legs apart, his hands upon her thighs, stroking. She wanted more of the wild unrestrained pleasure she had just known.

"Hadden, I should..." She swallowed hard. His thumb moved against her swollen flesh, and once more her body jerked wildly. She should what? She'd forgotten all thoughts.

"Hush. I want this just as much as you do."

She couldn't believe what she was doing, but she did want him to touch her, to make love to her. In another moment he was between her legs, and she felt him touching her, stroking her again with his cock. His hands touched upon her breasts, then settled at her waist. Then he drove hard and he was buried deep inside her.

At that same instant, Storm cried out her astonishment and her pain. A sob tore through her and she twisted, shoving at his shoulders, trying to dislodge the burning weight of him between her legs.

Poised to drive one more time, Hadden froze suddenly. "Bloody hell, I'm so sorry. It's my mistake. I lost all thought. Can you forgive me?"

Still, she couldn't speak. She was shaking her head in a state of denial but not regret. So much had gone wrong. It wasn't supposed to turn out this way. She should have known, should have stopped him, should have..."

Once he touched her, kissed her, held her gently in his arms, she could never have denied him anything. Yet to stop him would have been like telling her heart to stop beating.

He was so very deep inside her. He filled her and made her whole. He completed her and she didn't understand. "I've no regrets. I want a baby, your baby."

A lone tear slipped down her cheek even as the pain ebbed and she moved beneath his weight, this time in silent invitation for him to finish what he'd started.

"Darlin' if you don't stop that, I wont' be able to stop myself." He emitted a masculine groan. His body flexed and he began to follow the rhythm she set.

He kissed her eyes, her cheeks, the corners of her mouth, her nose, then deepened the kiss. Nibbling on the tender flesh, playing chase with her tongue, he kissed her hard and she wanted more. He kissed her again and again but it wasn't enough.

"Hadden..." Pleasure exploded within her, liquid fire raged through her. "Hadden," she whispered his name even while she spiraled higher, ever higher. Moonglow danced in her head, and the stars, dear God, the stars burned deep and bright.

He drove into her, stroking longer, deeper, harder, until he cried out. The sound of his voice against the magic of the evening was masculine and primal, evocative in nature. She raked her fingernails over the taut muscles of his back, learning the texture and the feel of his strength, the essence of the man.

Long, quiet seconds slipped by, and he braced his weight on his forearms and held himself away from her. He seemed to study her then, and she wondered what he must think of her. With gentleness that belied the power of the man, he lifted her hair and buried his face within.

"Lavender. Even your hair smells of your sweet and gentle nature." Hadden traced her collarbone, then down farther. His touch to her nipple brought it to a rapid and sudden peak. He laughed softly, the sound of a man well satisfied.

"Hadden."

"Next time I won't hurt you. I promise."

She didn't know how to respond to his easy promise. What she'd felt had been a small flash of pain amid burning pleasure. "Promise?"

His grin made her ache all over. She longed for the man and for the heart-wrenching desire he so expertly gave.

Without another word, he rose. The washstand and pitcher were nearby. "This will be cool."

"You're beautiful," she told him.

He didn't turn but wrung the cloth out. "Men are not beautiful."

"You are."

He chuckled, and with an economy of movement that surprised Storm, he was beside the bed, his weight pressing down the mattress. Without asking, he nudged her legs open and began to bathe her. His intimate touch surprised her and embarrassed her. He was looking as well as touching.

She trembled and tried to close her legs, pushing at his hands.

"It's all right, darlin' girl. You didn't object a minute ago when I buried myself deep inside you, and I promise you, I'll be there again very soon. I want to erase the evidence of innocence. If you thought it would be a good idea, we could display the sheets for the Robertsons to see I deflowered you, but I don't think you would want that."

She didn't know how to answer him. She needed to convince Henry even more than Charles that they'd consummated their marriage. But...

"You're doing it again." His hand tried the weight of her breast, caressing the soft underside, until his thumb finally reached the crest. "See, your nipple is like a rosebud, taut and ready for my tongue. Every little move you make sends your breasts swaying and begging. Touch me, kiss me, they say. They're lush and beautiful, absolutely perfect for my hand, for my touch and my lips." He brought her hand to his mouth, kissed each knuckle then brought her fingers close to him, so close she touched his cock. "I've never before felt this instant fire, a passion so strong I didn't have a clue how to control its power. You do this to me, darlin'." He tossed the cloth to the pitcher. It landed dead center in the bowl.

"I'm going to make love to you again if you'll have me. Will you, my sweet passion?"

"Yes." She could not believe what she'd just said and done. Still, she wound her fingers in his hair and pulled him close for a kiss. She could not find the words to refuse him. She wondered if sex with him would be this way for the rest of their lives.

Morning light stretched in through the window in the master bedroom. Golden beams slanted across Storm's face, highlighting the golden sun lightened streaks in her hair and her soft delicate features. The word fragile came to mind every time Hadden looked at Storm. And that, he laughed ruefully, was most of the time.

Ever since he'd seen her marching down the fairway, his thoughts had revolved around her. She drew him, calling his name with just a look.

Storm lying naked on the large bed was an aphrodisiac he couldn't refuse. She was under his skin, her fire blazed a trail within that he couldn't douse. He wanted her still.

Storm's passion. Yes, Storm's passion ignited an inferno within. *Fiery little piece of femininity*. She was all of that, and yet her virtue he'd seen and felt first hand. She'd been so innocent. Not any more.

Thoughts of Charles making love to her, abusing her sent a punch to his gut that left him nauseous.

He stretched lazily and rose from the bed before striding to the window. Peering outside, he sucked in his breath. Just getting out of a carriage were Larena and Fayth.

What the blazes were they doing here? The girls weren't due back for two more weeks. After last night he'd hoped to have several more delicious evenings with his new wife.

He soaked in the quiet of the house. It wouldn't stay that way for long. Even as the girls made their way up the walkway to the house, laughter and chatter followed them. He sighed, knowing the solitude was coming to a quick end.

Lavender. As long as he lived, the scent of lavender would haunt him, remind him of Storm.

Guess he'd have to meet the sisters. He glanced in Storm's direction. She still slept, so he pulled on his pants and the shirt he'd worn the night before, determined to maintain the privacy of their relationship. Storm could tell them what she wanted to, when she wanted to tell them.

Padding toward the staircase, he reached the top just as the girls were starting up.

"Mr. Johnston? What are you doing here?" Fayth questioned.

A grin spread across his face. "I live here now. Thought you girls were going to stay with the McLellan's a little longer."

"Oh my," Larena said.

"I-I just didn't think..." Fayth stopped then smiled. "We want to talk to our sister."

"Don't think that would be a good idea right now." Hadden didn't want Storm to be embarrassed. Her innocence and probable discomfiture were factors he had to consider, and he could just imagine the red staining her beautiful face when her sisters barged into the bedroom.

"Why not?" came from Larena.

"What did you do to her?" Fayth asked.

Before Hadden had a chance to answer, the girls pushed past him and started down the hallway to the master bedroom. "I don't think this is a good idea." He followed them, determined to play interference when he could, unsure of what they would encounter when they opened the door.

"Storm, we're home. You won't be able to guess what happened." Fayth stepped inside the door.

"Storm?" Larena ran into Fayth's back when her older sister stopped suddenly.

Hadden stepped past the girls, hoping to block their view.

Storm held the covers tight, her cheeks flaming and her hair in beautiful disarray, falling around her shoulders.

~ * ~

With an unusual disinterest, Henry Robertson watched the spring thunderstorm as it seethed outside his stately home. Lightning bolts hit the ground and farther out to sea. The ships anchored at the docks rolled and dipped with the incoming waves. Wind curled and moaned around the eaves. The rage he felt inside could not have been more violent.

Damn the little chit to hell. How could one tiny piece of work like Storm Graham-Johnston find a way out of the contract he'd thought secured when Bradford signed the piece of paper?

Charles was worthless too. He could have had her long before she'd had a chance to worm her way out of the agreement, but he'd been off playing and whoring under the guise of hunting.

Anything could happen now. His spies had told him Hadden spent the night. That could mean anything.

And if they hadn't slept together, relatives in London would welcome her with open arms. Her sister lived in Maryland. He should have kept a closer eye on her.

Candlelight flickered and wavered as Charles opened the door to the library. An instant later, all was dark. Not wanting to talk to his son without light, he lit the candles then walked to the sideboard and poured them both a drink. He could use one right now.

"I want the girl." Charles voice was harsh and insistent. "What are you going to do about it?"

"Shouldn't you woo her, sweep her off her feet so she'll change her mind?" Henry's was bitter, his plans now in violent upheaval.

"You know that's never going to happen."

A light flickered in the semi-darkness of the room. Embers from Charles' cigar glowed in the eerie light. Thunder boomed overhead. Coldness swept through him and settled deep in his gut.

Robertson understood damn well he had best secure Storm or perhaps one of her sisters, or his own fortune might be in jeopardy. Funds from the stables and races would take years to cover the money Bradford Graham owed him.

He turned, a smile sneaking out beneath his well-groomed mustache. He walked to the safe and pulled out his copy of the legal document that stated Storm or the money was his. He could live with the money, but Charles wanted the girl. A sudden and violent end to Hadden might be the very thing that would solve all his problems. The fire had not accomplished what he'd hoped but there were always other ways.

"Perhaps you should try a bit harder. Take her for a carriage ride." Henry shrugged.

"I'd have to kidnap her to accomplish that." Charles drank the shot down then poured another.

Henry stared hard at his son, trying to tell him without words that perhaps he should try it. "If you put your rod in her maybe Hadden won't want her."

"If I have the little chit, Hadden might want to put a bullet through me." Charles drank again.

Henry emitted a snort of disgust at his son's cowardice. "Nothing ventured nothing gained has always been my motto. You should try it."

The dreary room depressed him, the night attacking as if the tempest was on Johnston's side. Dim candlelight bathed the room, shadows dancing and fluttering across the walls. He swore under his breath.

Chapter Twelve

For a moment and with her eyes closed, Storm's thoughts lingered in that peaceful time between waking and sleeping. She heard the familiar chatter of her sisters as they walked around downstairs. She stretched lazily then brushed her hair from her face. Everything seemed so normal.

The lone sheet covering her slipped to pool around her hips. A brief second later, she plucked the material with her fingers and sighed softly. Her eyes slightly closed, her vision fuzzy, she wanted nothing more than to snuggle into the warmth surrounding her and go back to sleep.

She fought for control, trying to remember the night and what had happened. Her thoughts were crystal clear. She recalled all Hadden had done to her and what she'd done with him—the mercuric sensation within her that drove all rational thought and years of moral teachings out of her mind. God, but she was married so why would that matter?

His touch had been so right, so perfect. The way he'd caressed every inch of her body, so magical.

She had not understood, had wondered at the feelings.

The wine they drunk had made her feel relaxed and confident. She'd been so frightened of the sex and all that incurred, but Hadden had soothed her frayed nerves. He made her feel cherished and well loved. She paused in her thoughts, shaking off the feelings of apprehension swirling around her like a dark fog. Had this been enough to keep Charles at bay? Or did she really have to get pregnant first?

Hadden, she needed to fix breakfast or had he already left for the docks? Wouldn't he have told her, woke her up before he left?

The scent of her husband was still on the sheets and pillows.

Slowly, she brought the fabric to her cheek, last night's memories still so strong. He'd touched her so very intimately and she'd been just as eager.

"Hadden." She'd given him her innocence. She'd not wanted him to stop kissing her, ever.

Memories raced chaotically through her mind. Shared kisses, a tender caress, a sweet intimate touch and she'd desired him above all else. She'd never thought to feel this way, never thought to have a man cherish her so.

Hadden...

Fayth's voice resounded outside the door, then Hadden's brought her wide-awake and alert. Belatedly, she realized she was naked. The heat of embarrassment rushed through her.

"What are they doing here?"

"Oh, my God, they're at my door with Hadden. They don't mean to come inside?" She bolted to a sitting position.

The door swung open, both sisters stood in the opening.

"Fayth, Larena?" Sheets wrapped around her, she jerked off the bed only to fall back, her head pounding. Breathless, she clung to the sheet, holding it beneath her chin. "Aren't you supposed to be somewhere else?"

The girls started backing from the room. "We're sorry."

"Didn't know..."

Hadden stepped in front of her sisters. "I tried to stop them, but they were determined to see you and didn't listen to what I was trying to tell them. They said they had to talk to you."

My God, she was in this bed nearly naked with her husband making excuses to her sisters. What would they think? *That I'm truly married and that perhaps it was about time we made love.*

She didn't understand her jumbled emotions. She knew she'd be able to think better if she could dress but she didn't think jumping from the bed right now to don garments would be practical.

Mortification swept through her.

The door swung shut behind Fayth and Larena as they left the bedroom. The echo resounded in her head.

"They understand you're married." Hadden sat on the edge of the bed and watched her with his usual charismatic style.

"I thought you'd be at work by now." She pulled the sheet tighter, not understanding how to act in front of him and feeling the heat rise to her cheeks.

"I was on my way when the girls arrived. I thought I should run interference but it didn't workout that way. There is no need for you to be embarrassed." With the back of his hand, he touched her face.

She moistened her lips and watched his knowing gaze travel the length of her. "I can't help what I feel."

"You're a beautiful woman Storm and you're my wife. The girls understand that fact." He retrieved her dress from the night before. "Perhaps this won't do for making breakfast. But I'm always going to have fond memories of this red satin dress."

"I need my clothes. I need to get up and fix breakfast." She tried desperately to ignore him.

"If that's what you want, I'll go downstairs and entertain them, and we'll meet you when you're ready. You don't have to explain anything to them." He smiled before he stepped from the room leaving her alone with her thoughts.

The door clicked behind him as he left the room. With haste and before anyone could find their way back inside her room, she rushed to dress. Fumbling with buttons and ties, she was finally clothed.

Downstairs, the girls and Hadden sat in the parlor quietly chatting away. She didn't want to know what the conversation entailed, and she prayed it wasn't about how they'd found her upstairs in the bedroom—naked.

As she passed through the parlor to the kitchen, she nodded but didn't say a word. She didn't know what to say. Hadden looked at her with a strange expression on his face, and the girls were grinning.

Good God, did they know what she'd done? How she'd acted? She tried to think of something else as she cracked the eggs into the frying pan and set the bacon to cooking in another.

"Can I help?" Fayth stood beside her, a hand on her shoulder. "I don't understand why you're embarrassed. It's what you wanted to happen. You wanted sex with your husband. You wanted a baby so you could prove to Charles the marriage was real."

Could she be anymore blunt, and when had sex become an easy discussion between her and her sister? She set the fork down and turned to Fayth. "It's all so new and when my sisters burst into the bedroom taking me by surprise, I didn't have time to sort through all my thoughts."

"Was it the first time?"

Storm nodded. "Not that it's any of your business." She turned back to the eggs and bacon.

"I'll put the kettle on for tea."

Storm needed to deflect the conversation from her to the girls. "Why did you come back so early? I thought you had plans to stay the summer."

Fayth tied an apron around her waist. "It seems Blade and Aiden had a falling out. She thought she caught him with another woman. It wasn't the truth, at least that was Blade's short story, but when Aiden is miserable everyone is miserable, so we decided to come home."

"I see, trouble in paradise, and I thought those two might be the next to wed. Aiden has loved him half her life."

"True but Aiden isn't going to settle for Blade unless he returns that love, and I don't know if she'll ever really know for sure."

"I think she will once she learns to trust him."

Bacon sizzled, eggs cooked and the milk was poured. Tea simmered in the pot and the kitchen table had been set, and all Storm needed to do was call them for breakfast.

"Larena, Hadden breakfast is ready."

The two walked through the doors and into the kitchen, their lively chatter stopping the moment they sat down.

Seconds ticked by, silence darkened the room and left a hollow feeling in the pit of Storm's belly. She couldn't eat, yet she tried to choke down a little food. She couldn't wait until everyone left.

The moment felt awkward.

Hadden wiped his mouth with a napkin and rose from his chair.

"I'll be back for dinner." Then he turned to the sisters. "Will I see you then?" Yet he waited at the door of the kitchen.

Fayth was the first to speak. "No, I think we'll visit some friends, maybe stay the night somewhere else."

So they felt the discomfiture too. "You don't have to do that." Storm was quick to say even though relief had swept through her at their words.

"I think we do." Larena rose from the table and took hers and Hadden's dishes to the sink. "We will help you clean up first."

Fayth cleared the rest of the table while Larena heated water for the dishes. "You go say goodbye to your handsome husband while we take care of this." She motioned to the sink and the dishes.

"You sure?" Storm didn't know who she was more apprehensive to be with, Hadden or her sisters. Both had questions she didn't know how to answer.

"Of course. Now go." Fayth said, motioning for her to leave.

Storm nodded and joined her husband, walking him to the door. He grabbed his hat from the table by the entrance then pulled her into his arms. "You have nothing to be embarrassed about."

"I can't help the feelings. You didn't see the shock on their faces when they stumbled through the bedroom door."

"No, but I almost ran into them when they jerked to a sudden stop. Now give me a proper kiss."

He pulled her into his arms and kissed her softly at first then deepened the touch, reminding Storm of last night's passion and the way her body responded to him.

When they pulled away, he smiled at her before touching the tip of her nose with one fingertip. "I'll see you tonight."

Storm watched him walk down the pathway toward the docks. She leaned against the doorframe and sighed softly. After last night, she realized how deeply she wanted Hadden, more than just for a baby. He meant so much to her. Despite his initial anger over their marriage, he had acquiesced to most of her wishes, even agreeing to give her a child when she'd asked him. But he had told her he wanted a child.

Perhaps she'd conceived last night. It wouldn't be the first time a woman had become pregnant with the first lovemaking. She touched her belly, wondering if it were true and wondering too, if he'd stay away from her bed if she were pregnant.

She hoped not.

That seemed such an odd response from someone who'd feared the act for the longest time. *You weren't really afraid, just apprehensive.* It was Ravyn who feared the marriage bed.

She turned back to the kitchen only to find her sisters making the finishing touches on cleaning. "You're done."

"We are," Fayth said, drying her hands and untying her apron. "If all goes as planned we will see you tomorrow afternoon. I'm not sure how we will deal with living in the same house, but I'm sure we will find a way to give you and your new husband the privacy you deserve and want. Won't we Larena?"

Larena grinned. "Of course, and we could always return to the Mclellan Castle."

"Or we could go to London." Fayth giggled. "I'd like the excitement and the balls."

"And the suitors," Larena chimed in.

"No you don't. The two of you aren't ready to be paraded like cattle for unscrupulous gentlemen to vie for."

"It's not that bad," Larena said with coquettish flair then dancing around the kitchen.

"It is according to both Ravyn an Christel. The two of you be off. If you get a chance, send a message as to where you are."

As storm puttered around the kitchen, she heard the lively chatter of her sisters as they donned their wraps and left the house. She hoped to have one last cup of tea before she went to the stables. A few hours ride on Fiacre would be wonderful. Riding relaxed her and after a good ride, she could put her life in perspective.

She closed her eyes for a moment inhaling the sweet aroma of her tea. When she opened them, Charles Robertson stood in front of her. Her heart lurched to a sudden stop and she couldn't breathe. Everything seemed to turn dark as if the clouds passed in front of the sun.

"Good morning," he said, as pleasantly as if she'd invited him into her home.

"Get out of my house," she hissed. "Right now—before I call for Hadden."

"Now, why would you want to do that, Storm?"

"Don't call me Storm."

"Pardon me," Charles said with exaggerated politeness. "I repeat, why would you want to call Mr. Johnston? It's not as if he would find time to come here." He shrugged then. "And why would he want to? There is nothing between the two of you except a sham of a marriage, Miss Graham."

"I'm Mrs. Johnston and don't forget that."

"Well yes, we all understand you reneged on your father's word and married Hadden Johnston." Charles tossed his hat on the kitchen table, then pulled out a chair and straddled it. "An unfortunate mistake, my dear. Your actions have made everything so problematic."

"I don't understand what you're trying to tell me." Storm's composure slipped another notch. "There is nothing difficult about this. I'm married and there is nothing you or anyone else can do about it."

"That's not really true." Charles smiled, his boyish blond handsomeness belying the menacing note in his voice. "Your father, as you well know, signed a contract stating very clearly that in return for monies received, you'd become my wife. And never doubt it, Storm. You will live up to his promise."

"You're wrong," she blurted. "There's no way you can make me marry you. Haven't you heard a word I've said? I'm already wed. We've consummated the marriage."

"A minor and very temporary inconvenience, I assure you."

Storm's heart slammed against her ribs, but she forced herself to remain calm and expressionless. She didn't want to give away her fear. Somehow she had to stay relaxed and brazen this out. Trying for a bright, confident smile, she said, "I believe Hadden might have something to say about that."

"If you don't cooperate with my plans, Hadden Johnston might not be around to have a comment about anything."

"Are you threatening me, Charles?"

"Oh, my did you think that? Of course it's not a threat," he protested throwing Storm a hurt look. "Would I threaten the woman I love?"

"Love? You don't know how to love anyone but yourself."

Charles' confident expression disappeared, replaced by an icy hostility. "I'll let that pass, Storm, but don't allude to that again. Do you understand? You and I will marry, and you will learn to love me."

"Never. There is no you and me and there never will be."

"Of course there is. You're going to marry me, we're going to live together in my father's home, we're going to have children together, then we're going to get old together."

Storm sipped from her tea, peering at him over the rim of the cup. "Charles, listen to me," she pleaded, switching tactics in a desperate attempt to make him see reason. "I'll pay you the money I owe you. I can sell the stables or you can take them over, it's up to you."

"I don't like dirty stables nor do I want to run that type of business. Even if you sold the horses and the stable, it wouldn't be enough." Charles smiled. "It wouldn't be you."

"Perhaps not. I don't know how much Bradford owed your father. "But the stables do turn a profit. I have some of the finest racehorses in the British Isles. You and I can come up with a payment plan."

"Oh my Storm, Storm." Charles sighed as if dealing with a petulant child. "When are you going to get it through that pretty little head of yours that I don't want your money, what little of it there is? Even if you pay back every dime your father borrowed, it won't make any difference, no difference at all. I want you and I mean to have you."

Storm swallowed hard as the reality of his words settled in the pit of her stomach. The day became darker. "Well, you can't have me," she told him with a bravado she didn't feel. "I'm married to Mr. Johnston, and you're just going to have to accept that fact."

Charles tossed her a grin that made a chill run down her spine.

"My darling, I don't have to accept anything. As I just told you, your marriage to Mr. Johnston is a temporary set back, nothing more. A few months and the matter will all be cleared up. Indeed my father thinks we should be wed in no time."

"Well Henry doesn't know what he's talking about."

Charles dropped all pretense of civility and leaned forward until his face was inches away from hers. "My father is never wrong. Everyone knows that your marriage to Johnston is a farce. Why, he doesn't even live here with you. Marriages of that kind are easily annulled in the face of prior legal agreements."

Storm had the urge to slap his nefarious grin from his face but held onto her teacup instead. "Where Hadden sleeps and lives is none of yours or anyone else's business. We have agreed it would be easier for him to spend the weeknights on his ships. Especially in lieu of the arson attempt on his ship the *Wind Walker*. One can never be too careful. He plans on coming home on the weekends and leaving Perkins to stand guard on whatever vessel is in port."

Charles' laughter had a nasty ring to it. "You're either a very bad liar, Storm, or you're the only person in town who doesn't know that your loving husband is in Berwick this weekend."

"What?" She gasped but realized he must have gone to see the Widow Stewart, but staying for the weekend? That was absurd. "You're wrong. He went there for today but will be home tonight. I know all about his relationship with her."

"Ah, so you admit there is one, a relationship, but you didn't know a thing about Johnston's plans, and he obviously doesn't care enough about you to bother to tell you. And that tells me your relationship isn't quite so cozy as you want me to believe. Why don't you just get an annulment and we can be married by the end of the summer."

"Don't you ever give up? I'm not marrying you, not if you were the last man on this earth. And what my husband does or doesn't tell me is none of your business."

Charles sighed, a long, dramatic exhalation that made Storm shudder. "I told Father you would be difficult. I guess he and I will have to go back to the original plan."

"Just do that," Storm challenged, heedless of the danger she might put herself and Hadden in, "but in the meantime, I want you out of my house."

Amazed, Charles nodded and stood up. "All right, I'll go. I didn't come here this morning to upset you. I just came to let you know that plans for our wedding are proceeding on schedule."

"Get out!" Storm leapt up from her chair and wrenched the door open. "And don't come back. The next time I see you skulking around here, I'll shoot you myself. I swear I will."

Charles picked up his hat and sauntered toward the door. "See you soon, my darling," he cooed, reaching out and chucking Storm under the chin. "Real soon."

~ * ~

Only a few hours later and after a quick lunch, Storm saddled Fiacre and headed out of town toward Berwick. Letting the Stallion race down the road, she enjoyed the wind in her hair. The day was sunny and bright, filled with the redolent scent of spring flowers.

Five minutes later, she pulled up on the reins and slowed her horse to a trot. Fiacre whinnied his displeasure at the abrupt end to his gallop. Charles probably wasn't lying this morning but he didn't know the entire story. Hadden had promised to introduce her to the Widow Stewart and his children but would he appreciate a surprise visit. Misgivings assailed her and she was tempted to turn around, go back to the house and wait for an explanation.

She trusted him explicitly. And yet...

Did she have doubts?

What if she found the widow's home? He had just told her an approximate location and what if he didn't want her to show up there? What if his relationship with the widow was more than platonic? What if he ran to her after their lovemaking because she was lacking in some way?

She could make herself sick, and she sure as hell didn't lack confidence, or did she?

Second-guessing everything didn't make her feel any better. Didn't she just tell herself she trusted her husband? Then why was she headed down the road to find out if Charles, a man she despised and did not trust, was telling her the truth?

With a long sigh and a heavy heart, she turned Fiacre around to go home, understanding she needed to rethink her mission. But she warred with herself, she needed to talk to Hadden; needed to tell him Charles had entered her home without her permission and threatened Hadden's life.

Storm sat on her horse for several minutes, staring off at the panoramic vista in front of her and pondering what to do. Damn Hadden, anyway, for leaving her and putting her in this position. If...if what?

Last night she'd given him her heart, her soul and her body. She felt bereft at his lack of concern and his hasty flight. Maybe if she'd treated him like a normal husband from the beginning, he wouldn't have left her this morning under the guise of going to work. She frowned at her admission, realizing that although there was probably a thread of truth in her self-castigating thoughts, there was nothing she could do, at least at that moment, to rectify the problems in their marriage. And she admitted, she made a start last night. Now all she had to do was seduce him into her bed again. Determinedly, she put the matter out of her mind, intent on concentrating instead on how to handle the immediate situation.

Perhaps she could send a message to the docks. Perkins, she was sure, would handle the missive with consideration and if, by chance, Hadden wasn't there she wouldn't be faced with the embarrassment of showing up at the widow's home.

Storm shook her head dejectedly and urged her horse back to the stables. It was too big a risk to take. She just couldn't hand Charles and Henry Robertson the weapon of knowing she was insecure in her marriage. She needed to wait until tonight or whenever Hadden turned up again. Good God, but she hated waiting and not knowing.

She was his wife, didn't he owe her a thought or two? Shouldn't he tell her if he was leaving town?

At least she could get an estimate on the value of the stables and the horses residing within. Although Charles had said this morning that repaying the loan wasn't an option, Storm clung to the hope that if she presented Henry with a sizeable check, he could somehow stop Charles from carrying out his threats.

Moisture filled her eyes as she thought of selling her horses. She rubbed Fiacre's neck, hoping he'd understand, knowing he wouldn't. Fiacre was hers and would always be. But she knew she had no other recourse, short of asking Hadden for the money, and that she would never do.

She touched her stomach, a wan smile filling her. Perhaps she was pregnant and none of this would matter. Yet with the resolve that was so much a part of her character, Storm nudged the big stallion into a canter, never slowing her pace until she reached home.

It was dinnertime, following the longest afternoon of Storm's life. She had spent the entire time baking cookies and trying to figure out what to cook for dinner, then wondering if he'd be here to eat it. She changed her mind at least a dozen times before finally settling on roast chicken with spring peas.

She had walked out the door and stared at the docks at least a dozen times then retreated back to the confines of her house. She wished her sisters had not been so polite and stayed away. But if he did turn up for dinner, she hoped the evening would end the same way it had the night before.

Storm looked at the big grandfather clock in the hallway then walked into the dining room. It had just chimed six times. Carefully she folded the napkins and placed them beside the plates.

Storm jerked in surprise at the sound of someone beating on her front door. She hadn't even realized she'd been so lost in thought. For a moment, she placed her hand on her heart as if she could stop the rapid pounding that threatened to stop her breath.

She raced to the oven and took the chicken out, setting it on the counter. "I'm coming, I'm coming," she called as the knocking became even more insistent. But when she reached the foyer, she hesitated, fearing who might be on the other side of the door.

"Who's there?" she called out, praying that she'd hear anyone's voice save Charles'.

"It's Perkins," came a gruff shout.

"Perkins?"

"Yeah, your husband's first mate."

Hadden's first mate? Why on earth would he be at her door? With a shiver of apprehension, Storm threw open the door. A glance at the man's distraught face told her more than she wanted to know. "What's wrong?" she demanded without preamble. "Has something happened to my husband?"

"Yeah." The man nodded. "There's been another fire."

"You have to come right away, ma'am."

"A fire? What happened? Was anyone hurt? What about the ship?"

"Yes, on board. The fire started this morning but it was a little one, didn't even bring out the fire brigade. We were ready for something like this and the crew got it out before it could do any damage. But your husband got hit by a beam."

"Got hit by a beam? How?"

"Well, you see, no one is really sure how it happened. One minute all was fine, the fire was out, and this here beam comes crashing down. We yelled but Captain couldn't get out of the way before it hit him."

Storm's head reeled as she imagined the worst, and blindly, she groped for the door. Anyone who had been raised near the docks had heard hundreds of horror stories about sailors being struck down by any number of things on the deck. She was just glad they hadn't been out to sea because he could have been washed overboard.

"What happened?" she whispered, "Tell me everything."

"Just did, but nobody really knows why that beam fell. It shouldn't have happened. The beams were all secure this morning."

"Secure, how did it get unsecured?"

"Well, that's the puzzle of it. It couldn't have."

"Then how did it happen?"

Perkins threw her an uneasy look. "It had to be some kind of sabotage."

"Oh, my God!" Storm gasped for air. "You mean someone intentionally tried to hurt Hadden." Her thoughts sped to the conversation she'd had just this morning with Charles.

"Kinda appears so." Perkins nodded, wiping the sweat from his forehead with the back of his hand.

"Is he...is he dead?"

"No, no, he isn't dead," Perkins said quickly. "But he's unconscious and the doc's with him right now."

Storm blanched, causing Perkins' eyes to widen with alarm. "You aren't going to faint or nothin' are ya, ma'am?"

"No," she answered, wishing she felt as sure of that as she sounded. "I'm fine. Do you think he's going to be alright?"

"Oh yeah, he going to live, all right, but I think you'd better come anyway."

"Of course." Storm nodded, recovering herself. "Did you bring a wagon?"

"No, I rode. Your stable boy has your horse saddled and ready."

"Good, do I have time to run upstairs and change?"

Perkins nodded. "Hurry."

Storm raced up the stairs and into her room, unbuttoning her dress as she ran. Was Charles really trying to kill her husband? He'd threatened as much, but she hadn't really believed him. Yet she'd had a strange feeling he'd set the first fire.

She hesitated, her hand involuntarily clutching her throat. It had to be Charles. He had meant those threats he'd uttered this morning, and he'd wasted no time in putting his plans into action. But how could she prove it?

She had to talk to Hadden. Somehow, they had to come up with a plan to keep him safe. When Charles found out Hadden was still alive, he'd undoubtedly try to kill him again. The reality of Charles' ruthless intentions made her stomach knot.

It was imperative she reach Hadden as soon as possible. With renewed fervor, she shimmied out of her clothes then raced to her armoire and grabbed a pair of riding britches and a shirt. Clumsily she stepped into the pants. She yanked on a blouse then tore out of her bedroom and down the steps, fastening buttons as she ran.

Perkins was still waiting by the door for her. Storm paused in the foyer long enough to tuck in her blouse and pull on her riding boots, then joined him.

"Let's go," he commanded.

Storm answered the order with a quick nod. Outside she mounted Fiacre and started for the docks.

Chapter Thirteen

Storm charged through town on Fiacre as if all the demons in hell were after her. Reaching the ship in record time, she flew up the gangplank. Perkins followed huffing and puffing as he tried to keep time with her.

"Where is he?"

"Captain's cabin," Perkins bent over at the waist as he wheezed the words in short little bursts.

Bursting through the open door, she looked around frantically for her husband, then nearly fainted from relief when she saw him propped up in the huge double bed, looking at her with vague surprise.

"Hi, Storm," he greeted, his voice weak and slightly slurred.

"Oh, Hadden!" At his bedside, she pulled up a nearby chair and sat down, quickly assessing the white bandage wrapped around his head. "Does it hurt?"

To her complete surprise, he slanted her a funny grin. "I'm kinda numb. Don't know what they gave me, but I'm also a bit groggy."

"Groggy?"

"From the medicine," came a clipped voice behind her. "Couldn't really give him anything for the pain, might make him go to sleep. No, can't give him that much pain medication, not yet. He can't sleep."

Craning her head around, Storm saw the doc standing at a small table, shoving a rounded tube into his black bag along with several other instruments. With a nod of his head, he motioned Storm from Hadden's bedside.

"How is he?" she asked when she reached his side.

The doctor stared at her. "Your husband took a serious blow to his head. He was unconscious for about ten minutes. Now it's imperative you keep him awake. Do you think you can do that?"

Storm closed her eyes, putting her hand to her chest as if she could keep her heart from racing. "Yes. Yes, I believe so...keep his eyes open."

"I'm sure Perkins will help. I want you to keep him awake for the next six or seven hours."

"What will happen if he falls asleep?"

The doctor shrugged. "The sleep might be permanent. Concussions are tricky business."

"When he does go to sleep, I want you to wake him after a couple of hours, then let him go to sleep and wake him up again. Make sure you look at his eyes every time you wake him up and ask him questions to which he should know the answers. If anything seems strange, send Perkins to get me."

Fear settling in the pit of her stomach, Storm nodded at the doctor's instructions. "Would it be safe to move him to my house? I can take better care of him there."

"I'll tell Perkins to get a wagon. Some of the crew can carry him, and we'll make a nice bed for him for the trip home. I'll stop by your house tomorrow morning and check on him. If he runs a fever send for me right away."

Storm promised she would then saw the doctor to the gangplank, thanking him for his assistance. After he departed, she turned back to the crew who were hovering around her and tried for her best tone. "All right sailors, here's what we're going to do. You, sir," she said, pointing to a great bear of a man with a huge black beard, "go find the best wagon you have and bring it around. We're going to move Mr. Johnston to my house. After that I think you'd best clean up the deck and make sure no one else gets hit by anything falling from above."

"What?" the men gasped in unison, staring at her as if she were crazy. "You can't do that—move him. The Doctor said he needs his rest."

"This isn't a discussion. Doc said it would be fine to move him, and he'll be more comfortable in our home. Now you in the blue shirt, what's your name?"

"Jackson," the man answered, whipping a battered cap off his head and stepping forward.

"Well, Mr. Jackson, I'd appreciate it if you would go find a some soft padding and a few blankets for the wagon."

"Not much of that around but I'll scrounge up the best for the captain." He turned and left on his mission.

"Now I know all of you are concerned about my husband and if you wish, you can all come see him. One at a time, of course. I do appreciate all of the help you can give me right now."

~ * ~

The journey from the docks to Storm's home was made without incident. Thankfully it wasn't very far. Several of the sailors took it upon themselves to ride in the back of the wagon and keep Hadden's jostling to a minimum.

Two men rigged a crude stretcher and helped Storm get Hadden into the house and to a downstairs bedroom.

"Is there anything else you need, ma'am, before we leave?" Jackson asked. "I'd be pleased to help."

"If it isn't too much trouble, would you come by the house sometime before dark just to make sure he's doing all right? My sisters might not be home and if he's in any kind of trouble, I won't have anyone here to send for the doc."

"Sure, no problem. We'll take turns and try to get by your place every few hours," Jackson said.

The others nodded, agreeing.

"Thank you so much. You've all been very kind. I hope the person responsible for this is caught." Her thoughts went to Charles and his earlier threat, and she prayed he wouldn't show up here again.

"Maybe I should just stay. I won't be any problem and I can camp out on the porch." Jackson ran his fingers through his hair and looked hopefully at Storm. "If the mast was sabotaged, there's no telling something else won't happen."

"Of course, that would be nice. I would feel a lot better if I knew someone was here to protect my husband."

"That's just what I plan on doing. Whoever tried to kill Mr. Johnston might try again and you would be helpless in those circumstances. I'll just stick around until the captain is healed up enough to look out for himself."

Storm stared at the big man for a moment, then nodded. "Thank you," she whispered. "I'm very grateful."

With an embarrassed grunt, Jackson sat down on the top step. "Just go about your business, ma'am," he directed, "nobody's gonna bother you tonight."

But what about the back door? Charles had come in that way only hours before the fire and Hadden's accident.

~ * ~

"I don't want any more foolish conversation. I just want to sleep, Storm. I need about twelve hours." Hadden leaned back and closed his eyes, his brows wrinkled together.

"Doc said no more than a couple of hours sleep then I have to wake you. You're going to have to put up with my foolish conversation until doc checks you out in the morning."

"Maybe, but I need sleep. This isn't rest. He said I needed rest too."

Storm stared at her irascible husband and determinedly held out a glass of water. She didn't like being told her efforts were foolish. "Drink this. You'll feel better." The glass of water shook in her hand. She told him in a tone she hoped meant business.

"Did he say I couldn't eat?"

"Well, no. He didn't mention food. I suppose you could have something. I'll get you some soup."

"I don't want soup, I want real food." Hadden shoved himself into a sitting position. "Right now, the pain in my head is going away. I've got a hard head and a mast ramming down on it, isn't going to do much damage."

"Even so, I want to make sure you wake up tomorrow morning. But if eating keeps you awake then I'll bring you some roast beef and potatoes."

"Thank you."

Storm smiled. "I'm glad to see you so cranky. It's a sure sign you're feeling better."

"No I'm not." Hadden acted like a petulant little boy. "My stomach is growling and I won't feel better until I eat."

"Oh, come on," Storm cajoled. "Men are always hungry. I don't see how this is any different than usual."

"I haven't eaten since early this morning, that's how it's different."

"Fine," Storm's patience with his ill temper was coming to an immediate halt. "If that's what you want, I'll fix it." Turning, she started out the door. "Cooking the food will take some time." She handed him a book. "Read this."

"Storm?"

"What do you want now?" She sighed, stopping in front of the door and waiting for the next demand but left before he could say anything else.

~ * ~

She walked back into the room a half-hour later, carrying a tray laden with roast beef, mashed potatoes and green beans. "This should fill the void left in your stomach for a little while."

"Storm, I wanted to say thank you, but you didn't give me the chance."

"Well, I needed to get out of the room before I bashed you in the head, against doc's orders." She set the tray on his lap and tucked a napkin under his chin. Perching on the edge of the bed, she picked up a fork and speared a piece of meat, lifting the food to his mouth.

"What the bloody hell are you doing?" He looked at the fork

poised in front of his lips.

"Feeding you of course."

"I'm not an invalid and it's my head that was hurt, not my hand. I can feed myself." He picked up a spoon and scooped potatoes to eat. "See?"

"Fine." Storm threw down the fork. "Go ahead. I was just trying to help." She didn't know why but her pride had just taken a direct hit.

Hadden picked up the fork and shoved food into his mouth. "You don't have much patience, do you?"

"Well, I'm not the one who won't follow doc's orders," she shot back. "I'm trying to keep you alive, and you're doing your best to... to..." She couldn't finish the unthinkable sentence. "I'll come back for the tray. Enjoy." She didn't want to be in the room with him for one more second.

"You're leaving? I thought you were supposed to keep me awake," Hadden told her, his mouth full of food.

"I'm tired of talking with someone who doesn't have anything positive to say."

Before he could stop her, she marched from the room and slammed the door shut in the process.

"Thanks a lot. Leave me lying here hour after hour by myself. A man could die here and you'd never notice," he spoke to the empty room.

She rested against the door, listening to his words and smiling and waiting. She counted, wondering how long it would take him to call her back and maybe apologize. But then she thought, he really didn't need her to eat. She decided to take a much needed rest and leave him to his own devices.

An hour later, she opened the door and stepped inside. He was lying on his back, his tray of empty dishes on the floor. Hadden's hands were clasped together and his eyes were closed. She didn't want to wake him, but she did want the tray. Deciding she could get it later, she started to back from the room.

"Don't go. Stay and talk to me until I need to sleep. For some reason I'm wide awake and bored silly."

A jolt of pleasure rippled through her. Maybe he didn't think their conversation was foolish. "If you'd like." She nodded, moving to the chair beside his bed. "How is your head?"

"It's throbbing and hurts like hell. When the crew yelled for me to get out of the way, I didn't have time."

"Didn't you hear the crack when it broke?"

"That's the funny thing. There was no noise. It just came out of nowhere." He reached out and took her hand in his.

Storm gazed at him, curious, but enjoying the contact. She liked the feel of his calloused hands. "That is unusual, isn't it?"

"Never seen or heard anything like it," he admitted. "What I can't figure out," Hadden said, pausing, "is who started the fire and set all this in motion."

"I might know the answer to that question."

Hadden's eyes lifted to hers with surprise registered in their depths. "How?" he lifted her hand to his lips and placed a gentle kiss on the back.

"Charles Robertson came to visit me this morning. He barged through the back door and I couldn't get him to leave."

Jerking to a straighter position, Hadden groaned and put his hand to his head. "Are you telling me you think Robertson is trying to kill me? Why would you think that?"

Storm's voice was strangled when she answered. "He doesn't like the fact I married you. You know that but when he talked to me this morning, he threatened your life."

"Charles was my first suspect with the fires. I just thought he was attempting to ruin my business. But murder?"

With little hesitation, she filled him in on the details of her confrontation with Charles, but leaving out her desperate offer to try to repay the loan. Hadden didn't know about the amount of money Bradford had borrowed from Henry and neither did she. Storm didn't want him to feel obligated to pay it back so she'd always steered their conversations away from the monetary and toward the sale of the stable. At this point, she didn't think Charles would accept any amount of money because he'd made it abundantly clear that he wanted her.

Hadden listened without comment to her rendition of Charles' visit. When her words trailed off, he said, "I think it's time to have a chat with Charles."

Storm put a hand over her mouth to hide a gasp and unconsciously tightened her fingers around his hand, terrified of what he might do. "Please don't do anything foolish. Charles is crazy. He won't stop at anything to get what he wants. We both know he never has."

Hadden squeezed her hand and kissed the back once more. "Don't worry. This time he's dealing with me, not some naïve school girl."

"You know about his past and the things he's done?"

Hadden nodded. "I've always suspected there was more to the rumors that have circulated ever since he turned fifteen. And are the rumors about your friend Ella true?"

"Yes," she said.

"Did you go to the authorities?"

Storm shook her head. "There wasn't a reason to do that. Lawrence knew and loved her enough to raise the baby as his own."

"That bastard! An innocent young girl like that. And he wouldn't do the right thing by her."

Storm faltered. "Ella wouldn't have married him. By the time she knew she was pregnant, she also knew what kind of person Charles was. She hated him, his father and everything he stood for."

"Did he rape her?"

"Not exactly. But in a way yes. She didn't really say no but she didn't say yes either. She told him to stop but he wouldn't."

Hadden's eyes narrowed and darkened with rage. "That son of a bitch. And now he thinks he's going to have my wife?" With an abrupt movement, he flung the blanket aside.

"What are you doing?"

"I'm getting out of this damn bed and going to see that bastard." His voice was filled with rage.

"You can't! I won't let you. Your head? What if you blacked out and he killed you?"

"I'm bloody fine, damn it. You act like I'm dying when all I've got is a small bump on the head. Now move out of the way, Storm. I have to get dressed."

But Storm didn't move. "Hadden please, listen to me. We have no proof of anything, and if you go over to the Robertson's now, there's no telling what could happen. If Charles gets violent, and you can't see straight, how will you defend yourself? Please don't go. I don't think I could bear it if you got hurt again because of me."

He paused and for a long second stared at her. Then he slowly sat back on the bed, pulling her down next to him and wrapping his arm around her shoulders. "Why do you mean because of you?"

She tried not to cry but hot tears welled in her eyes. All her frustrations and fears were becoming so apparent. "I forced you into a marriage you didn't want. If I hadn't done that, you wouldn't be involved, your ships wouldn't have been set on fire and you wouldn't be lying in bed with a concussion that nearly killed you." Her eyes filled with tears and it was all she could do to hold them back.

Hadden lifted his hand to the side of Storm's face, gently guiding her head down to his shoulder. "You're right," he murmured, placing a gentle kiss next to her nose. "If you hadn't asked me to marry you, I wouldn't be involved. But, the fact is, I did marry you, and no one threatens what is mine."

Storm raised a tearstained face to look at him. "But you can't confront him tonight. You're hurt and the doctor said..."

"Hush," Hadden said, his lips close to her ear, "I know what the doctor said, and you're right. This isn't the right time. I need a plan."

"Oh, God, I'm so sorry about all this. But if I could change anything, I wouldn't. What I did to you was so wrong. I understand that now, and I won't fight you if you want to have our marriage annulled. I didn't realize Charles was so set on having me that he'd come after you." Her voice shook with heartache.

"When did I say anything about an annulment?" Hadden whispered.

"Hadden?"

"Hush."

Before she could say anything else, Hadden's mouth covered hers. His lips were soft and warm, intoxicating in their sensual allure as they enticed her own to open and allow his tongue entrance. Storm felt a mercuric heat spiral down her spine, and with a small, surrendering sigh, her lips parted beneath his.

Hadden gathered her closer, deepening his kiss as he laid her back on the bed. Sweetly his fingers traced a path from her neck then trailed lower, skimming across the upper swell of her breasts. Storm was aware of the path his hand was taking, but she didn't want to stop him. Instead, she twined her arms around his neck, threading her fingers into his thick, dark hair and arching her back.

Hadden moaned low in his throat, his hand cupping her breast, sweeping his thumb back and forth across her nipple. He twisted his body, throwing a leg over hers and pressing his hips against her thigh.

Storm felt his heated erection, even through the layers of her skirt and petticoats. An overwhelming need to move closer so she could feel his arousal and the insistent pressure against her core swept through her. Mindlessly she allowed herself to sink into the heady swirl of desire, she shifted her hips and remembered the feel of him from the other night's lovemaking.

With a strangled gasp, Hadden slowly broke the embrace. "Oh my God, not now sweetheart. I can't think straight and my head is throbbing. I want our lovemaking to be unhurried, and I want to make each moment perfect for you."

"I thought that was my excuse, a throbbing head. I heard mother say it so many times but it never stopped Bradford." She sat up, pushing her hair from her eyes but not embarrassed they'd almost made love. "I know it's too soon. I'm a bloody fool."

"No, you're not a fool." He set her aside and touched her lips with a fingertip. "I'll make this up to you. I promise."

She nodded, squishing her lips together, unsure what to think. God, she'd just about pushed him into something that might hurt him. Doc said he needed rest.

"I'll take the tray to the kitchen." Her voice shook from the passion he'd elicited from her. Trying to calm her racing nerves, she picked up the tray.

"I'm done and I think I'll try to sleep."

"All right then, you have two hours, and I'll be back to wake you up and check on you. If there is anything else you might need, call me."

"I won't and I think you should try and get some rest. It's been a long day for you too, and I know you're tired."

Storm didn't want to leave him, but he'd made it clear. He needed to sleep and even though she knew that fact to be true, she hesitated. "Yes, yes I am tired. I'll try to sleep." The door closed behind her, and she was left with her turbulent thoughts.

~ * ~

The next few days passed in a blur. Doc visited every morning and each time, he pronounced Hadden nearly recovered, and he spent the bulk of his time resting.

Finally the doctor told her there was no reason for him to visit and Hadden could get back to doing whatever he wanted. This was a major relief to Storm, who was exhausted from taking care of all his needs, and she was thankful for her decision to keep him on the first floor. She could not have imagined running up and down the stairs every time he wanted something.

She opened the door to the room he was occupying and set the breakfast tray on the table near his bed. "Here you go." She smiled at him, wishing he would start acting normal. He had been solicitous and careful with every word. She just didn't know what to think.

"Thanks, I'm ready to get up and help out around the house. Did I tell you how much I appreciate all you've done for me?"

"You just did." She pulled up a chair, wanting to visit for a while. Her sisters had spent most of their days and some of their nights with friends, telling her they wanted her to have time alone with her new husband and not wanting to make extra work for her.

"I want a real bath and real clothes."

"Then that's what you should have." She wondered if he'd given any more thought about confronting Charles but she didn't want to bring up the subject. His crew had stopped by several times and told her there was no evidence pointing Charles' direction. Evidently he'd done an admirable job covering up his crime.

"Well then," Storm nodded, "I'll fix a tub after you finish eating."

"You don't have to fix anything. You're not my slave. Just show me where everything is and I'll pump and haul the water."

"I'd be happy to help. It's no trouble. You bring the water and I'll get the tub ready."

"Sounds good," Hadden told her then returned to his eggs and bacon.

When he was done with breakfast, Storm heated several kettles of water on the stove, adding them to the buckets. Hadden poured them in the tub until his bathwater was warm. "All right, that should be enough. Here's the soap and two towels. I'll see you when you're finished."

Storm hurried out of the kitchen. She started to close the door, then changed her mind and pulled it open a few inches. *Just in case he does need me.*

Sitting down in the dining room and sipping on a cup of tea, she waited for him to finish. She heard a small splash and knew he'd sat down. Then everything was quiet—too quiet. Then she heard small noises, a grunt or two. Her imagination sparked. She was left with the need to look in and see what was going on but she didn't dare.

"Bloody hell."

His curse sent her nerves spinning. Visions of Charles walking in the back door and killing him sent shivers wracking her body. She bolted upright not even thinking that if Hadden couldn't defend himself what could she do.

When she rushed through the kitchen door, she was brought to a sudden and very abrupt halt.

A gasp escaped her as she watched Hadden's wet, gleaming muscles grow taut with his efforts to retrieve a bar of soap, which must have slipped through his fingers. Even though they'd made love it had been dark and she'd never taken the time to look at his body. Now, mesmerized, she couldn't stop staring. When she finally realized she was holding her breath, she let her air out in a loud whoosh.

Despite her efforts to look away, she didn't move, finding it impossible to tear herself away from the fascinating sight of her magnificent husband in all his bronze and naked glory.

Her gaze lowered to where sparkling droplets of liquid beaded in the dark hair covering his chest. God, but he was so muscular and coppery that looking at him made her yearn to run her hands along his body.

Without thought, she stepped closer.

He smiled at her, finally noticing her appearance. "Could you get the soap for me?" he queried. "Or I could get up and treat you to a view of my very naked body."

Storm suddenly felt as if there wasn't enough air in the kitchen to allow her to take a deep breath or do his bidding. But she regained her composure and stepped close enough to retrieve the soap. "Here." She held the soap out to him.

I need to leave now. Leave now before I do something I'll regret.

But her feet wouldn't move.

"The soap?"

"A, yes..." She picked it up and handed it to him but still she stared and waited—for what she wasn't sure.

Chapter Fourteen

In that moment Hadden forgot everything he'd been thinking. Watching Storm stare at him while he bathed made him decide on a spur of the moment decision. Standing, he sluiced water over his body to rid himself of the soap. Then, without a second thought, stepped from the tub and strode across the kitchen toward his beautiful wife.

Frozen, Storm watched him move in her direction. She didn't have time to blink before he'd wrapped her in his arms, naked, dripping water and fully aroused. His hot sexually charged body pressed against her, his mouth plundered hers. Her response was immediate and passionate. With a small cry of surprise, she circled his neck with her arms and opened her mouth, welcoming his invading tongue.

He felt the fabric of her dress mold against his chest and he longed to rip it off and feel the soft flesh beneath. She rubbed her now wet body against him, and he cursed the fabric separating their heated bodies. The barrier was something he didn't want to deal with.

"I want you right now, and I want to see every inch of you. Do you want that too?" he rasped, breaking their scorching kiss and gazing at her. Her eyes sparkled and beckoned him.

She nodded. "I do," came her whispered reply. "Right now, not a minute later." Her hands pressed against his chest, her fingers gently caressing.

The soft whisper in her voice was like an aphrodisiac to his soul and again Storm lifted her mouth for his kiss then moistening her lips with her tongue.

But Hadden didn't kiss her. Instead, he placed his forefinger beneath her chin and silently waited until she opened her eyes. "I want you so much. Will you have me again?"

"I want you more."

"Good." He nodded, scooping her up and into his arms before heading for the staircase. "Now, I hope your sisters don't decide to come home until I've thoroughly ravished you." He trailed kisses down her neck and gave his attention to the delicate shell of her ear, loving the way her body shuddered against him.

He carried her up the stairs as easily as if she were a child but stopped halfway down the hall and set her on her feet.

"Are you hurt?" she asked. "Is it your head?" Her hands were braced on his shoulders, her breasts touching his torso.

"No, none of that." Hadden pulled her up hard against him. "I just can't wait to kiss you again and it's too bloody hard to do while I walk."

Storm started to speak, but her voice was trapped by Hadden's mouth descending on hers. His kiss was hot and searing in its demand and she loved it. She responded wildly, letting him ravish her mouth.

He wrapped his arm more tightly around her and stepped forward, pinning her between the wall and his body. Storm moved against him, spreading her feet. She wanted to feel him against the center of her core.

Hadden reacted to her body's invitation, lowering his hands and pressing her hips tight against his. "You're driving me crazy." And once again he swept her into his arms, continuing to kiss her as he carried her down the hall.

He kicked open the door to the master bedroom then set her on the bed. His body so hot with desire he thought he might burst into flames.

"Do you know just how beautiful you are?" he whispered as he pressed gentle kisses down her neck.

"Thank you," she blushed and reached up to sweep her fingers across his damp chest.

Overjoyed with her initiative and liking the feeling of her soft caress, he ran the backs of his fingers down her cheek, reveling in their softness. "You know this is the second time and I do believe our agreement for a marriage of convenience will be null and void by the time we're finished here."

"Good."

"And that doesn't bother you?"

"Absolutely not. Hadden I want a child, and I want to be free of Charles and his threats."

He leaned over her, bracing himself on his arms. Lowering his head, he kissed her eyelids then slowly moved his lips over to the sensitive skin near her ear, wishing she'd also spoken of a need for him. "I want a child too, and I will do everything I can to make Charles understand that we are not afraid of him. You are mine."

Storm turned her head until her lips brushed his. "You," she said, " I want you now. I need you inside me."

Hadden began unbuttoning her dress and watched as she closed her eyes, shifting her body to arch closer to his questing fingers. When her dress was open to her waist, he reached up and quickly untied the ribbon on her light chemise, drawing in a deep shuddering breath, as he feasted on the sight of her beautiful breasts. Storm opened her eyes and smiled at him.

Hadden felt her softness and her eager response. "I think I want you more than you want me. Remember, I'm not going to hurt you this time. All you will feel is pleasure." He knew this to be true but he needed her to know it too.

Storm nodded, and he felt her relax even more. "I know, only pleasure... so much pleasure. I trust you, Hadden."

With a gentleness he didn't know he possessed, he caressed her and kissed her, but when she parted her lips beneath his, he responded with a passion that threatened to steal the very breath from his lungs.

Still kissing her, he slipped his arm behind her neck and raised her to a sitting position, peeling her dress off her shoulders and skimming the material down her arms until she was free of the bodice. Then he lowered her back to the bed and stood.

"Raise your hips," he told her, and when she did his bidding, he skimmed her skirts and petticoats off, letting them pool on the floor by the bed. Then he took her shoes off and they joined her clothes.

"God you're beautiful."

A blush spread over her as she watched him gaze at her naked body. He wondered what she was thinking and if she liked what she saw. "Should I take my stockings off?"

Hadden shook his head. "No, I don't think there's anything in the world quite as intoxicating as a woman wearing nothing but her stockings. Leave them on for now."

With the unmistakable sensuality of a woman born to be a lover, Storm raised her knees and crossed one slim leg over the other. "And I, Mr. Johnston, don't think anything in the world is quite as intoxicating as watching you take a bath. Can I do it again sometime?"

Hadden tossed her a slow, seductive smile. "You won't be saying that when we're finished here, my passionate one," he promised, lying down next to her and pulling her over on top of him. "I'm going to show you something that's a lot more exciting than bathing but maybe later we can take a bath together."

Storm stretched out full length atop him. Nestled between her thighs and pressed against her core, his cock pulsed with impatience.

"The way you feel against me sets my heart racing," he whispered, skimming his hand up her body until his fingers reached the side of her breast. "Every night I was recovering, I'd lie in bed and remember how you felt that first time we made love, and I longed for one more time."

"Really?" Storm braced herself on her elbows and stared down at him. "You thought about me the last few nights?"

"I did."

"I thought about you too, and I wanted to come to you but I was afraid I'd hurt you."

"You told me the second time there would be no pain and I believed you. Did you really want to make love to me again?"

"Oh yes I did," he chuckled, taking advantage of her new position to slide his tongue sensuously down the cords of her neck. "I also think about you when I'm on the fairway, when I'm in my office, when I'm walking to your home, or when I'm unloading and loading my ships and when..." He paused, his brows drawing together in startled recollection. "You know, I was thinking about you when that damn mast hurtled down to land on me."

"That's awful. I wish you hadn't been thinking about me." Storm stiffened her arms and lifted herself off his chest. "I thought you didn't get out of the way of the mast because you didn't hear it coming."

"I didn't hear it coming," he laughed, "but I would have heard it if I hadn't been daydreaming about you." And raising his head, he buried his face in the softness of her breasts. Cupping his hands around her bottom, he nudged her upward, causing her to lift her breasts until his mouth closed around her nipple. He sighed with pleasure.

Storm let out a moan and moved against him. "You have no idea what that makes me feel inside."

"I think I do." He rolled her over and seized her mouth with another kiss.

She responded by reaching up and running her fingers over his chest. He let out a groan of pleasure as her fingers skimmed his flat nipples. "Does that feel good?"

"Everything you do to me feels good."

Storm grinned, threading her fingers though his thick hair, then arching her back and rubbing her nipples against his. "And this?"

Hadden suddenly shot to his knees, gulping in a great draught of air. "You've got to slow down or this will be over before it has even started."

"Storm stared at him, seemingly bewildered by his last statement. "I'm sorry. I didn't know."

"Bloody hell," he moaned, his eyes riveted at the point where the sheer stocking clung to her slender thighs, "I do like it. That's the problem. I like what you were doing too much. That's why we've got to take it slower or I'll explode."

"I don't understand. What do you want me to do?"

He closed his eyes, thinking of a couple thousand things he'd like her to do, none of which would do anything to slow things down. "Just lie still. Don't move and don't touch me for at least a minute."

"I don't know if I can do that. If you touch me then I know." She moistened her lips. "I know I'll want to touch you too. And I thought you told me you wanted a woman who wouldn't just lie still. You wanted a partner not a statue."

He grimaced. "I did but I guess I've changed my mind."

Storm sighed. "If it's what you want, I'll try not to touch you." She dropped her hands to her sides and closed her eyes.

Hadden tossed an annoyed look to the ceiling, thinking he must have lost his mind to make such a crazy request. Then he focused his attention on his throbbing cock and knew if he hadn't, he'd never be able to control himself long enough to give Storm the pleasure she deserved. And he wanted, no needed her to reach a climax today.

Kneeling, he lowered his head and kissed the sensitive skin on the underside of her breast, then trailed a path downward with his tongue, finally pausing with his mouth against the soft skin of her belly.

Despite her promise, Storm shifted beneath him, seemingly unable to lie completely still as Hadden wove an intimate path down her body. He grinned inside when she parted her thighs, opening herself to him in ultimate invitation.

Hadden smiled in unabashed male exultation at his wife's response to his intimate attentions. Slowly he trailed his forefinger down her belly, pausing when he reached the soft down at the juncture of her thighs before continuing on his seductive quest.

He glanced down and found Storm gazing at him, her eyes wide with a combination of desire and nervousness. He held her gaze, binding them together in a silent lover's communication as his finger dipped into her hot, wet depths, touching her intimately.

Storm's eyes flared at his invasion and Hadden deepened his touch, exploring and seducing. She moaned as he withdrew his finger then pushed it in again, then nearly bucked off the bed when his knowing fingers touched her sensitive bud, massaging.

"Please," she gasped, her head moving back and forth on the pillow, "Please let me touch you. I have to be part of this."

The battle was lost long ago. He moved over her, pushing back the hair at her temple. "Kiss me."

With a long whispering sigh, Storm put her hands on either side of his face and raised her lips to his. Hadden covered her mouth with his then he slipped inside her.

With strength he didn't know he possessed, Hadden clamped down on his skyrocketing lust, forcing himself to hold back, making the moment sweeter. He uttered a quick prayer that his starved passions wouldn't get the better of him.

"Hadden."

"What?"

"You don't have to be so careful. You won't hurt me."

A shudder running through him at her softly voiced words, he increased the pace.

Hadden felt her response soul deep and deepened his thrusts. Together they climbed toward the pinnacle, breathlessly reaching the summit at the same moment and hurtling over the other side.

Hadden closed his eyes, trying to keep the weight of his body from resting on top of hers and smothering her. Silence reigned and the pleasure and passion he felt with his climax became a part of him. Then Hadden broke their intimate contact and rolled to his side, taking Storm with him. He gently stroked, caressed her flushed cheeks. "How do you feel?"

"Wonderful." She sighed and touched his face, a smile on her face, her eyes sparkling. "Can we do it again?"

Hadden chuckled and wrapped his arms around her, hugging her close. "A man could get used to this."

"So could a woman," Storm responded.

"And yes, my darling, we can do it whenever you want." Hadden grinned, very pleased with his wife and his marriage. He had not thought he would ever feel this way.

~ * ~

Hadden strode through town, stopping in front of the Robertson's home then striding determinedly up the walk and knocking on the front door. The encounter with Charles was necessary for his life with Storm to continue without fear. He couldn't live with himself if she lived in terror for his life, and he didn't want to come home someday just to find an empty house.

Thank God, Storm had believed his tale about going to the docks to check on his ships and the cargoes. Not that he'd lied to her. It was just an omission of facts that would keep her from worrying about him. And he had gone to the docks, but he hadn't stayed for as long as he intimated he would. Instead, he'd had a quick talk with Perkins, reviewed the past week's inventory and shipments then returned to town.

Long past time for him to have a man-to-man chat with Charles, he decided there was no time like the present. His nerves stretched tight, he collected his thoughts and decided what needed to be said to Charles.

As he touched his hand to the knot on his head, Hadden's brows furrowed with tightly controlled fury. No doubt in his mind who was responsible for the accident and the two fires; that fact was not the main reason why he stood in front of the Robertson's home anticipating a confrontation. He'd deal with the arsons and the attempted murder later after he gathered incriminating evidence against him. He wanted the courts to have no doubts about Robertson's guilt.

Today he was here to issue a warning and to make sure Charles understood that if he ever threatened Storm again, he would pay with his life.

Hadden had never thought of himself as a violent man. But the idea of Robertson forcing his way into her house and confronting Storm with veiled threats and innuendos of what he would do if she didn't keep the promises Bradford had made threw him into a furious rage.

He stood here now to make it clear to Charles it would never happen again. The marriage was consummated and Storm was his, period. He would brook no further interference from Charles or Henry or anyone else for that matter.

Receiving no answer to his first summons, Hadden raised his fist and knocked again, this time louder than the first.

The door swung open as if someone had been standing behind it and had just decided to respond. Henry Robertson, looking flushed and anxious, stood on the other side. A drop of sweat slid down the side of his face.

"Good morning, Johnston." His voice was curt and a little shaky.

Hadden ignored the greeting. There was nothing good about standing at the Robertson's home. "I'm here to see Charles."

"Charles isn't here." Henry started to shut the door but Hadden blocked it with his foot.

Hadden gazed at the old man in silence, trying to gauge the truth in his tense words.

"He isn't," Henry said again. "He'll be gone for a couple weeks, business you know. Went to London."

"Well isn't that just coincidental?"

Henry shook his head, trying hard to adopt a look of innocence. "I'm afraid I'm not sure what you mean by that."

"Really? It was most likely your idea. If you say he's gone, I'll believe you, but give him a message for me when he returns."

Robertson nodded, wiping the sweat from his forehead with the back of his arm. "If you like."

"Tell him the next time he threatens me, my wife or anyone I care about, he's a dead man."

Henry's eyes widened at the dangerous tone in Hadden's voice. "Now see here, Johnston, who do you think you are to be speaking to me in that vein? I'm an upstanding pillar of the community."

Hadden smiled, a dangerous scowl that made Henry pale. "Who am I, Mr. Robertson? I'm the man who has every intention of killing your worthless son if he's stupid enough to go near my wife."

"You're not above the law. I can have the magistrates carry you off just for talking to me like this."

"Try it," Hadden challenged.

Henry drew a strangled breath and his eyes bugged out. "Get off my porch, now." With a shaky finger, he pointed to the road.

"Make sure you give Charles my message."

~ * ~

"Storm? Storm, I'm back? Are you home?"

Met with silence, Hadden's heart lodged in his throat and his mind hurtled to a place he didn't want it to go. He'd just threatened Charles. Bloody hell, what had he done? Put Storm's life in more danger?

Trying for a calm he didn't feel, Hadden walked through the foyer and stood at the bottom of the stairs. "Storm!" he called up to the second floor. "Are you there?"

Silence darkened the room and intensified Hadden's fears. "Storm!" he tried again.

"Where the hell are you?" Pushing through the swinging door, he strode through the kitchen and out to the back porch. "Storm are you out here?" Calmness was overrated. She'd told him she planned to stay home today. She wasn't going anywhere.

So where the bloody hell is she?

Still he was met with an eerie silence, except for the twitter of the birds and the croak of a frog.

Anxiety made the hair on the back of his neck stand up and hurriedly he retraced his steps to the house, searching for a note, for some clue that would tell him where she was.

Nothing.

Suddenly, Henry Robertson's words surged through his head. *Charles is away on business...*

He was a fool to have believed Henry.

"Bloody hell!" Hadden swore, his breath coming in shallow pants and his nerves frayed as he raced up the stairs. Tearing into the master bedroom, he looked around, searching for anything that might indicate that Storm had packed a bag, looking for possible signs of a struggle.

Nothing, no drawers hanging open, no clothes spread around, and her valise sat on the floor of her armoire, where she always kept it. The furniture all in place as it should be.

"Keep calm!" Hadden commanded. "She's probably visiting Ella." She changes her mind frequently.

Relieved by that notion, he raced down the stairs to the stables and ordered the stable boy to saddle a horse. He leapt on the horse, excepting the fact that he hated riding with an unexplainable passion and flew down the road toward the Lawrence household as if all the demons in hell chased him. This moment overshadowed all his fears.

Vaulting up Ella's front steps, he beat fiercely on the door. It opened almost immediately, and he looked down to see a small child gazing at him, eyes wide with interest.

"Is your mother here?" Hadden commanded, careless of the fact that his size and loud voice would frighten the child.

The child nodded.

"Can I see her, please?"

Again the child nodded and left for the kitchen, leaving him on the porch.

"Mama, there's someone here to see you."

Ella stepped through the kitchen doors wiping her hands on her apron then pushing errant strands of hair behind her ears. "Oh, Mr. Johnston, what brings you here?"

"Mrs. Lawrence," he began. "Have you seen my wife?"

"Today?" Ella asked, looking surprised.

"Yes, today." He didn't mean to put such emphasis in his voice but he was terrified for his wife.

"No, no I haven't. She hasn't been by to see us in over a week. Is there something wrong?"

"I haven't figured that out yet," Hadden told her. "I came home a little while ago and she wasn't there and she didn't leave a note. She said she'd be home all day."

Ella smiled. "I'm sure she's out riding her horse or shopping, nothing to worry about."

Hadden shook his head. "She's not shopping. I was in town and I'm sure I would have seen her."

"You sound worried as if there is something wrong. Did you check to see if Fiacre was in the stable?"

"I am worried and I hope everything is fine. It's just that when I left this morning, Storm said she was planning on staying home." He sounded like a bloody fool, repeating himself. "And no, I didn't check on her horse. You're probably right, she's out riding." God, how he wanted to believe that nonsense.

"Oh, well there has to be some logical explanation. You know she's not really accustomed to telling people where she is going and what she is doing."

"You're undoubtedly right. It's just that Charles Robertson left this morning..." Hadden's voice trailed off, his nerves strung tight.

"Oh, my God," Ella gasped, her hands clutching at Hadden's arm. "You don't think he..."

"No, I'm sure it's just a coincidence, " Hadden interrupted quickly, wishing he felt as positive as he sounded. "I'll just keep looking." Turning, he started down the porch steps.

"Mr. Johnston?" Ella called after him.

"What?"

"If it isn't too much trouble, would you let me know when you find her?"

"Of course, Mrs. Lawrence."

Hadden strode to his horse and vaulting into his saddle, tore off down the street, leaving a trail of dust behind him.

Hadden stopped for a moment at the house, just in case Storm might have come home. He stuck his head in the front door and called her name, but wasn't surprised when there was no answer.

Walking his horse to the stables, he handed the reins to the stable boy, hoping to ask the lad if he'd seen Storm today. He found the stables deserted and was forced to rub his horse down and take care of him before he left. Fiacre was in his stall, munching his food and looked at him with soulful eyes. When he was finished, he cursed, "Bloody hell!" He hit his fist against the wall of the building in angry frustration. "Storm, where the hell are you?"

He didn't have any ideas left as to where he could look for her. Wandering through the tack room and down the walkway through the stables, he found himself outside and gazing into the training area. Shielding his eyes with his hands, he saw two small figures in the distance, both mounted and exercising the horses. Hadden's heart slammed against his ribs.

He strode to the training area and climbed on the fence, straddling the wooden bars and watching, so relieved to see his wife he wanted to shout. He wanted to ask her what the bloody hell she thought she was doing. *Calm myself you idiot, just calm myself. I don't want to frighten her.*

He drew a deep breath then let it out again. Now that he knew Storm was safe, he was suddenly furious. Why hadn't she left him a note telling him where she was going?

Jumping off the fence, hands fisted by his sides, he strode toward them.

"Hadden, I didn't expect to see you yet. It's not dinnertime." Then seeming to sense his anger, she asked, "What's wrong? What are you doing here?"

Without a word, he reached his arms to her and pulled her off the horse, clutching her to him in a desperate embrace. "Where the bloody hell have you been?" he demanded, his voice coarse with fear and relief.

"There's a race in a few weeks and the horses needed to be put through their..."

His mouth cut off her words as it descended on hers in a scorching kiss.

"What is going on?" she gasped, pulling her mouth away and trying to loosen his bone-crushing grip.

Hadden's story tumbled out incoherently as he continued to kiss her eyes and cheeks and neck. "Robertson...business...thought he'd kidnapped you..."

"What are you saying? You thought Charles Robertson kidnapped me?" She felt him nod against her neck.

To her surprise, he raised his head. "Why didn't you leave me a note telling me what you were going to do today? I came home and you weren't there, and you weren't in town or at Ella's."

"I'm sorry. This wife thing is still kind of new to me. I'm not used to having you keeping tabs on my whereabouts." Storm apologized when he released her lips. "I thought I'd be home before you."

Lacing his fingers through her hair, he tipped her head back until their eyes met. "Don't ever do that again," he said, giving her a tiny shake. "Do you understand me? Don't ever do it again!"

"All right." She nodded. "I told you I'm sorry. I never thought you'd be worried about me."

Hadden looked at the stable boy. "Take the horses and leave us alone. Don't let anyone out here."

Hadden didn't release her, and Storm's eyes widened as she felt her hairpins slipping from her head. "What are you doing?"

"Just shut up and kiss me." He pulled her into his arms and headed for the trees beyond and the little brook behind her house, kissing her all the way.

"We're outside!" Storm gasped, trying to wiggle out of his arms. "We can go home, you know."

"I don't think so. I can't wait that long," he said, setting her on the ground, his hands sweeping downward to cup her breasts. "I want to do it here with the sound of water soothing all the frayed nerves I've experienced in the last few hours."

"But, Hadden, what if someone sees us." Horrified, she looked down to see his fingers flying across the buttons on her bodice. "Stop this, stop right now!" she demanded, trying unsuccessfully to bat his hands away. "We can't make love here—outside."

Hadden grabbed her hand and placed it over the bulge in his buckskins. "That's why we can make love here—outside."

"Well, we can't. It's not proper." She wrenched her hand away from his erection. "We can't do this here. Someone might see."

"This is your property, and it's almost dark. No one is going to see us." He slipped out of his jacket and spread it on the ground then he pulled her back into his arms and onto the jacket.

"Hadden, you're crazy," she protested, still not able to believe he intended to make love to her in the woods by the creek.

His grin widened. "I know. But this spot is beautiful and romantic. And I need you now."

"Just because it's romantic doesn't make it proper."

"I don't know, a friend of mine made love with his wife in a loch."

"Did they get caught?" Storm asked, her eyes suddenly dropping to his midsection as he began unbuttoning his britches.

"Nope," he answered, pulling his pants down his lean hips.

She moistened her lips, her heart racing. "Well, now what?" Storm asked, her eyes riveted on his erection.

"I will take your clothes off."

"Okay," Storm murmured, reaching out and wrapping her fingers around his cock.

Hadden groaned and moved a step closer. He spread open her gaping bodice and dipped his head, pulling a nipple into his mouth as he worked her dress up her thighs.

"We have to be very quiet so we don't attract any attention," Storm warned, as her fingers fumbled with the ties on her pantalets.

Hadden nodded and brushed her hands away, hooking his fingers into the waistline, he ripped them all the way down the front.

"Hadden!" Storm gasped. "You didn't have to do that. I could have just taken them off."

"Not fast enough." He pulled the ripped pantalets down until they lay at a pool by her feet. He laid her back on his jacket, wrapping her legs around his waist.

Storm tossed her head back and closed her eyes, shivering in anticipation as she felt Hadden's rough fingers skim up the insides of her thighs.

Hadden lowered his lips to hers, his fingers toying with her budding nipples as his tongue dipped erotically in and out of the soft interior of her mouth. Suddenly he could wait no longer. Grasping her by her hips, he entered her.

Storm let out a tiny shriek of surprised pleasure and undulated beneath him to the rhythm he set, thrusting her hips forward to meet her husband's passionate assault. Nothing she had ever experienced had excited her as much as the raw sexuality of this frenzied coupling. With a deep throaty moan of ecstasy, she answered his every thrust with one of her own, moving with him until they came together.

For an endless moment, they were motionless, panting and spent. Then, slowly Hadden withdrew as Storm unwrapped her legs from where they still gripped him and rolled to one side with her in his arms. He grinned and gazed into her eyes.

"I thought I would die when I believed you were gone, that somehow Charles had taken you." He kissed a nipple then the other, slowly making his way to her lips.

"I'll leave a note next time. Kiss me again."

Chapter Fifteen

"How is your head feeling? Storm asked one Sunday morning as she brushed Fiacre, and Hadden leaned against the side of the horse's stall. With a smile on her face she turned to watch him.

"Just dandy," Hadden acknowledged, rubbing the spot where the mast had landed. "Get a headache every once in a while otherwise I'd never know I'd been hurt. Doc says the pains will go away."

"Good, I'm glad about that." Storm laughed. At least a portion of the guilt she felt about Hadden's accident had been lifted with the knowledge he hadn't sustained any permanent damage.

"Do you have anything planned for today?" Hadden asked, his smile touching Storm's heart.

"No, nothing special. Do you want to do something?" She had hoped someday he'd ask her if she wanted to meet the children, so she kept her fingers crossed thinking this might be the day.

"I do. I want you to meet the widow and the boys and girls she takes care of. We're going to have to go shopping first though. The kids are growing so fast they will need more clothes."

Storm laughed, pleased with his invitation. "Do you always bring them something?"

"Yup!"

"You're going to spoil them, you know that don't you?" The way he cared for the people he loved always made her happy. He was kind and generous, considerate too.

"That's the plan," Hadden answered, wiggling his eyebrows.

Storm laughed at his outrageously lecherous look, already thinking about what she might buy his children that would be practical yet fun and wondering what kind of toys they liked.

The past few weeks had passed in a blissful haze. She and Hadden had been together almost constantly, spending the long, lazy summer days getting to know each other. During the evenings, they took long walks, strolling hand in hand through town as they talked about their childhoods, their families and their dreams and hopes for the future.

One sunny day, he took her to the golf course where he played and tried to teach her how to golf. That was a disaster. All she could do was roll the ball along the ground.

Their newfound friendship made each new day an adventure, filled with the promise of new pleasures as they discovered how much they had in common.

And the nights... Never would Storm have believed she could find such rapture in a man's arms. Hadden was the gentlest of lovers, yet at times virile and so demanding their lovemaking would last only a few minutes, yet be followed by another amorous adventure at a slower pace.

As the days passed and their intimacy grew, Hadden encouraged her to explore the carnal side of her nature, whispering words of encouragement and delight when she boldly responded to his scandalous suggestions.

Hadden never mentioned Charles Robertson, although Storm suspected the vile man was never far from his mind. Several times he had left the house alone, returning hours later wearing a look of grim determination Storm found a bit terrifying. But despite the lurking threat hovering over their heads, she cherished the time they spent together.

Storm had long ago admitted to herself she loved her husband deeply. Regardless of the bizarre circumstances that had brought them together, she realized that in Hadden, she had found her soul mate. Basking in the warmth of his growing affection, she began to blossom, her newfound happiness evident in her every smile and gesture. For the first time in her life, she experienced a feeling of completeness.

It was late morning before they were ready to leave for the upcoming adventure. Storm stepped onto the porch and watched as Hadden pulled a wagon in front of the house. "I thought we were going to ride."

Hadden shrugged, looking a bit sheepish. "Just couldn't bring myself to mount a horse again. I'm saving that torture for emergencies and I'm praying no more of those will occur."

She couldn't help but smile at her husband. She really wanted to rid him of his crazy dislike of horses but didn't think it would happen anytime soon, so she resigned herself to riding in the wagon beside him.

They headed into town, their first stop the general store. Inside she delighted in buying candies and a few toys for the children as Hadden told her a little something about each of them. She decided she'd send her stable boy to the widow's house so he could give them riding lessons. Their taking after Hadden was not going to be an option.

After the general store, they headed to the drapers where Hadden purchased enough fabric for Adele to make something new for each child, then Storm picked out something special for Adele to fashion a dress for herself. She touched her hand to her stomach, knowing she was with child and wondering how she would tell Hadden. She was pregnant, and it wasn't for lack of trying on both their parts. She closed her eyes, a small sigh escaping her lips. She'd never thought attempting to get pregnant could be so pleasure filled.

"How far is it?" she asked, as they rumbled along the bumpy road toward Berwick.

"Another fifteen minutes," he answered, looking at her with a smile. "You're really eager to meet them aren't you?"

"I know how important they are. I want them to like me."

"They won't like you. They'll love you." He laughed and nudged the horse to keep going.

Later they turned on to a well-worn path leading over a rise then he stopped the wagon. He leaned forward, resting his forearms on his thighs.

She inhaled a swift breath at the sight in front of her. A large white house was nestled in the valley below. Children played in the large yard and the sounds of their laughter floated on the summer breeze.

"It's beautiful, Hadden. No wonder you're so proud of this."

"Thank you but I want to make it bigger, better. I want to find a way to help more abused children. But Adele can't do it all. She's going to need help. See," he pointed to a large structure adjoining the house, "I'm building two more rooms."

"You have found more children?"

"I have, two young boys. These young men, Perkins found in Hyde Park. You might say, they were perfecting their craft."

Storm looked at him puzzled. "Their craft."

"They were pickpockets."

"Oh," she hesitated. "And you think you can trust them with Adele and the others?"

"Yes and no, but I'm willing to give them the chance, and they've sworn they will not go back to their nefarious ways."

"And I repeat, can you trust..."

He put a finger over her lips. "They have a different life here. They don't have to steal for their food—to live. Adele was willing to give them a chance and they understand fully that if they do anything against the law, they will make up for it with labor. They've also been told that when they come of age, I will help them find work."

"And they agreed."

"Yes."

Storm looked at him, reading the hope and the love he had for the children in his eyes and falling even more in love with him if that were possible.

He reached over and took her hand, raising it to his lips and kissing it. "I love you, Storm," he whispered. "I want us to share the love of these children while we make our own. I want to fill our lives up with children and grandchildren and spend my old age sitting on a porch with you. But I need to know if you want this too, if it can be part of your dreams."

"It is, Hadden, I know it is." Storm's throat was thick with joyful tears she was trying to contain. "I couldn't ask for anything more."

Before she realized his intent, he was off the wagon and wrapping his hands around her waist to lift her from her seat. "Kiss me," he murmured when she was on the ground. "Kiss me and tell me you love me too."

"I do." Storm's eyes filled. "Oh, Hadden, I love you so much..."

They kissed, and it was a long heart-pounding caress full of love, promise and excitement.

Hadden finally broke their embrace and sat down, pulling her next to him and wrapping his arms around her shoulders. "Just look at the children, sweetheart, all of them and the land, there is so much and it's ours. We can do make dreams come true with it," he paused and pointed, "all the way from the edge of those trees over there to that rise on the other side...," he swung his arm in a huge arc, pointing to a spot in the shadowy distance far to the west, "is ours. It will be the perfect place to raise our family and our extended one as well."

Storm nodded so full of emotion she couldn't speak. When she finally did find her voice, it was shy and a bit tentative. "Hadden?"

"Yes?"

"How long will it take to build this dream?

"It's a work in progress. It won't take very long to build our house. I've drawn up some rough plans but I want your input too. I'll hire a crew and they can get started right away. We should be able to move in before it starts snowing."

"Is it all right with Adele?"

"I'm sure it will be. We can talk to her today as soon as we give the children their treats."

Placing a finger under her chin, Hadden tilted back her head until their eyes met. "What's wrong?"

"Well, nothing really." She ducked her head and blushed.

Hadden cocked his head to one side, staring at her. "Storm, what is it? Talk to me."

She gazed at him, her eyes filled with light and happiness. "I just want to be settled before our baby is born."

"Did I hear you right?" Hadden's voice boomed across the valley and echoed off the surrounding hills. "A baby? So soon? But honey, how do you know? It hasn't been that long."

Storm blushed more deeply. "It only takes a few weeks to know."

She put her hands to her face. "I wasn't going to tell you until I was certain but I missed my woman's time, and Ella says I have all the signs." She blushed again despite her efforts to stay calm. Confiding such intimate things was so new to her.

"The signs? Hadden queried. "What signs? Are you sick? Bloody hell, woman, you let me take you out in that damn wagon with all the potholes and..." his voice trailed off as he roughed his hair back from his face. "You've got to take better care of yourself. You have to let me..."

"I'm fine," she laughed, pushing playfully at his shoulder, "and I only feel nauseous in the morning."

"You should stay in the house and away from the stables. I'll admit the wagon is probably safer than riding, but you're on Fiacre every day."

"I won't fall. I've been riding since I was a child and you know it."

"I don't care. Anyone can fall. Now, after we see the children, we're going to take the ride back to town real slow. And we're not going to do anything like this until next spring. I won't take any chances with this child."

"You're being ridiculous but I do understand, really I do, and I never thought of you as the overprotective kind."

"You're right. When it comes to your's and our baby's safety I'm always going to be overprotective," he muttered, laying her back in the grass and bending close to look into her eyes. "That's my baby you've got in there, and I'm not taking any chances with her or you."

"Her?" Storm teased, pushing back a lock of hair that had fallen over his forehead. "What if it's a him?"

"Him...her...it doesn't make any difference to me, and I don't want you to feel as if all I want is an heir. I'm not like your father. The point is that you have to take care of yourself, and if you won't, I will do it for you."

"Does that mean we can't make love until after the baby is born?" Storm asked, pursing her mouth in an innocent little moue.

Hadden frowned, staring into her eyes. "I hadn't thought about that. I guess we'll have to ask the doc."

"I can't believe you just said that." Wrapping her arms around him, Storm pulled him down on top of her and buried her head in his neck. "Ella told me that it's perfectly safe to make love—right up until the end."

"I'm not sure about that. I don't want to take any chances. So despite the fact that you think I'm overprotective, I'm still going to ask the doc."

"Hadden Johnston," Storm protested, pushing him away, "if I had known you were going to be such a fool about this, I wouldn't have told you until I absolutely had no choice."

Bracing himself on an elbow, Hadden smiled at her. "You're right. I'm a fool when it comes to your welfare. Now come on, let's go see the children."

When they rose, they were greeted by some of his extended family.

"Mr. Johnston, Mr. Johnston." Two of the young boys from Adele's home rushed up the hill. "Were you going to sit there all day?"

"No, we're coming down."

"Do you have presents?" the oldest asked.

"Of course I do and I've got someone I'd like you all to meet." Hadden pulled Storm into his arms. "Will you boys take the wagon? I'd like to walk the rest of the way." He wrapped an arm around Storm's waist, making sure that if she mis-stepped he would be able to support her.

When they reached the bottom of the hill, the children circled around them yelling and clapping their hands with delight as Hadden handed out the gifts.

"Is she your new wife?" Mary the youngest of his children asked.

"Yes, Storm is my wife, and I hope you will all welcome her with open arms."

"I thought you were going to marry Adele."

~ * ~

Mary's words haunted Hadden as he walked into the tiny café in town to meet with his lawyer. He'd never given Adele any encouragement they might become a couple, and he'd thought he'd always been up front with her when it came to their relationship. So why had Mary thought he was going to marry Adele? He pushed those thoughts aside, determined to deal with them later and concentrated on the present.

He'd been surprised to receive the brief note from James Walters, his attorney, asking him to join him for lunch, but had quickly sent the young boy delivering the message on his way with a quick affirmative response.

Hadden had employed James for a very long time and on every occasion where he'd needed a good lawyer, the man had come through for him. So he wondered why the urgent message. Yet something in the back of his mind made him believe this had something to do with Charles.

Spying Walters sitting at a table at the back of the café, Hadden nodded a greeting and walked over to join him.

"Good afternoon, James," Hadden greeted, thrusting out his hand.

"Ah, Hadden," James returned, rising and shaking his employer's hand. "I'm glad you could see me on such short notice."

Hadden sat down and picked up the menu, ignoring his quest to discover the reason for this meeting. "What's good today?"

James laughed. "Oh come now, you know everything is wonderful here. Liza can make a miracle out of anything. But I heard the oysters are particularly good and the catch of the day is cod."

Hadden joined in the laughter. "Yeah, but I'm not really fond of seafood, maybe I'll try the pot roast."

"The waitress recommended the chicken pot pie so that's what I'm having."

"Sounds good to me." Hadden nodded, setting his menu on the table. "So," Hadden began, motioning the waitress to bring him a cup of tea. "Why did you call this meeting? I know it wasn't just for the food."

James sobered. "Actually, yes. There are a few things about your wife you should be aware of before Charles returns from his business trip."

Hadden nodded, but remained silent as the waitress put his drink on the table and took the order. She sauntered away then turned to throw Hadden an enticing look over her shoulder.

"Does that happen to you often?" James asked, shaking his head.

"Hadden shifted in his seat, a bit embarrassed that his prudish lawyer had noticed the girl's attempt to lure him. "Yeah, sometimes."

James grinned, "You're just too charming a fellow."

"What? It never happens to you?"

James shrugged. "On occasion but never quite so blatant."

Hadden grinned back at his lawyer. "Yeah I'm not surprised." Clearing his throat, he went on to say, "You were about to tell me why you asked me here today about my wife. If you don't tell me soon, my curiosity will get the best of me."

James straightened and drumming his fingers on the table, seemed to be trying to figure out what to say. "I thought we needed to figure out a way to repay the debt to Robertson."

Hadden froze, his tea half way to his mouth and a lump in his throat. "I know there was a debt but what I don't know is the amount. Storm hasn't wanted to talk about it. Besides, Charles has been adamant he doesn't want to be repaid. He only wants Storm."

James set his drink on the table. "I thought you knew about the massive amount of money the Grahams owed the Robertsons. My apologies, I should have contacted you sooner. I just assumed your wife would have explained the family's financial situation to you sooner than later," he said, his voice heavy with trepidation.

Hadden set down the glass. "Well, she hasn't, so why don't you tell me what this is all about."

I'm not all that sure she knows how much is owed.

James wanted to stall for time but didn't dare. He recognized the anger and the shock in Hadden's expression. He'd seen if far too many times to discount the emotion. He was going to have to tell Hadden Johnston that, as Storm's husband, he owed the Robertson's either the deed to the stables, including all of the horses within, or seventy thousand pounds.

Drawing a deep breath, he said, "A long time ago, Bradford Graham borrowed a great deal of money from Henry Robertson. I'm not sure exactly how many pounds but with interest it now comes to a staggering figure of seventy thousand pounds. Apparently, Mr. Bradford was never able to pay Mr. Robertson back, and for many years, nearly until the time of Mr. Graham's death, Mr. Robertson let the payments slide. He merely continued to add interest to the amount owed, but never pressed Mr. Graham for it. Then, when he heard Mr. Graham was dying, he demanded either the loan be paid in full, the deed for the stables signed over to himself and his son, or..."

"...Or Storm marry Charles and bring the stables into the family that way," Hadden finished.

"Yes." James nodded.

"So," Hadden continued, his voice soft, "Storm, in order to keep her stables and save herself from having to marry Charles, decided to seduce me into marrying her instead, figuring that once we were married, I would repay the loan." He didn't want to believe the worst-case scenario. Storm had been upfront from the beginning with the knowledge she had at her disposal. So far James hadn't told him anything new.

"I have no idea but from what I've ferreted out about this situation, Storm had no real knowledge about the extent of what was owed," James said.

"I didn't think so but even if she did know, would she have told me?"

"Her father was never forthcoming about his financial status, considering the women in his family beneath him and his money. I represented Bradford too."

"So you don't believe she knew how much was owed." Hadden searched for more information as he tried to piece everything together.

"She knew he owed money by the very nature of the contract, but I'm sure she didn't know how much. It would take decades of earnings from her horses to pay back the money owed to Henry."

He sighed, thinking of Storm and the fear she'd been harboring all these months. "Why didn't she tell me?"

"You can't blame Storm, and I'm not sure why I'm defending your beautiful wife."

"No, I don't understand it either but I've got a lot to think through before I confront Storm with this new information."

Hadden walked out on the docks then up the gangplank to the *Serendipity*; the only ship in port at the moment. Leaning on the rail, he watched the waves ripple against the bow. Yesterday all seemed right with the world and his new life. He was going to be a father and he'd never been happier. At this moment now, he was so confused his head pounded.

Storm, what had she known? He thought back to that first day on the golf course when she shockingly proposed a marriage of convenience to him. Had it all been manipulation or had she possessed an ounce of sincerity?

Thoughts of Elizabeth swarmed in his muddled brain. No, he refused to believe she was anything like that woman. Storm was fresh and honest. She didn't have a deceitful bone in her body. So why hadn't she told him about the money? Could it just be a lie of omission or was she afraid to tell him?

He needed to find out but in this mood he was afraid to confront his pregnant bride. The journey to find love had been long and filled with potholes, all of which they'd seemingly navigated with success. This new rut in the road felt like a sinkhole.

Even though he felt shocked and deceived by Storm's omissions, he was going to face this and together they would solve the problem. Storm was his wife, his responsibility. He had to stand by her no matter what.

Hadden's jaw tightened as he thought about everything James had told him. His anger was not directed at Storm, however, his fury settled on three people, Charles and Henry Robertson and Bradford Graham as well.

The beginning of their tenuous relationship had been rocky, but he was able to overcome all of the obstacles once he'd realized how desperate she'd been for his protection. And with everything they'd shared in the past months, he would have thought she'd been secure enough to tell him all of the truth. He knew first hand how treacherous Charles Robertson could be and he needed information in order to defend and protect her.

Considering how he felt about her, all she would have needed to do was ask and he'd have given her anything. Bloody hell, seventy thousand pounds was a pittance. He'd have given her ten times that much if she'd just asked him. So what was his problem now? His gut tightened. He'd always wanted total truth, he hated lies, even lies of omission and this one was huge.

That thought made him stop and think. How had Storm intended to pay the debt Bradford had accrued? She had talked about giving all of her horses to Charles but that wouldn't come close to covering the astronomical debt. It would take years of earnings from the track to even come close.

If someone had punched him in the gut, he wouldn't have felt so confused. Now he had to find a way to confront his beautiful wife and discover the truth.

$$\sim * \sim$$

Hadden spent the night on his ship, shifting through all of the things he wanted to say to Storm as well as the things he needed to ask, but couldn't decide on an approach that wouldn't leave her defensive or hurt. It wasn't until after ten that he sent Perkins with a message telling Storm he would stay on the ship tonight.

When the sun came up, he was dressed and on his way home, determined to discover all of Storm's secrets. Yet when he entered the kitchen and saw her standing by the stove making breakfast for him, his resolve vanished. Caught between frustration and love, he didn't know how to react to the sight of her.

She turned and brushed hair from her face, her eyes with huge dark circles beneath, cheeks red and splotchy. In one hand she held a spatula and she looked as if she wanted to give him a good whack with it.

He could kick himself, he'd done that to her. So calling himself a fool, he stepped toward her. "Storm."

"I didn't know what to think. You just disappeared. Perkins didn't get here until after ten and you never said why, just that you weren't coming home. I didn't know if Charles was part of this or you were angry with me. What I didn't know frightened me more than if I'd known the truth, whatever that might have been."

"It won't happen again."

"How do I know that? I was frightened then angry, and after that, confused. We had such a beautiful day together, and I thought everything was good between us."

"It is all good." He swiped hair from his face and stepped forward to wrap his arms around her. "I'm sorry if I hurt you."

"No," she held her hands in front of her to stop him. "Not until I find out why? Whatever kept you away is a problem that needs fixing, and I don't want to spend another night like the last one."

"There is no problem." He'd decided to pay the debt and not tell Storm what he'd done. She was pregnant and didn't need any extra stress.

"How can you say that?"

"Because the reasons I stayed away no longer matter."

"But they do. And I don't know what those reasons are. Don't you think you owe me an explanation?"

"I believe you owe me one." He could have bit his tongue but hours of brooding had clouded his judgment.

Storm swallowed and stepped back, bumping into the stove then jumping away. "Regardless of what you seem to think," she said softly, "I don't know why you seem to be angry with me, so please tell me."

"Can we talk about this after breakfast? I'm famished." Delaying the inevitable was probably not the best idea he'd had, but he was exhausted and hungry and really thought he would deal better with this after he had food in his stomach.

"If that's what you want." She turned away from him and focused her attention to the bacon simmering in the pan. After a few minutes, she scooped out the potatoes, forked the bacon onto a plate and dumped out the scrambled eggs. She set the plate in front of Hadden, poured him a cup of tea, and grabbed her hot chocolate.

"Aren't you going to eat?" He asked with his mouth full.

"Not hungry." She sipped her drink and held the cup so she could see him over the rim.

"But you were cooking breakfast. Am I eating yours?" Guilt swept through him. He was an inconsiderate fool.

"I was cooking in hopes you would show up hungry."

"But you have to eat."

"I had a piece of toast earlier and will eat more as my stomach allows it. Now finish eating so we can talk."

He suddenly didn't feel like eating. Pushing his plate away, he set his fork on the table. "Well, let's talk. I don't think I can eat anything else until this is cleared up."

"So you admit there is a problem."

He didn't answer, couldn't. He had hoped they wouldn't have a confrontation.

"Hadden!" Storm's voice demanded his attention. "Talk to me, please."

"All right." Hadden sighed. "It was the money."

"Money?" Storm asked. "What money?"

"The money your father owed Henry Robertson."

Storm inhaled a sharp breath. "The crux of the contract. I'd hoped... I don't know what I'd hoped."

"Did you have any idea what the bloody figure was?" Hell but he hated the pained look he saw on Storm's face. He felt as if he'd hit her, and he never wanted to hurt her.

"No, I don't know how much my father owed. Bradford said Henry wanted the stables and me. He never mentioned a set amount of money."

"James found out that the other provision of your father's agreement with Robertson—the one you didn't tell me about—was that if you didn't marry Charles, you had to pay him seventy thousand pounds. They never really wanted the stable, knowing full well it would take decades for the horses to pay out."

"Seventy Thousand pounds!" Storm gasped, her look of surprise so real Hadden's heart went out to her.

"I'm sorry but someone has to pay it."

"I thought all I had to do was turn over the stables or pay rent to him. I had no idea Bradford owed that kind of money to Henry." She hesitated for a moment,

"James told you Bradford owed seventy thousand? He was our attorney too."

"He thought I knew."

He looked at her for a long moment, trying to assess the truth in her words. Uncannily he believed all of what she said but instinct told him there was more. "I've paid the debt and I've reconciled my feelings about it."

"You didn't. I was going to pay it."

He tossed her a dubious look.

"Okay," Storm admitted, meeting his chilly gaze squarely, "I confess I knew there was a payoff clause in the agreement, but I never intended to ask you for the money."

"Really? How did you plan on paying Henry?"

"I had it figured out. I was going to sell Fiacre to him then pay off the rest with the winnings from tracks."

"Seventy thousand? Fiacre must be worth a hell of a lot."

"He is," Storm returned.

"So why didn't you sell him?"

Storm looked down at her tightly clenched hands. "I wrote Charles a note offering..."

"But you didn't sell him." He inhaled a deep breath. "Never mind, I understand why you couldn't part with him. I would have never wanted you to lose your favorite horse."

"I'm so sorry, Hadden." Tears ran down her cheeks, and she tried to sweep them away with her hands but they kept coming. "I know I forced you into marrying me, and my reasons were far from honorable, but I can't stand to have you think it was your money I was after."

"I have to sort through all of this. But it doesn't matter. We're married, and I will come to terms with Charles and the money you owe Henry. You have my name, you have my protection, you have my money."

"Do I still have your love?"

Hadden didn't want to answer that question. She would always have his love. But right now the feelings were just too raw for him to tell her how he felt.

Chapter Sixteen

"Help! Everyone, we need you out there fighting the fire!"

The townsfolk stood, unmoving, in the general store, heads turned toward the docks where fire billowed from several ships before turning their attention to a smoke-blackened Perkins who was gasping for breath.

"We all thought the crews from those ships out there had the fire controlled," a man from the back of the store said as he strode to the door to look outside.

"Yeah, the rain from the storm passing through should have put it out." The man appeared unconcerned about the fire.

Perkins gaped at the people as if they were crazy. "What's wrong with all of you? We've been fighting this thing for the past couple of hours. Mr. Johnston and our crews have been trying to get the fishing boats as well as the merchant ships out to sea but the wind's blowin' in the wrong direction and the process is taking longer than we'd planned. We need help if we're going to save this town. Usually when there's a fire, you people come out to help, pretendin' it's a party, but today no one is helpin' and now it's spreading. It's gonna threaten the town."

He wiped the sweat from his brow before continuing. "If you men don't get out there and help us fight this thing and get it under control, you're all bloody well gonna lose your homes and maybe your lives. As it is, three men have died and a whole bunch more are hurt."

"You mean it's not contained at the docks?" Ella asked, racing to the door and peering outside.

That's what I've been trying to tell you," Perkins said as he gestured with arms outward to all of the shoppers.

"Good God, he's right. We have to help, come on. Don't just stand there gaping."

"Thanks, maybe the ladies can set up a place where we can bring the injured," Perkins said.

"Nonsense," Storm intervened, stepping forward from where she stood near the ribbons. "Ella and I helped haul buckets at the last fire and we're willing to do the same this time."

"She's right," Ella said.

"If we get enough men out there, you'd do more good tending to those who get hurt," Perkins spoke to Storm and Ella. "I'm going from store to store trying to get the men to go haul water. This town's livelihood depends on those vessels out there and we've got to save them."

"Perkins, you go back to fighting the fire. Ella and I will go to the stores and spread the word."

The store emptied as the shoppers scattered in all directions. Storm hurried out with the rest of the crowd, stopping to grab Perkins by the arm. "Is my husband all right?" she asked, terrified of his answer.

"He was when I left the docks." Perkins' smile as well as his words gave her the assurance she needed.

"Thank you," she said then headed for home, stopping at every house along the way to alert her neighbors of the impending disaster and encourage them to get out and help. Ella did the same, racing in the opposite direction.

By the time Storm reached her house, the streets of the tiny village swarmed with people. Wagons careened down the Main Street laden with ropes, buckets and medical supplies. Men raced by on horses, galloping toward the docks. Little children stood in fenced front yards, crying over being left by their mothers but in the care of elderly neighbors.

Storm sprinted through the front door and into the kitchen, throwing open cupboards and tossing liniment, bandages, baking soda, into a large bag. Then she hurried outside to the back porch, grabbing all the buckets she could carry.

Racing outside, she hurried down the street, rounding the corner on the Main Street and flagging down the first wagon she saw. "Can you give me a ride?" she yelled at the driver.

"Of course, Mrs. Johnston," he said, working to control his spooked horses. "Toss that stuff in the wagon and climb on board."

Storm did and was just settled in the seat before he whipped up the team, sending them into frantic gallop.

"I'm Steven Brown," he told her while he drove. For a second, he looked her way to slant her a bucktoothed smile, then focused his attention back to the horses.

"Good to meet you," Storm told him, clinging to the lurching wagon seat.

"Does your husband know what you're doing?"

Storm gaped at the man in surprise, astonished at his question. "No, no, he doesn't."

"He's not going to be too happy. You're supposed to be takin' care of yourself. Restin' if you know what I mean."

Storm focused on the road ahead in embarrassment. Was there anyone in town who didn't know she was pregnant? She'd never seen this man but he knew.

"Have you lived here very long Mr. Brown?"

"Nope, moved here from London. Arrived in town a couple of weeks ago on one of those merchant ships on fire down there." He nodded in the direction of the docks. "Lookin' for a job and hoped your husband would hire me. Crewed for a warship during the last war with the U.S. Thought if I helped put this fire out, I'd stand a better chance. What do you think?"

"You'll have to talk to him."

"Been trying but he's a hard man to find."

"After the fire is out, I'm sure Mr. Johnston is going to need help and if he doesn't, some of the others will. You'll find work."

Steven Brown grinned. "Thanks for the encouragement."

The smoke wasn't as thick and heavy close to the docks where the wind had been able to whip it away, and Storm stared at the damage the fire had wrought, flames licking skyward.

"Bloody hell," Steven muttered, "Perkins wasn't kidding when he asked for help. This is real bad."

Storm nodded before she was seized by a fit of coughing.

Untying the scarf that was around her neck, she wrapped it around her face before she climbed down from the wagon, watching as the townspeople formed a bucket brigade and wondering how they were ever going to control the fire that seemed to find new fuel with every passing second.

~ * ~

The day turning into the night seemed to last forever. Hour after hour, Storm bent over the wounded firefighters. Some were near death and all she could do was try to make their remaining hours less painful.

By evening she was exhausted but she continued to work. Ella came to relieve her and handed her a glass of water.

"You need to take care of yourself, Storm." Ella looked pointedly at her before continuing. "I shouldn't have to tell you that in your condition. You can't risk losing your child."

"I know. I'm going to sit and drink this water, but I will come back and help." She wiped away the tears sliding down her cheek while she tried to catch her breath and slow her heart rate. A few drops of rain sent the girls beneath the shelter the men had made from canvas.

"The wind has shifted and the storm clouds have decided to dump rain on us. Maybe the fires will get put out with the help of Mother Nature." Ella sat down beside Storm.

A loud clap of thunder filled the sky with light while fat heavy drops of rain pelted from the sky. Storm had never seen it rain so hard. It seemed the gods above were lending their hand. Despite the icy drenching rain, people were dancing in the streets and on the pier, clapping and whooping with joy. The ground outside the tent turned into a quagmire of mud.

The sound of sizzling wood was a godsend. She stood, putting her hand at the small of her back and stretched, easing the pain. Blinking rain off her eyelashes, she inhaled a fresh breath of air and said a silent prayer of thanks. Then she closed her eyes, allowing herself the luxury of a moment's respite. Her rest was short-lived. Suddenly she felt a hand clamp down on her shoulder. With a startled scream, she opened her eyes and turned to stare into the furious visage of her soot-covered husband.

"What in bloody hell are you doing here?"

She swallowed the lump in her throat and tried to ignore his obvious anger before hurtling herself against the rocklike wall of his chest. "Oh, Hadden," she clung to him not wanting to leg him go, "I was so worried about you. No one could answer any of my questions about where you were or if you were all right. Except Perkins and that was hours ago."

"I'm all right. Now answer my question. What are you doing here?" He gently traced a droplet of water down her cheek.

Storm released her hold and stepped back, focusing on her husband. "I'm helping the injured."

"Bloody hell, Storm! Are you crazy? You're pregnant."

The people around them seemed to turn and focus on what they were saying to each other.

"I've had enough. I'm pregnant, not on my deathbed." She tried to keep her voice low enough that she was sure no one could hear her. "And I'm tired of being treated as if I'm an invalid. There is nothing wrong with me. If I thought I was doing anything to endanger our child, I wouldn't be here. Now move out of my way, I've work to do."

"Storm," Hadden's voice was low and frightening. "You're going home."

"Don't tell me what to do or where to go." She turned, putting her hands on her hips and glaring at her overprotective husband.

"You'll do as I say."

Storm inhaled a steadying breath, trying hard to block out the sight of the crowd that seemed to be circling them. "I'll go home," she told him. "I refuse to argue in front of the entire town. But when you get home, we're going to talk about this."

"You're damn right we are." Hadden took her firmly by the hand and led her to the wagons. "Perkins, take her home please."

Hadden put his hands on her waist to help her into the wagon but he stopped and turned her to face him, a tender expression on his hard, chiseled face. She stared at him bewildered. "Kiss me before you go," he whispered close to her ear. "Please kiss me."

"In front of the town?"

"Absolutely."

She reached up to place a kiss on his smoke-blackened cheek, but he turned his head and for a second their lips melded. When he pulled away, Storm looked at him, wondering if his caress meant he forgave her for coming to help with the fire. With that, he put his hands on her waist and helped her into the wagon.

"Now, sweetheart, go home and go to bed. I'll be there later."

"I'll see you when you get home. Be careful," she told him as Perkins set the wagon in motion.

Hadden nodded, waving at her, a grim expression on his handsome face. "I will, but the worst is over."

Thank god."

Hadden opened his mouth as if to say something further, then closed it, settling for a quick squeeze of her hand. "Get her home safe, Perkins." The man nodded and turned the wagon, heading to Storm's house.

A strange sense of foreboding swept through Storm, as she looked over her shoulder. Her last vision of Hadden was the heartbreaking sight of him standing in front of the docks, his hand wearily kneading the back of his neck as he stared at the simmering debris floating on the ocean's waves.

~ * ~

Yes, she was going to go to bed, but what she needed most was a hot bath. She pulled the tub into the kitchen while water was heating on the stove. A few minutes later, she was soaking in a tub full of bubbles, the hot water soothing her strained muscles. She set her head on the rim of the tub and closed her eyes, relaxing in the soothing feel of the water.

Her thoughts drifted back to the fire. Today had been a revelation, proving to her material things didn't matter when compared to human lives. The lost ships weren't important. What was most important was that she loved Hadden and he loved her. If everything were lost, they'd rebuild. She placed her hand on her stomach. Yes, she was pregnant but she refused to be treated as if she couldn't do anything. She was healthy and capable and she had a long time before the baby would be born.

Storm smiled. Despite today's tragedy, or maybe because of it, she was sure for the first time that Hadden really did love her. She'd seen it in his eyes when he'd helped her into the wagon and squeezed her hand, and that simple gesture meant more to her than just the saying of the words, although she had to admit, she wanted him to say the words again—and again.

They loved each other and that was all that mattered.

Exhausted and not wanting to fall asleep in the tub, she quickly finished washing and toweled dry. Donning the nightdress she'd set by the tub, she walked upstairs to their bed.

In a state between dreams and reality, Storm felt the covers on Hadden's side of the bed move then the mattress dipped with his weight. "I didn't expect you home so soon," she murmured, reaching out to run her hand down his arm.

A strange grunt was all she heard. Thinking he must be exhausted, she decided to not pursue further conversation. But she wanted a good night kiss. "Are you awake enough to give me a kiss?"

She felt him lean toward her and drew a quick breath in anticipation of his lips touching hers. It was then she noticed an unfamiliar sweet scent she'd never smelled on him before.

"When did you start wearing cologne?"

"Ever since I can remember." His mumbled words sent a blind panic sweeping through her head.

Storm screamed, her heart pounding beneath her ribs. It wasn't Hadden. Her fingers curled and she struck out, blindly trying to scratch the intruder's face.

A heavy body covered hers, and a pain shot all the way up her arm as strong hands grasped her wrists, forcing her arms down and behind her.

"I'm the man you were supposed to marry. Remember me?" came a snarl close to her ear. "And I'm going to give you that kiss you just asked for."

Storm's scream was cut off by Charles Robertson's smothering mouth. She tried to wrench away from him as he ground his teeth against her lips, but he was too strong for her. She thought to scream again but when she opened her mouth, his tongue invaded, choking her as he thrust it in and out.

She struggled, trying desperately to rid herself of the cloying weight of his body. She dug her heels into the mattress and bucked him off. For a split second, Charles released her arms, freeing her enough for her to rake her nails down the length of his face.

He pulled back, and Storm used her advantage to make an attempt at escape. She scrambled to stand, but he caught her by the collar of her nightdress, throwing her back down on the mattress and dealing her a sharp blow to the temple.

Storm's head exploded in pain, then all went black.

When she woke, she was lying on the bed. She touched her head, closing her eyes. The room spun and danced eerily in front of her, nausea rolled in her stomach. A slight clearing of her vision showed her Charles sitting on a chair next to the bed.

"You made me do that to you. Why? I never wanted to hurt you." He smiled at her, shrugging his shoulders as if he meant what he said.

Her mind racing and her nerves shattered, she swallowed hard. "Hadden will kill you for this."

"No." he shook his head. "That won't happen. You see I've taken care of everything. My plans never go awry. Mr. Johnston isn't going to be doing much of anything let alone seeing to my demise."

"I don't understand what you're saying." She blinked then stared at Charles, searching his face for some knowledge.

Charles' smile was smug and self-satisfied. She felt her blood drain from her face. "He's a hard man to get rid of. Heaven knows I've tried a couple of time to no avail. The first two fires didn't even have an impact. But a blow to the back of the head did the job."

Once again the room swirled and spun. Storm had to grab hold of the bed to steady herself. Drawing several deep breaths, she struggled to keep her eyes open. "Did you kill my husband?"

"Oh, my no." He crossed one leg over the other and leaned forward. "Now that wouldn't be fun. I wanted to watch him suffer and if he were dead that wouldn't happen. If you want the truth, his life is now in your hands."

She knew she had to stay strong, find a way to discover everything Charles wasn't telling her. "What do you want me to do?"

"It's very easy. You get dressed, pack a bag and go with me tonight and your husband will stay alive. You refuse and I'll send a message and he dies tonight."

"You're crazy," she said with a calm she didn't understand, knowing that Hadden would come after them once Charles had his men let him go. They couldn't keep him imprisoned forever. Hadden's crew would find him and free him.

"Don't call me crazy again. I don't want to hurt you because I love you, but if you force my hand, I'll have no recourse."

Storm nodded her head, understanding all Charles was capable of doing. "Why? Why are you doing this? Hadden told me he paid the debt to your father."

Charles snorted and wiped the sweat from his forehead with an embroidered handkerchief. "The agreement means nothing to me. All I ever wanted was you and because I knew you couldn't raise seventy thousand pounds I went along with the agreement, knowing it was easiest way to have you. But when you married the wealthiest man in town..."

Storm gazed at him, genuinely confused. "When did you...fall in love with me. I barely know you?"

"True but I've fantasized about having you since I was a teenager. And I always get what I want."

Nausea swept through Storm, her skin prickled. When she spoke again, her voice was so low Charles had to lean in to hear her. "If I agree to leave with you tonight, will you let Hadden go?"

"Of course I will. Where we are going, he'll never find us."

Storm understood how limited her choices were. She would go with him and find a way to escape and get a message to Hadden. "Okay, I'll go with you, as long as you give me your solemn word Hadden will be released unharmed."

Charles' face lit up with the easy, boyish smile that so belied his true character and Storm, at that moment, wondered if he truly did have Hadden imprisoned somewhere. Whether he did or not, she still had no choice but to go along with his irrational plan.

"Quit worrying about your husband and get packed," he demanded, sounding frustrated with her line of questions. "We have a long trip ahead of us, and I want to be out of here before daybreak." Rising, he stepped away from the bed, allowing Storm to stand.

She drew in a deep breath and walked to the other side of the room. "Would you give me some privacy to dress?"

"Not a chance in hell. I've waited what seems like a lifetime to see you naked." He leered at her, his eyes focused on her and his eyebrows raised.

Clutching her hands and trying to stay calm she asked, "What do I need to pack?"

"Just some riding clothes. We'll buy whatever else you need when we get to Edin..." he broke off, "before we leave the country."

Storm nodded, turning to do his bidding and hoping her face hadn't betrayed the fact she'd noticed his slip. Edin...Edinburgh. *We must be going to Edinburgh.*

Not for one moment did she believe Charles actually had Hadden in his clutches or if he did have him would release him. But on the off chance either of these scenarios was true, she had to find a way to let her husband know Charles' plans. But how was she going to do that when he wouldn't leave her alone?

She searched the room for some clue, realizing she needed a distraction. Her gaze settled on her dressing table and she had an idea.

Turning her back to Charles, she cemented her plan in her mind. Praying for the needed courage, she acted before she could back down. Lifting her nightgown over her head, she unveiled every inch of her body to him.

"Bloody hell..." he groaned, his gaze raking her body. He darted a quick glance toward the window. "It's almost daybreak. We have to get going."

With a calculated swing of her hips, Storm sashayed to her armoire, angling her body to give him a tantalizing view, then squatting down to pull out her valise. Walking to her dressing table, searching through the articles lying on top of it, she prayed he was in too much of a hurry to risk acting on what he'd implied he wanted. God she felt dirty, but she knew this was her only chance.

She had to do this quickly or risk discovery. Furtively she tipped over her box of powder, spilling part of its contents. With the tip of her finger she spelled out the word Edinburgh in the scented dust then the initials...C.R.

"Hurry up, Storm. We have to leave." Impatiently he tapped his fingers on the bedpost.

Storm gulped a lungful of air and slipped into her clothes. As she closed the door behind her, leaving with Charles Robertson, she prayed to every god she could think of that Hadden was alive and would find the clue she'd left for him.

~ * ~

Hadden stepped in the front door and was greeted with an eerie silence that propelled his thoughts back to another day, one that sent him frantically racing through the town to find Storm. He tried to tap down the feelings of uneasiness that seemed to be rising from his gut.

"Storm!" he called. "Storm are you here? I need to see you." He started for the steps leading to their bedroom then stopped to stretch his muscles before deciding to look through the first floor of the house before he ascended the stairs.

"Bloody hell, I'm dying." He raked his fingers through his hair and walked to the kitchen. "I must have used every muscle in my body yesterday." He gazed at the empty room in surprise. Even though she hadn't answered, he'd still hoped to see Storm cooking his breakfast. The darkness in his mind he'd felt when he first stepped into the house returned.

"Storm!" he called again, retracing his steps then looked up the staircase. "Are you still in bed." There was no answering response. "Where the hell are you?" Storm never seemed to be where he expected her to be, and he hoped she wasn't in the stables, exercising Fiacre or any other horse. With a deep steadying breath, he climbed the stairs, praying he'd find her still in bed.

The moment he stepped through the door to their bedroom he sensed something was wrong. Bright morning light slanted through the window, but Storm wasn't in bed. He walked the perimeter of the room, gazing at everything.

"What has happened here?" He saw the rumpled bed, the clothes strewn over the back of the chair, and the nightgown lying in the center of the floor. He shifted his gaze to the armoire and his breath caught in his throat. Unlike the first time he'd panicked, Storm's valise wasn't there. He closed his eyes, praying for strength, knowing Charles had to be behind this. But he couldn't tamp down the rising terror. He sat down on the bed, his hands holding his head as his eyes filled with unshed moisture.

He lay back on the bed, his hand over his eyes, trying to think, trying to remember. Reaching out, he picked up a pillow and pressed it to his face, inhaling deeply. "What the hell?" It smelled like cologne.

"Charles..."

With a bellow of rage, Hadden hurled the pillow at the wall. "You're dead, Charles." Jumping up, he grabbed on to the bedpost and squeezed until his knuckles turned white.

Once again, he searched the room for a clue. "Calm down. You've got to think." With an effort of will, he fought back his rage and his terror. He walked to the bureau and stared into an open drawer. Nothing out of order there, then he walked to the armoire, trying to remember all the clothes in her wardrobe. The only thing missing was an old riding habit. "They were on horseback, but where were they headed?"

He searched the room again, his gaze riveted on the dressing table. He noticed Storm's powder jar lying on its side and investigated. Her combs, brushes, and mirror hadn't been disturbed. Hadden picked up the jar then leaned closer, noticing writing in the dust. He drew in a sharp breath as he realized what she'd written. Edinburgh and C. R.

A jolt of terror whipped through him. The son of a bitch was taking her to Edinburgh. Was he planning on taking her out of the country?

"Over my dead body." Hadden's voice was clouded with emotion. He rushed from the bedroom, down the steps and out the front door.

He had to catch them before he lost their trail. It would take days to reach the Scottish city and he hoped Storm would be able to slow their progress. In Storm's condition there was no way she should be riding that distance. Bloody hell, she could lose their baby.

Reaching the stables, he gestured for the stable boy to saddle a horse for him. When that was done, he raced from the stables and straight to the Robertson house. Henry might know where Charles would stay in the city, and Hadden intended to use whatever means necessary to pry the information out of the old man if he did.

At the Robertson's home, he was off the horse before it had come to a complete halt and striding to the front door. He ignored the ornate knocker and beat on the door. "Open the door, Robertson. Open the damn door! Now!" His voice was so loud and so harsh it caught the attention of several people strolling past the home. "If you don't get here and open this door, I'll kick it down."

"I'm coming. I'm coming!" came Henry's irritated sounding response. "Hold your damn horses."

A few seconds after his response, the door swung open and Henry stood with a scowl on his face. "What the bloody hell do you want now?"

"I want your son. Where is he?" Hadden pushed his way into the house, searching the rooms the best he could, hoping Charles hadn't had time to leave.

Henry glowered at Hadden, his face turning a beet red shade. "What the hell do you think you're doing pushing your way into my home? I don't keep tabs on my son. He is a grown man."

"Son of a bitch, your son kidnapped my wife." Hadden grabbed Henry by his shirt and nearly lifted him off the floor. "You'd be wise to tell me everything you know about this."

"I don't..." Henry yelled back. "I don't know anything."

"When did you see him last?"

"Yesterday afternoon."

"What time?"

"About two, I think." His voice wavered and he pushed the few strands of hair dangling on his forehead behind his ear.

Trying to stay calm, Hadden let Henry go, giving his a him a little push as he sent him away. "It must have happened last night. He entered our home without permission before. Bloody hell, that means they've a huge head start. I was so occupied by the fires and I thought she was safe."

Henry stepped back, adjusting his shirt. "Why do you think Charles kidnapped your wife? He has no reason to have anything to do with either of you. The debt is paid."

"I'm aware of that fact. I was the one who paid it."

"Then why?"

"Because your son is crazy. You know it, I know it, the town knows it. He hates me, and he's obsessed with Storm. How many more reasons do you need?"

"My son is not crazy. And I need a lot more information from you before I can believe any of your insane accusations."

"Now listen here, I don't have time to argue with you. Every second they get farther away and my wife is in danger. Charles broke into my house last night, went to our bedroom and kidnapped her. But sometime before they left, she managed to leave a message."

Henry's mouth gaped open and his eyes widened. "A...a message?"

"She told me they were going to Edinburgh and she also wrote your son's initials—C. R.

Moisture welled in the old man's eyes, spilling over onto his reddened cheeks. "My son, my dear son, I don't know what I did wrong to make him like this. So he really did take your wife. I knew he was obsessed with her but I never thought he'd go this far."

"I don't care, and I don't have time for this—for your lies. All I want to know is, where you think he might have taken Storm in Edinburgh. Do you have contacts there? A place for him to take refuge. Do you have friends in another country where he might go?"

"Well, Edinburgh yes, I've a cousin who lives there, and I think he might be taking her to North Carolina. He spoke of a friend who has a plantation there. He thought he could make money growing tobacco."

Hadden's mind raced with the implications. All his ships were at sail to various parts of the world. It would be at least a month before one of his boats would return home. He ran his fingers through his hair, pacing, thinking and feeling the desperation of a man whose options had disintegrated to nothing. There were no ships left at the docks to book passage. He had two reasons now to believe they would travel overland.

"Give me the name of your cousin and his address." Hadden's heart filled with hope.

Henry paused, rubbing his hands on his pants. "What will do to my son when you find them?"

Hadden's mouth thinned into an ominous line. "What would you do to a man who has tried to kill you, burned your livelihood and kidnapped your wife?"

Henry stepped back. "I know he started the first two fires but the last one?"

"I suppose you had something to do with that?"

"Only the first two, we wanted to scare you into paying up or letting Charles have Storm. I knew your men would put it out before it caused major damage."

"My God, you're both insane. And you, old man, are going to help me find her."

He sighed. "Come into my office and I'll give you the information you will need."

Henry sat down and wrote out his cousin's name and address. "I hope you find your wife." While he was handing the note to Hadden, a slip of paper fluttered to the floor.

Hadden picked it up and read. The Carolina. Out of Edinburgh. With the morning tide in two weeks.

Chapter Seventeen

"I'm exhausted and I'm stopping." Storm reigned in the horse and dismounted. The area was enclosed with trees and bushes. This time she was truly tired. Before now she'd been trying to slow his mad pace through the back trails by faking her fatigue and whining about anything that came to mind.

Charles' lips thinned with irritation as he shot a pointed glare at Storm who was now standing beside her horse. She walked the animal to a small bush and looped the reigns around the plant.

"We're not stopping—don't have the time." His voice roared through the tiny space, yet the sound didn't seem as commanding as it once had.

"Maybe you aren't going to rest, but I am. The horses need a break too, unless you mean to kill them before we get to wherever it is you're taking me."

"We stopped two hours ago." He turned his horse around and rode back to Storm. "Don't think I don't know what you're trying to do, but it's not going to work."

"It doesn't matter what you think. I'm staying here for a while and you can certainly feel free to ride on without me. If I were to sit on that horse another second, I'm sure I'd fall off."

"It's not going to do you any good to stall. Your husband doesn't have any idea where we're headed. He could be on his way to London."

"Then your men let him go?"

"Of course not," he told her. "Why would they do that?"

"What if he escaped?" Charles was right. Stalling for time in hopes Hadden had been set free was exactly what she'd been doing but this time she wasn't. Bone weary, she didn't think she could remain in the saddle any longer. "Since Hadden doesn't know where we're going, and he's still imprisoned by your men, why can't we rest? In my condition and without rest, I'm sure to lose the baby."

"Because I can't take that chance and that condition of yours is something I'm going to take care of as soon as possible. I'm not about to bring up someone else's' brat."

Storm jerked to attention. "What do you mean, take care of?"

"You heard me. There are ways to end your pregnancy."

"Don't you try it, Charles." Storm's voice was deadly. "You try to force me to take anything that will end my pregnancy and I'll kill you."

"You could try but I'm a lot bigger and stronger than you are. Once we get to North Carolina, you won't have anywhere to go or anyone to depend on."

"So that's our final destination?" Did he know her sister Ravyn lived in Maryland? A small measure of relief swept through her. Somehow, if Hadden didn't catch up to them before they sailed, she would find a way to get a message to Ravyn. At the moment, she didn't have the energy to spar with Charles. She meant every word she'd just said, but she felt sure it wouldn't come to that. Yet she still looked for a way to escape him and antagonizing Charles would not allow him to let down his guard. "I apologize. I could never kill anyone. But I won't let you hurt my child."

Charles laughed, his face a sneer. "Too bad its father doesn't care about the baby as much as you do. Have you seen him or any sign of him?"

"He cares. And I'm betting your men aren't still holding him. You and I both know he'll find me as soon as he can." In the back of her mind she feared the worst. Two days had passed and all her hopes had begun to vanish. If he was dead, or he didn't find her and their child, what would she do? She couldn't live her life with Charles but she could find her way to her sister's home, knowing Ravyn would help her.

Don't think about those things. He'll come. He's alive. Nothing will keep him from finding me.

With great determination, she focused her attention on the situation at hand. Storm found a soft mossy spot and sat down, leaning against a boulder and closing her eyes. God, it felt good. She could go to sleep here she was so tired.

She opened her eyes and watched Charles dismount. He stood by his horse, reigns in his hand. "How long this time?"

"An hour, just an hour." She prayed he'd give her that long, but he'd never allowed more than a ten to fifteen minute rest before this.

"No," Charles said. "I'll give you ten minutes and not one second more, then we'll move forward."

Her tears weren't fake this time, they pooled in her eyes, rolling down her cheeks. "I'll try but I don't know if I'll be able to stay in the saddle. I'll die if you keep pushing me so hard."

"I'm beginning to have second thoughts about you, you know. You're not at all like I thought you were. You can't do anything, not even saddle your horse. You can't cook and all you do is cry. You're so sick all of the time, I don't even want you. But things will be different when we get to the States."

"Please, we both know Hadden isn't coming for me. Just give me a half hour."

"Thirty minutes, but we're going to have to make up the time. If we don't the ship will sail without us."

He paced half of the thirty minutes, hitting his leg with his riding gloves. Storm didn't sleep but she did get rest and she knew she was giving Hadden thirty more minutes to catch up to them.

If he was free from Charles' men and if, he was able to come for her.

"Time's up," he commanded, "Get on your horse."

Storm let out a weary sigh, but she did what Charles told her to do. Drained, she hauled herself into the saddle and followed behind Charles. They crested a hill, and she could see the valley below. She turned to look behind her in hopes of seeing Hadden.

No one was there.

Charles must have noticed her and laughed. "He's not coming for you. He doesn't even like you. He's probably celebrating the fact you left him and now he's a free man."

She shuddered, under the circumstances of their hasty marriage, that thought had crossed her mind more than once.

They rode for several more hours, the sun sinking in the west. She knew she couldn't go any farther. The jostling made her sick and her head pounded, falling off was an option she didn't want to risk because of the baby, but at this point if that was the only way to make him stop, she might try it.

"It's getting dark. How much longer are we going to ride? In a few minutes we won't be able to see and I'm starving."

He wiped sweat from his forehead and looked at the trail they were taking. "Maybe you're right. I can barely see my hand in front of my face."

"You don't want to get lost do you?" God, she didn't want that either. Lost in the Highlands was a completely, insane foolish thing to let happen, no way.

"We're going to miss the ship if we keep stopping."

"There will be another one. There is always another ship."

"We're going to keep going. We have to. Who knows how long it will be until I can book passage on another vessel headed for North Carolina?"

"No, this time I'm not getting back on my horse." Storm dismounted and dropped the reigns. Her heart pounding, she stared defiantly at Charles, challenging him to make her do what he said.

"Get back up."

"I told you no. I should have insisted last time we stopped. If you don't kill me, you're going to kill the horses then we'll be on foot. Do you want that Charles? Do you want to walk to Edinburgh?"

"Don't make me punish you, Storm."

Storm was too tired and hungry to worry about his threat. Her stomach rumbled its discontent. "Go ahead punish me," she tossed back to him. "You've already done everything you can to hurt me, what could be worse?"

"Want to make a bet," he spoke slowly, clenching his fists, his eyes narrowing. "I haven't done anything to you yet."

"Really?" she asked, controlling her emotions the best she could. "You kidnapped me, threatened my husband and my baby, and now you tell me you'll punish me if I don't keep riding. So do it. Punish me."

Charles ran his hands through his hair and looked to the north. Then with a big sigh told her, "We'll camp here for the night."

Relief swept through her, glad he'd not found a way to force her onto her horse. She sensed he wouldn't carry out his threats. He might get mad enough to hit her. She didn't want that but he wasn't going to really hurt her.

He wanted sex with her and that gave her some leeway. Thank God for her nausea. She'd never thought she'd think that but her sickness was keeping him away. Now that she was convinced Hadden was still imprisoned she was going to have to find a way to escape.

Waiting until they reached Edinburgh was prudent. She didn't want to be stranded in the Highlands without some protection. Even though she deemed Charles meager protection. The one thing she did fear was if Charles got her as far as North Carolina, he would find some way to destroy her baby. So she had to escape him before they boarded the ship.

Until she could formulate a workable plan, she would continue to employ the tactics that had worked for her today. She'd found that alternating between whining at him and standing up to him left him so confused he didn't know how to deal with her. Maybe she could be so unpleasant he'd decide he didn't want her enough to put up with her. She doubted that would happen but thinking about the possibilities encouraged her.

She closed her eyes and focused on Hadden then she let her mind drift to pleasant summer days with cool breezes off the ocean. What was Hadden doing right now?

Had he found a way to free himself, had he seen the clue she left behind on her dresser or had Charles killed him. A shiver ran down her spine but she forced the fear from her head.

"He's alive and he'll come for me."

~ * ~

After Hadden had left the Robertson household, he'd ridden as faster than he'd ever thought possible, hell-bent to make up the time and the distance advantage Charles had on him. He'd stopped only at inns along the way to exchange his exhausted horse for a fresh one.

Sixteen hours of riding and Hadden knew he had to sleep or risk falling off the horse from fatigue. He stopped at a roadside inn, paid for a meal and a room then asked the innkeeper to wake him in a couple of hours. The next morning he was in the saddle again and more determined than ever to find his wife.

By the second day, his inquires at every inn paid off. They had stayed at one, leaving early in the morning. They were only a few hours ahead of him. He'd catch up before the sun set.

His instincts told him he was getting closer, but it wasn't until the sun was hanging on the horizon and he saw smoke from a campfire curling heavenward that he felt a small measure of success.

"They're only a few miles away." He didn't want to alert Charles, so he dismounted and led his horse along the road until he was about a quarter mile from their campsite. Tying his horse to a bush, he made his way by foot until he could see them.

He sat down only a few yards from Storm and waited until dark. The growing storm clouds overhead would make the night pitch black, giving him a decided advantage.

The hours passed, time ticked away and still Hadden waited. Holding his breath, hearing his heart pound, he watched the scene. God, but he wanted to pull Storm into his arms and tell her she was safe with him, that he loved her more than he could say with words.

"I've got to get more wood for the fire," Charles announced.

Storm remained silent.

"Get over here so I can tie you up."

Storm didn't respond but when Hadden heard the accepting

submission in her voice, a deep-seated fear swept through him.

"I'm not going anywhere. I'm just too tired. Charles you don't need to tie me. All I want to do is go to sleep."

"I don't trust you. Get over here."

Hadden's fists clenched at his sides and it took all of the control he could find within to not kill Charles where he stood. He hoped to use the time while Charles was gathering wood to rescue Storm and get her to a safe spot before he returned and confronted Robertson. He watched as Charles trussed Storm then Hadden saw him stride in the opposite direction into the woods. He waited a few more seconds, then surveyed the perimeter of the camp, approaching Storm from the front his finger to his lips to make sure she didn't make a sound.

"Hush..."

He stopped by her and squatted to rid her of the knots binding her hands then pulled out a knife and deftly slit the ropes. "Shh...don't make a sound," he whispered close to her ear. I'm getting you out of here."

Tears of relief filled her eyes. "I thought you weren't coming. I thought he killed you."

"Hush...we can talk about this later." Hadden pulled her into his arms. God, he couldn't live without her. Yet her thought that he wouldn't come alarmed him. Why would she think he wouldn't search for her and save her from Charles? "We've got to get out of here before Charles returns."

"Just like that? We're going to leave? Hadden, he'll follow us. I know he will."

"Don't worry. My horse is tethered a little ways from here. I'm going to bring you that far then I'll double back and have a chat with Robertson."

"Okay, but you've got to be careful. He's evil and crazy and he despises you. He'll try to kill you. He's the kind who would murder you in your sleep if he had the chance."

"I won't give him the chance. Come on, let's go." He helped her to her feet, praying all would turn out in their favor.

Under the cover of darkness, they walked the short distance to his horse. He kept his arm around her, understanding she'd been through so much and needed his strength.

"Thank you," Storm said when they reached the sanctuary of the copse of trees. "Thank you for coming for me."

Hadden tipped her chin up with his forefinger, and wishing there was enough light that he could see her face clearly and knowing their reconciliation would have to wait.

"Thank you?" he parroted, confused for a moment.

"For not dying, for believing in our love enough to follow me." Tears fell from her eyes and she clung to him.

"Be strong. I'll return as soon as I've dealt with Charles." He smiled and gave her a gentle kiss. "We'll have lots of time to answer each other's questions. Now, I want you to wait here for me. Stay hidden if you can." He had her scoot backwards into a thicket and covered her entrance with branches. "Don't go anywhere."

"What if there's spiders? I don't like spiders."

"I won't be long and they're better than Charles."

"Promise."

"I promise," Hadden encouraged her.

"Be careful and come back to me."

"I intend to do just that. Now take my gun." From out of the darkness, he handed her his pistol. "If you see Robertson coming for you, shoot the bastard. Take a steady aim, you've only got one shot."

Storm nodded.

"And don't for any reason leave these bushes until I come back and tell you to. Understand?"

He left and, for what seemed an eternity, only silence filtered through into her hiding place. Her heart thundering in her ears was the only noise.

Then...

Pressed back in the bushes, Storm heard the clang of swords and the shouts of the men, then a shot. She knew Charles had a pistol and she had Hadden's. She waited terrified, heart racing, sweat beading on the back of her neck and still she waited. In front of her hiding place she heard the snap of a twig. "Hadden," she whispered into the black night. "Hadden?" *Talk to me please, just talk to me.*

Silence surrounded her and with no answering response, she thought the shot must have killed Hadden. She had to see for herself and she had to help Hadden if possible. Pushing away the branches covering her hiding place, she crawled from her shelter. Sticking the pistol into her waistband, Storm stood and tried to see through the blackness of the night. Hearing and seeing nothing, she raced forward and burst into the clearing to see Charles standing over Hadden with a huge boulder aimed at her husband's head.

"Bastard!" Storm charged toward Charles. "Stop or I'll kill you." Pulling out the gun, she held it in front of her and took aim.

"Don't shoot. He's not dead." Charles held the rock above his head then slowly lowered it. "Don't shoot."

"Liar." Storm stopped only two steps away from him to steady her shaking arms. She wanted the shot to kill Charles.

Charles dropped the boulder and put his hands in the air. "Please..."

"No, you deserve to die, Charles. You...you killed him...the man I love...the father of my child."

They stood close to Hadden, and just as Storm started to pull the trigger, a movement on the ground stopped her. In that brief second, Hadden tackled Charles and dropping to the ground, they disappeared into the darkness. The sound of their punches and grunts followed.

Hadden...you're alive...

Fighting, arms entwined, they rolled into the light the tiny campfire emitted.

As she stood and watched, Hadden pummeled Charles' face, then they rolled and Charles seemed to have the advantage. They were evenly matched. She pointed the pistol at Charles, hoping to shoot, but she'd couldn't get a true aim.

"Run, Storm!" Hadden yelled, dealing blow after blow into Charles' bleeding face.

"But..."

Hadden looked at her. "Run."

Charles took advantage of that brief lack of concentration, pulling up his feet, he kicked Hadden in the stomach, bucking him off then rolling over and over together as the men fought, neither with an advantage.

Somehow Charles had found a moment to pull the knife from Hadden's belt. He tried to stab Hadden, but Hadden caught his hand. They wrestled for control of the knife.

Storm screamed as the knife slowly lowered to inches from her husband's neck.

~ * ~

Hadden rolled, taking control and sent the knife into Charles' heart. He sat back on his haunches stealing a long breath of air, his heart racing. God, he'd almost died here and what would have happened to Storm? His gut rolled, nausea hit him hard but he cleared his mind.

"Storm?" He looked to his wife. "Storm, no." Racing to her side, he felt for her pulse. The heartbeat he felt was strong and steady. He breathed a sigh of relief, praying she would wake soon.

Holding her in his arms, he rocked her gently, cooing nonsense as he waited for her to escape the sleep that had overcome her. After what seemed an eternity, Storm slowly opened her eyes.

"Hello, there baby."

"I—what happened? I remember..." she swallowed and looked to the place where Charles lay unmoving.

Hadden moved his fingertip along her hairline, gently pushing hair away from her face. "Everything is fine now. He can't hurt you any more."

"Is he... Did you kill him?"

"Baby, you saved my life. If you had done what I told you, stayed in hiding, I'd be dead and you'd be on your way to Edinburgh with Charles."

"God, I remember." She closed her eyes for a moment.

"It's okay. We don't have to talk about it now." Hadden pulled her closer, wishing he could protect her form all harm and knowing he would die trying.

"When I saw Charles pull your knife and it was over your head..." she shuddered, gulping for air.

Hadden stopped her with a soft kiss. "It's over, sweetheart. He's not ever going to bother you again."

Storm opened her eyes, noticing that his right eye was turning color. She touched the bruise. "Does it hurt?"

Hadden touched her hand and brought it down to hold it in front of him. "I didn't know he made purchase. Is it black?" He needed to laugh. Such a minor injury compared to what could have happened to them.

"I'm so sorry..."

"Hush, sweetheart. There is nothing for you to feel sorry for. It's done and now Charles is a bad memory, nothing more."

Storm lowered her eyes. "We killed someone. I don't know if I can live with that. He would have killed you, wouldn't he?"

"Yes, he would have."

"Then we didn't have a choice."

Hadden drew his eyebrows together, not liking the sound of her voice. He had to try to lighten the mood and pull her from thoughts of murder. "Why didn't you stay where I put you?"

Storm's focus sharpened as her eyes flared with annoyance. "Isn't it obvious?"

Relieved by her response, he knew it was the right ploy to challenge her. If there was anything that could bring his wife back to her normal state, it would be to question a decision. Even if he didn't like the fact she'd left her hiding place, he did need to admit that she saved his life.

Maybe I should stop telling her what to do.

He knew in his heart that would never be possible. His basic instinct was to protect her and their child, yet he continued and said, "You told me you'd stay in the bushes."

She pushed away from him, staring into his eyes. "I lied and I didn't like the spiders and other bugs crawling on me." She shivered, wrapping her arms around her body.

"I'm glad you lied, sorry about the spiders." Hadden pulled her back into his arms. "You saved my life."

Storm moved away and stared at him in confusion. "Why do you say that? What did I do?"

"You distracted Charles. I don't think I could have beaten him. You're an incredible woman, Storm Johnston."

"I am?" she whispered with a tiny smile.

"The sun will be up in a few hours. With a little rest do you think you'll be able to ride?"

"If I could see my hand in front of my face, I'd start right now. I want to get home and sleep in our bed with you holding me tight."

"But I thought I heard you telling Robertson you were too exhausted to ride any farther."

Storm shrugged her shoulders. "Guess I lied again."

"I'm going to have to curb you of that sin." Hadden laughed and kissed her on the forehead.

"I wanted to slow down Charles in case you were coming after me. I didn't know if you would even look for me or see the clue I left."

Hadden's brows drew together. "Storm, did you really doubt me?"

"I hoped you would follow but I didn't know if Charles was lying to me. He said his men had you imprisoned and wouldn't let you go unless I came with him. He told me if I didn't cooperate, he'd have you killed."

Hadden's heart dropped. "His men never kidnapped me. He lied to you."

"I did think at one point he was lying but I couldn't risk your life."

"Oh, baby, none of that matters now," Hadden wrapped his arms around her and pulling her down to lay on the sweet highland heather, "none of that matters. You're my wife and I love you. That's all that counts."

"Is it true? You love me?" Unshed tears brightened her eyes.

"Sweet, sweet heaven, if you only knew how much I love you. You will never know how I felt when I discovered you were missing and when I found your clue. I thought the earth had dropped out from beneath my feet."

"Hadden, will you be truthful about something?"

"Of course."

"If you had discovered that I'd left you of my own accord, would you still have come after me?"

"Why?"

"Just answer me, please."

A long silence followed before Hadden nodded. "Yes, I would have found you no matter how much time and money it took. Even if I thought you didn't want me, I would have found you."

"Because of the baby?"

"No, because I love you."

"I love you too," Storm whispered, tears once again pooling in her eyes.

"Sweetheart, I don't want you to cry again."

"Well I don't want to cry again either but I don't seem to be able to stop."

"Maybe it's because you're pregnant."

They laughed then lay quietly together for a few minutes. Hadden propped himself up on an elbow and looked down at her. "Storm, you know what I said a minute ago about the baby not being the reason I came after you?"

"Yes."

"You see, I don't want you to think I don't care about our child. I love her already."

"You mean you love him?"

"It doesn't matter. I want children, your children as many as you want. If it's just one, I'll be happy if it's five or six, that's okay too. It's your choice. But you are the most important person in the world to me, and I want you to know that baby or no baby I would have searched the world for you until I found you."

She touched his cheek, shaking her head as if in disbelief. "I love you so much." She leaned forward and kissed him. "In fact, I couldn't have chosen a better man to force into a marriage if I'd had the pick of anyone in the world."

~ * ~

Several days and nights had passed since Hadden rescued Storm. The travel had been slow and the nights passionate. They arrived home to lit candles in all of the windows. Lorena and Fayth rushed down the walkway to greet them.

"You're back and safe. Hadden rescued you. I knew he would." Fayth chattered non-stop.

Hadden slanted the two girls a pointed glare. "Your sister is tired."

"Oh my, of course she is. We can talk tomorrow," Larena said. "Although waiting is hard."

"Thank you," Storm said. "It has been a long exciting and depressing trip. I'm going to take a bath then go to bed, and Hadden is going to report the death of Charles Robertson." Storm gave her sisters both a huge hug then walked to the kitchen to get her bath ready. When she finally settled into bed, sleep claimed her quickly.

Storm woke to the sound of Hadden's laughter. A smile in her heart, she turned to watch him, wanting to share in the humor and good feelings.

"What makes you so happy this morning?"

"I'm in love." He flashed her a boyish smile that would have made her heart melt if it hadn't done so when she first looked at him.

"You say that now. Who's the lucky girl?"

"Come here, you little minx," He pulled her on top of him. "Kiss your husband and tell him how much you love him and how you can't live without him."

The sleepiness she'd felt when he first woke her vanished, and she leaned down giving him a chaste kiss on the cheek.

"That's not a kiss. Kiss me like you mean it."

"You haven't answered my question."

"What question?" Hadden's voice became husky as she ran her tongue across his lips.

"Exactly who is it you love, Mr. Johnston?"

He rotated his hips against her, insinuating his stiffening cock intimately between her legs. "Who do you think?"

"There have been stories, rumors, innuendos." She reached down and caressed his erection.

"Oh really?"

"Yes really."

Hadden's moan of pleasure gave her encouragement to continue. She ran her palm across the hot, wet tip of his shaft. This conversation needed to come to a quick and immediate end. Sensuously, she moved down the length of Hadden's body, pausing to gaze at his cock. "I know who you love."

"Who?" He groaned.

"It's that Storm Graham girl."

"You're a bright girl. How did you know?"

"I just know." Storm ran her tongue around his shaft. "I've heard she'll do anything you ask, anything at all."

"You heard right." Suddenly all their easy banter stopped as Storm took him into her mouth.

For several seconds, she didn't move then Storm shifted her body up his, and swinging one leg across his hips, eased herself on his rigid cock.

Storm felt his hands on her waist. He drove into her, fast and furious. She accepted him and reveled in their lovemaking. She felt him touch the center of her core, again and again. Unable to slow this and in any case not wanting to, her body spiraled in ecstasy. Throwing her head back, her body convulsed around his until she collapsed against him, hearing his groan as he too reached that pinnacle. It was over and she felt replete, sated, her heart pounding a rapid staccato.

"Is this why you love me?"

"Oh, yeah," he said. "That and about a million other reasons."

~ * ~

Hadden knew the minute the girls woke in the morning and visited all of their friends, the word would spread that the Johnstons had returned. No one knew for sure where they had been, but there was speculation something had been wrong.

By the time the sun was beginning to set, everyone in town had heard some version of the events of the last week. Rumors ran rampant. Some insinuated Storm had run off with Charles and Hadden had found the young lovers and killed Charles in a jealous rage. Others, remembering Charles' reputation, insisted Charles had kidnapped Storm and by the time Hadden found his wife, she was more dead than alive. Still others insisted it was Storm who killed Charles after freeing herself.

Storm and Hadden tried to ignore all of the gossip and remained in their home reconnecting in ways only young lovers can.

Much to Storm and Hadden's surprise, Henry Robertson, the next Sunday morning at church, strode to the pulpit just before the end of the service and, in a grief stricken voice, explained to the congregation what had happened. Making no excuses for his son, he just asked the town to forgive Charles and treat the Johnstons with respect. They had been through a grave ordeal.

Hadden had been at the docks that morning taking care of some of the havoc wreaked by the fire Charles started when he heard what Henry had said. Soon after, Hadden arrived at the Robertson home and spent a private time with the old man. No one, not even Storm knew what had been said but, from that point on there were no more incidents between the Johnstons and the Robertsons.

During the fire several ships were lost; two fishing vessels and one merchant ship. All of the other ships were restored to sailing perfection. Hadden spent money and time helping the fishermen and merchantmen recover their businesses.

His sanctuary for the children was coming along nicely, just as his new house nearby. Because of the fire two more children were left without parents. He quickly adopted them and sent them to Adele, making sure they were loved and would receive all of the necessities of life, including either an education or job experience when they were of age.

~ * ~

"Storm, what the devil are you doing? We're going to be late."

Storm pinched her cheeks and smiled into the mirror then grabbed her reticule. "I'm coming."

"Storm..."

"Yes, I'll be right there."

She raced down the steps, but paused when she reached the bottom, turning in a slow circle to show off her new dress.

"How do I look?"

"Beautiful, sweetheart, you always steal my breath when I look at you. Now, let's get going."

"Why are you in such a hurry?"

"The sooner we go, the sooner we can get back and..." He ran his hand down the front of her dress, pausing to stroke her rounded stomach.

"You're terrible, Hadden Johnston. I don't know what I'm going to do with you. Is that all you think about?" Storm slapped his hand away and picked her shawl off the table. "I swear you're incorrigible."

"Yup, I think about you naked in my arms every second of every day." He stepped closer and pulled her against him.

"Really?"

"God's honest truth." A smile curved the corners of her mouth and she lifted her face for a kiss.

The old grandfather clock in the corner ticked off a full thirty seconds while they kissed each other. Eventually Storm pulled away and stepped determinedly one step backward. "I thought you were in a hurry. If you keep this up, we won't get there at all."

"I know, I know." Hadden pulled her back into his arms. "We are late, so we better do this quick." Dipping his head, he sucked her lower lip into his mouth, his palms massaging her nipples until they were tight buds begging for his touch, his fingers frantically fumbling with her buttons.

"Where are the bloody buttons on this damn dress? I don't want to rip it."

"In the back." Storm gripped his wrists and pushed his hands away from her breasts. "And we're not doing this. I spent hours getting ready and I'm not going to arrive at this party looking like I just crawled out of bed."

"I won't let that happen." A familiar huskiness crept into his voice. Storm's eyebrows rose.

"Hadden. Don't! You're crazy. Now stop it." But even as she spoke, her hand dropped down and touched him intimately. "Now look what you've done." She laughed.

"No, look what you've..." his words trailed off into a pleasured groan.

"You're not going to stop are you?"

"No way. Not when I feel like this. Not when my cock is hard, pulsing and needing to be inside you."

"You're insatiable." Storm's fingers deftly unbuttoned his breeches. Reaching inside, she released him.

Then with one sweeping movement, Hadden lifted her full skirt up to her waist and shimmied her pantalets down her legs. "Quit looking at me like that."

Grasping her by her waist, he lifted her off the floor. "Can't help it. Put your legs around me and I'll do the rest."

Storm followed his instructions.

He strode into the dining room and set her on the edge of the table, again hiking up her skirts till the many yards of loose, flowing material pooled around her. Leaning toward her, he whispered, "I don't think we're going to get there on time." Thrusting his hips forward, he was inside her with one smooth stroke.

"We aren't. I know. On time."

"And, you—know—what?"

"What?" She clamped her legs tighter around him.

"I—ahh—don't give, oh a bloody hell."

They let out a simultaneous groan of ecstasy. Hadden's grip loosened and Storm fell back on the table, breathing hard.

"You know what?" she gasped.

"No?"

"I don't give a bloody hell either."

~ * ~

On their way to celebrate the unveiling of the new rooms that would start to make Hadden's dream of a sanctuary for unloved and unwanted children a reality, Storm knew it wouldn't be much longer before their new home was finished and they could move in. Living in the Graham home with her two sisters had been a challenge. She knew they spent most of their time with friends to give them much needed privacy.

"What are you thinking? Hadden asked as they drew closer to Adele's home.

"Not really thinking about anything. Just enjoying the fresh air.

Hadden nodded. "It's beautiful out here and I love the night sounds."

"I'll be so happy when everything is done. I want to move in to the new house where we won't have to dodge my sisters."

A little while later, they pulled up on a hill overlooking the spot where their home and the sanctuary were being built. As he'd told her, the sanctuary looked complete. To her surprise instead of turning toward Adele's home, he directed the team to the right, to their new home.

"You're going the wrong way."

"Need to check something at the house first."

"But we're already late."

"I know but this won't take more than a second."

Hadden stopped the wagon in front of their new house then jumped down. Walking to the other side he reached up to help Storm to the ground but she shook her head. "No."

"Let's go look inside."

"I don't want to. It's dark and you just go do whatever it is you need then we can leave for the party."

"No, I want you to see this too." He held his hands up again.

"I don't want to," she said but with a resigned air, she asked, "What is it you want me to see?"

"For me, please," he ignored her question.

Wiping an errant lock of hair from her head and slanting him an 'I don't really want to do this' look, Storm leaned forward and allowed him to lift her down. Arms linked, they strode to the house, but when they reached the door, Hadden paused, bending down and lifting her into his arms.

"Hadden, put me down. You can't..."

"Hush, I don't need any complaining while I'm carrying my bride across the threshold," he told her as he nuzzled his nose in the crook of her neck.

The door swung open and the room inside blazed with light.

"Surprise!"

Friends, family, Adele and the children surged forward, all holding lamps and candles and calling out greetings and congratulations.

Amazed, Storm gazed at the gathering then focused her attention on her beaming husband. "You knew about this?"

"Of course." He set her on the floor of their new home. "So did everyone here. I never believed we'd keep it a surprise and when Aiden and Blade arrived, I was sure the gossip would find you, but everyone kept the secret."

"Well, everyone did, including Ella and we all know she's never kept a secret from me since we've known each other."

"Now before we do anything else, I want to show you around your finished new home."

Like a kid in the sweet shop, Storm followed her husband from room to room as he pointed out the fabric for the curtains she picked out and wallpaper. She alternately clapped her hands with joy or sighed in ardent appreciation of the beautiful furnishings. But when Hadden showed her the nursery, her heart nearly stopped beating. The crib and the tiny pillows as well as the coverlet were so cute and cheery."

"Adele made those and Paul, the oldest of my children, built the crib and the dresser. He likes to work with his hands and loves to make furniture. I do believe he will make a fine craftsman."

When Hadden finished the tour, he ushered her down the stairs to the party.

"How do you like it?" Larena and Fayth were the first to greet her.

Aidan and Blade stood in a corner looking on, both with huge smiles on their faces.

"It's more than I ever expected. Ravyn...!" Storm raced across the room to give her older sister a huge hug. "When did you get here?"

Ravyn returned the hug. "Yesterday morning to be exact. It seems you've been through quite a bit these last few weeks."

"I have, and why didn't you come see me?"

Ravyn shrugged. "It would have ruined the surprise, don't you think?"

"I suppose but I don't really care. I'm so happy everyone is here. How long are you staying?"

"Just a month," Ravyn told her. "Aric and I will help you move then we'll stay in the house with Fayth and Larena."

"I'm so excited to have you here."

Mary tugged on Storm's skirt. She picked her up. "This is Mary."

"Glad to meet you, Mary. How are you?" Ravyn said, acknowledging the little red-haired girl.

"I'm fine. I helped make your baby's new things."

Storm tweaked her nose. "Why thank you. What did you do?"

"I took all the pins out."

Ravyn and Storm smiled. "Very good."

~ * ~

"I enjoyed the party and thank you for bringing my sister here. It's been so long since I've seen her." Storm snuggled into Hadden's arms before giving him a chaste kiss on the cheek.

"You're so welcome," he told her.

"Can we start again, a fresh beginning as if nothing in the past happened between us? I don't like to remember that first day I met you on the golf course and the crazy proposition."

"Without that crazy proposition we wouldn't be married, have a baby along the way and be so happy," he reminded her.

"No, I suppose not, but I wish our meeting could have happened in a different way."

"I don't." He pulled her down to give her a huge kiss, stroking her back then pulling her close. He started to nibble little kisses across her face and down her neck.

"No you don't. We have to get up. My sisters and cousins are coming for breakfast and if we make love again, they might arrive here and we'll still be in bed."

Hadden laughed. "If we are, maybe they'll make breakfast for us."

Storm pulled away from him, staring into his eyes. "I love you so much, Mr. Johnston. Everyday I love you more."

"You couldn't possibly love me more than I love you."

"Of course. I suppose you're right." Storm kissed him again, their tongues dueling for dominance.

When the kiss ended, Hadden touched her cheek. "Let's go make breakfast."

"Hadden, you are my passion—Storm's passion."

About the Author

achristay@aol.com

Born in Medford, Oregon, novelist Christine Young has lived in Oregon all of her life. After graduating from Oregon State University with a BS in science, she spent another year at Southern Oregon State University working on her teaching certificate, and a few years later received her Master's degree in secondary education and counseling. Now the long, hot days of summer provide the perfect setting for creating romance. She sold her first book, Dakota's Bride, the summer of 1998 and her second book, My Angel to Kensington. Her teaching and writing careers have intertwined with raising three children. Christine's newest venture is the creation of Rogue Phoenix Press. Christine is the founder, editor and co-owner with her husband. They live in Salem, Oregon.

Other books by Christine Young
Available at Rogue Phoenix Press

Catching Meara
Book One in the McKenna Clan Series

Meara Thorton was a feisty, world-class computer hacker—cornered by the FBI and shockingly given the chance to be their newly acquired technical analyst. Brilliant and intuitive, yet aching with the loss of everyone she has cared about, her restless heart led her to discover a love she fought and a world she didn't know could possibly exist.

Sweet Sexy Sadie
Book Two in the McKenna Clan Series

From the first time Sadie's eyes met those of Brody McKenna in the hot Sierra Madre Mountains, theirs was a potent attraction—not gentle, slow, and easy, but hot, hard, and all-consuming. The daughter of a dysfunctional family, Sadie had dreams no man could wrench from her with hot sex and an all-consuming passion. She'd challenge this alpha male with all the strength she possessed. But her red hair, fiery temperament, and indomitable spirit obsessed Brody...and he knew he had to find a way to show her he was more than he appeared and convince her to make a life with him.

Sweet Misbehavin'
Book Three in the McKenna Clan Series

Cast adrift after fleeing the home of Jokul, the ice demon, Atantsi, a firestarter, grew to womanhood as she moved through time to keep the demon from finding her. Though stubborn and courageous, she was ill prepared to use powers she had not been taught. Her first sight of the intoxicating Carr McKenna left her breathless, and her second encounter gave her hope for a future she never thought she had.

A playboy, a second son and a shifter, a man who thought his life would be carefree, Carr McKenna was shocked to discover the woman he'd paid as an escort is a firestarter who is running for her life. He is the leader of all the McKennas around the world and that he has multiple powers. His passion for Margo and the need to defend her might cost him his life as well as hers.

Highland Honor
The first book in the Highland Series

Willfully stubborn, innocently courageous, Callie Whitcomb braves a journey through the treacherous highlands to the Macpherson castle. Callie flees from an unwanted marriage as well as her ruthless half brother. Naively she believes Colin MacPherson, the head of the clan, is loyal to her father and will give her sanctuary, protecting her from the vile plans that have been made for her.

As hard and as unyielding as the winter storms that sweep through the countryside, Colin is irresistibly drawn to the impetuous beauty who has magically appeared on his doorsteps. Despite his vows of revenge against her father, she stirs his passion as well as his sense of justice...but to love her would violate all his vows of revenge.

Highland Magic
The second book in the Highland Series

Throughout the Highlands she is known as Keely, the witch woman. She is a great healer-a woman whose dreams come true. Ian MacPherson is a man who puts honor, loyalty and duty above everything. Their lives are entwined when Ian is sent by the Scottish King to bring Keely to trial for witchcraft. He is attacked and left for dead, but Keely rescues him. When he wakes, he discovers he has no memory. As he remembers his lost past, Ian finds that his need to protect the woman who has saved his life eclipses his duty to his king and country. He is a man torn between honor and duty to his country and the woman he loves.

Highland Song
The third book in the Highland Series

With her white-gold hair and azure eyes, Lainie MacPherson is as wild and untamed as the rugged Scottish Highlands where she was raised. Lainie vowed to avenge her rape. Recklessly, she defies English laws and the man who raped her puts a bounty on her head. The man who is sent to bring her to Edinburgh sets a dangerous trap. With nothing left to live for the beautiful Scottish spy steals the sealed documents the English soldier has tempted her with.

When the exquisite temptress takes the bait and runs off with not only the forged documents but the purses of the men in the tavern, Aaron Slade vows to hunt her down and bring her to justice, never dreaming she will tame his jaded soul. When Aaron discovers the truth about the tempestuous woman who stirs his passion to the point of madness, he dares not love her, but desires her with all his soul.

Dakota's Bride
The first book in the Lakota/Pinkerton Series

When Emma St. John received her brother's letter imploring her to escape her stepfather's vengeful scheme and to trust Dakota Barringer with her life, she was willing to chance it. But the handsome, brooding riverboat owner Emma found in Natchez a danger of another kind. For Emma soon found herself surrendering to an unrelenting desire.

Raised by the Sioux when his parents were killed, Dakota had been betrayed once before by a white woman. He wasn't about to trust another, especially one claiming that her stepfather, a powerful U.S. senator, had framed her as a murderess. But he couldn't let Emma's intoxicating effect on him. Now Dakota would risk his very life to protect the innocent beauty who had seduced him with her tender love.

My Angel
The second book in the Lakota/Pinkerton Series

A BEAUTY IN BUCKSKINS
When her father decided to send her to a finishing school back East, Angela Chamberlain refused to be confined to stuffy drawing rooms. Instead, the daring spitfire who could shoot like a man and ride like the wind longed for a life of adventure and romance—and she knew exactly who could give it to her. Devil Blackmoor was a hired gun with a dangerous reputation. But Angela was willing to go to the ends of the earth to capture the handsome devil's heart.

A DEVIL IN DISGUISE
He'd come to America looking for excitement, but Devil Blackmoor got more than he bargained for when he encountered a beautiful rebel who answered his kisses with a wild innocence that touched his very soul. Yet standing between them were more obstacles than either ever dreamed. For Devil had strapped on a gun for the wrong man. And that made Angela his enemy. Now he'll have to choose between his duty and the woman he loves more than life.

The Locket
The third book in the Lakota/Pinkerton Series

The year is 1894. Seeking revenge for crimes against his family, Misha Petrovich follows a path that leads straight to Ariel Cameron's boarding house in Mist Harbor, Oregon. A family heirloom in Ariel's possession leads Misha to believe she is guilty. The locket has been handed down to the oldest girl in the Petrovich family for generations. Ariel is innocent of wrong doing, but her father is not. Misha is torn by his feelings for Ariel and his need for restitution against her father. Knowing that the relationship between them is fragile, Misha does everything in his power to protect Ariel's father. His efforts are to no avail when her father is shot. Ariel comes to realize Misha's steadfast courage and determination to protect her and her father despite what has happened to his family. Ariel's love and devotion heals Misha's heart.

The Talisman
The fourth book in the Lakota/Pinkerton Series

Running from a marriage that lasted one night, Dr. Moriah McKeown discovers the land she has settled on is coveted by determined and lawless men. Yet the proud young woman who once vowed never to abandon her home has second thoughts when her adopted children are threatened. Her only recourse is to enlist the aid of a dark, dangerous gun for hire.

Haunted by the past and a betrayal he will never forgive, Ian Civanovich uses his fast gun and his reckless courage to forget the faithlessness of a woman in his past. He will trust no female—nor will he rest until the threat hovering over Moriah McKeown is put to rest.

Forever His
The fifth book in the Lakota/Pinkerton Series

Struggling to come to terms with the part she played in Jacob St. John's death, Etta Barringer resigns from Pinkerton Agency and seeks peace and solace in a Rocky Mountain Cabin.

Jacob has vowed to discover the reason Etta has betrayed him, sold him out to his enemy and left him for dead.

Isolated in their cabin, they discover their love for each other and learn to trust. But the trust is shattered when Jacob learns she is married to his sworn enemy; the man who left him in the desert to die.

Allura
The first book in the Twelve Dancing Princesses Series

Allura McClellan is horrified by her father's decision to take out an ad in the Times awarding her to the man strong enough and smart enough to win her hand and uncover her secrets. She's an intelligent young woman who takes great delight in the freedom allotted to her by her father. She's well aware that marriage would effectively curtail the adventures she's shared with her sisters and cousins.

Hunter Gray is nothing like the other men who've arrived to vie for Allura's hand in marriage and everything that goes along with it. However, he is the first to refuse to concede defeat and pursue her despite her attempts to disguise her true appearance. It's her temperament that is of more concern to him than her looks. Hunter has worked all his life with the hope of someday owning his own land. Now that it looks like there's a very real possibility that everything he's ever wanted is within reach nothing is going to deter him – including Miss Allura's disagreeable disposition.

The Wager
The second book in the Twelve Dancing Princesses Series

Amorica Hepburn was sent to London to find a husband. Finding a man was the last item on her agenda. With her two cousins, Amorica wagers she can dissuade her suitor before the others. Despite her efforts she discovers a chemistry that cannot be denied. Suddenly she is the arrogant man's wife, pledged to a marriage neither desire. But swept off to his ancestral home above the Dover cliffs and into his strong embrace, Amorica is soon possessed by a raging passion for the husband she had vowed to despise…

Damian Andrews couldn't afford to trust the emerald-eyed spitfire who happened upon his secret. Amorica's hatred of all men of his kind only inflames the war that rages between them. Still, he can not control the intense desire his stubborn bride inspires, or make her surrender to his will until he has conquered the headstrong beauty on the battlefield of love…

A Marriage of Inconvenience
The third book in the Twelve Dancing Princesses Series

A REGAL BEAUTY

When the duchess decides to wed her to a wastrel and a fop, Ravyn Grahm takes matters into her own hands and declares her engagement to another man. Instead of fessing up and telling her great aunt what she has done, she goes through with the pretense. Aric Lakeland is the bastard son of an earl and has a dangerous reputation. But Ravyn is willing to do most anything to keep the duchess from discovering the lie.

A DEVIL-MAY-CARE SMUGGLER

He'd bought land in America, looking to put down roots and end his life of adventure, but Aric Lakeland got more than he bargained for when he encountered a beautiful heiress who made a promise she didn't want to keep. But the promise could not be undone and standing between them were more obstacles than either ever dreamed. Aric had made plans to spend the rest of his life in America and that was at odds with Ravyn's plan of living in England and running her father's estate. Now, he'll have to choose between his dreams and the woman he loves more than life.

Highland Sunrise
The fourth book in the Twelve Dancing Princesses Series

He Made Her An Offer...

Life has thrown Christel McClellan some experiences that could have devastated a less determined woman. Beautiful, self-assured and fiercely independent, she is trying to forget the loss of her stillborn child. But is the child alive?

She Couldn't Deny...

Life is carefree for Ryder MacLaren who loves to see what is on the other side of the sunrise. Laird of Clan MacLaren, he is wealthy, handsome and happily unencumbered...until stunning Christel McClellan enters his life. When he hears her story, he believes the child she thought dead has been sold to a wealthy buyer.

Rebel Heart

HER REBEL SPIRIT DEFIED HIS OUTSIDERS SOUL...⸢SEP⸣She was velvet and silk, eyes the color of a summer storm and amber hair. Victoria DeMontville, because of a promise and a codicil to her father's will, was forced to marry one man to protect her from another. She hated Cameron Savage with a fierce passion. But to hold on to her genetic research and find a cure for the deadly Signe virus, she must pretend to love the enemy at her door, come with weapons of fire to melt her icy heart...

HIS OUTSIDERS TOUCH IGNITED RAGING PASSIONS...⸢SEP⸣He wore a mask, disguised as the Phantom, a true legend come to life. Even as war and debate over new genetic research engulfed them all, he would find his greatest adversary in the beauty who'd branded him an outsider and barbarian, the woman he was born to possess, his soul mate.

A St. Patrick's Day Tale
by
Christine Young, C. L. Kraemer, Genene Valleau

Tumble through time…

…to Ireland in 1817, when tensions are high between Protestants and Catholics and faey people guide the fate of villagers. A lovely Catholic lass stumbles upon the weakly ritual fisticuffing between Irish lads. She falls into the lap of a handsome young Protestant. Family ties, grudges, and two conniving faeries threaten their budding love. But the faeries outsmart themselves when they hijack a time machine that has mysteriously appeared in their forest and are whisked to…

…Eugene, Oregon in the 20th century, amid a property feud between the local faeries and night elves. The conniving faeries from Olde Ireland try to stir up more mischief. However, a warrior gnome convinces the magic folk to control their own destiny, and forces the intruding faeries to take refuge in the time machine again, spinning their way toward…

…A modern day castle in western Oregon. An eccentric inventor is determined to reclaim his wayward time machine and save his beloved wife from her latest misadventure. If only they can travel safely past the black hole…

A Valentine's Anthology

The Lending Library-a fantasy by Christie L. Kraemer
Faeries try to fit into the human world when the forest where they make their home is destroyed by a mysterious enemy.

Chasing Rainbows-a contemporary romance by Genene Valleau
An eccentric aunt, an inventive uncle, a mother who wears poodle skirts, and a brother who wears pearls provide a hilarious backdrop for the courtship of a young woman who yearns for a "normal" family.

The Gift-an historical romance by Christine Young
A man and a woman on opposite sides of the Civil War get a second chance at love after one final battle returns soldiers to their war-torn

homes to rebuild their lives.

Writing as AnnChristine
Safari Moon

Solo St. John, a wildlife photographer, is preparing for a trip to Alaska. Suddenly, Solo finds women of all sorts invading his privacy, his home and his office, all cooing nonsense words and blatantly throwing themselves at him. Solo doesn't know why, and he has no idea how to rid himself of the persistent women. He finally decides to beg a favor of his best buddy Nyssa Harrington.

In love with Solo for the past ten years and knowing he doesn't return her feelings Nyssa doesn't want to talk to Solo. She knows if she accepts his phone call, she will not be able to resist the temptation to hope again.

A Valentine's Anthology

Sharks byAnnChristine
Will Lily and Jacob, best friends forever, find love or will they discover friendship is not enough for a relationship to take the final step into marriage.

The House on Berkley Street by K. J. Dahlen
When Serenity is asked to find the truth in a forty-year old tragedy, someone in the town of White Oak, Texas doesn't want the truth told. Can they stop her before she finds out what they have kept hidden for so long?

The Placebo Effect by Solstice Stevens
First, there was the poison. Then, there was a four story jump and the basketball hoop. Jessamyn Hamhill's life has been one validation attempt after another . . . until now.

VISIT OUR WEBSITE
FOR THE FULL INVENTORY
OF QUALITY BOOKS:

http://www.roguephoenixpress.com

Rogue Phoenix Press
Representing Excellence in Publishing

**Quality trade paperbacks and downloads
in multiple formats,
in genres ranging from historical to contemporary romance,
mystery and science fiction.
Visit the website then bookmark it.
We add new titles each month!**